# PRAISE FOR JILL SHALVIS

"Bestseller Shalvis (*Love for Beginners*) launches the Sunrise Cove series with a charming, emotional romance featuring a cast readers will quickly come to see as old friends."
—*Publishers Weekly* on *The Family You Make*

"*Love for Beginners* is quintessential Shalvis, with humor and heat (whew, Emma and Simon give us heat), and a cast of characters you'll hate to leave behind when you turn the last page. But even so, we promise you'll finish this book feeling warm from the inside—and maybe the outside too. This is the summer's perfect beach read."
—Christina Lauren, *New York Times* bestselling author

"Jill Shalvis has a unique talent for making you want to spend time with her characters right off the bat."
—Kristen Ashley, *New York Times* bestselling author

"Sisterhood takes center stage in this utterly absorbing novel. Jill Shalvis balances her trademark sunny optimism and humor with unforgettable real-life drama. A book to savor—and share."
—Susan Wiggs, *New York Times* bestselling author, on *The Lemon Sisters*

"Jill Shalvis's books are funny, warm, charming, and unforgettable."
—RaeAnne Thayne, *New York Times* bestselling author

# The Summer Escape

# The Summer Escape

### A Novel

# JILL SHALVIS

### AVON

*An Imprint of* HarperCollins*Publishers*

THE SUMMER ESCAPE. Copyright © 2024 by Jill Shalvis. Excerpt from BETTER THAN FRIENDS © 2024 by Jill Shalvis. All rights reserved. Printed in the United States of America. No part of this book may be used or reproduced in any manner whatsoever without written permission except in the case of brief quotations embodied in critical articles and reviews. For information, address HarperCollins Publishers, 195 Broadway, New York, NY 10007.

HarperCollins books may be purchased for educational, business, or sales promotional use. For information, please email the Special Markets Department at SPsales@harpercollins.com.

FIRST EDITION

*Designed by Diahann Sturge*
*Title and chapter opener art © Danussa / Shutterstock*

Library of Congress Cataloging-in-Publication Data has been applied for.

ISBN 978-0-06-323581-6

24 25 26 27 28  LBC  5 4 3 2 1

# The Summer Escape

# CHAPTER 1

At the ripe old age of eight, Anna Moore decided she knew enough about engineering and physics to design a cape so she could fly. It went without saying that "flying" off her family's second-story deck into a pile of soft, spongy Tahoe snow—which had in fact been neither soft nor spongy—had gone badly.

As an adult, she understood the ridiculous plan had come from the part of her brain responsible for stupid ideas. Older now, and hopefully wiser, Anna had long ago locked that part of herself away and given up being a wild child. It'd definitely taken her longer than it should've, but eventually she'd accepted that it was safer to live life by the book.

Apparently though, she still had to learn her lessons the hard way. Or as in today's case, the *really* hard way. She'd told Mari, her entire support staff at her private investigations firm, that she didn't need backup today. So there she stood, alone in the alley of the bar she'd been staking out for a case, having run into the pissed-off ex-husband of a different client. The guy was as big and mean as the Sierra mountains behind him and, oh goodie, held a knife in his hand.

Some days it didn't pay to get out of bed.

Anna had her back pressed to the brick wall behind her and her hands out in front of her, signaling she came in peace, wondering how to reach the Mace in her back pocket without him noticing. Problem was, while he towered threateningly over her, he wasn't quite close enough for a well-aimed knee to the crotch.

So yeah, hindsight being twenty-twenty and all, she could've used backup. And where the hell was everyone anyway? It was broad daylight, and the bar, part of a beautiful little shopping village, sat right across the street from Lake Tahoe. Normally on a gorgeous July day like this, there'd be people swarming everywhere. But today . . . not a soul. Seemed her luck was on point as always. "Okay, Gerald, you've got my attention. Let's talk this out."

"You testified against me in court and Tish got custody of Brownie."

Brownie being a nine-pound Shih Tzu. "Yes," she said. "Because you went off the rails during mediation and threatened to bake Brownie like, well, a brownie."

Gerald's massive shoulders drooped, and a flash of shame crossed his face as he lowered his knife. "I'm sorry. But I never would've done it. Brownie's my baby. I rescued him at five days old and bottle-fed him for weeks. Tish didn't even want him." His eyes went misty. "He's all I've got left, and now he's gone too."

From inside her pocket, her phone buzzed an incoming text, and she knew from the air of superiority surrounding it who it was from. "Listen," she said. "That's my big sister, and trust me when I tell you that if I don't respond immediately, she'll send out the cops, SWAT, *and* the National Guard." This was probably not even a fib. Hi, she was twenty-eight, and her sister, only six years older, still tried to mother/smother her on the daily.

"I'm the baby of the family too," Gerald said sympathetically. "I've got four older sisters who never leave me alone. They're always bossing me around and telling me what to do."

"So you understand me," Anna said. "And I understand you. See, this is just a mistake, Gerald. Let me go and there's no harm, no foul."

He scratched his scruffy jaw as he thought so hard she could almost see smoke curling from the top of his head. "You'll call the cops on me."

She shook her head. "I wouldn't do that to you." Her most impressive investigator skill was lying. "You could just walk away."

He thought about that. "If you agree to talk to Tish about joint custody of Brownie."

"Sure. Consider it done." She would talk to Tish, not that she could guarantee anything.

When he nodded and walked away, she let out a relieved breath and sagged against the wall. Honestly, she understood some of Gerald's rage, if not his methods. If an ex had taken Clawdia, the feline love of her life currently shedding all over her bed, she'd be devastated too.

But the knife? No. She couldn't let that stand.

Giving up on surveillance, she called Gerald's ex, warning her about the weapon and the threat, letting her know that Gerald claimed all he wanted was Brownie. Tish said she never should've given him that knife for Christmas a few years back—*gee, ya think?*—and also she was tired of Brownie eating her shoes anyway.

With that handled, Anna quickly accessed her texts. One from Mari, checking in from the office. One from her friend Nikki, reminding her that it was Anna's turn to buy drinks that week. And . . . shock . . . three from her pregnant-with-triplets sister.

> **WENDY:** I need you.

> **WENDY:** ???

> **WENDY:** It's an emergency!
> And this time I mean it!

Heart kicking hard, Anna quickly strode to her car as she called her sister. "What's wrong?" she asked the second Wendy answered. "The babies?"

"They're fine, but I'm not. I need pickles."

Anna sucked in air as her heart settled back in her chest. "You've *got* to stop doing that!"

"I can't," Wendy said. "Not until you forgive me."

They'd had a fight. Yet another in a long line of fights that Anna didn't have time to deal with today. "Do you really need pickles?"

"More than anything except peace on earth and maybe for Ryan Reynolds to be single. Don't tell Hayden."

Hayden being Wendy's saint of a husband. "Fine," Anna said. "I'll bring you pickles after work."

"But . . . what are you doing right now?"

Besides dodging knife-toting dumbasses? "*Working.*"

"Okay, but the babies *really* need pickles."

Anna thunked her head on her steering wheel.

"I know, I'm being slightly bossy again, aren't I?" Wendy sighed. "Ignore me."

If only that were an option . . . "I'll be there soon as I can." Fifteen minutes later, she was in the store, heading toward the checkout with a massive jar of pickles, when a new stream of texts came through.

**WENDY:** I could use a watermelon too.

**WENDY:** And a steak!

**WENDY:** Oh, and Raisin Bran!

**ANNA:** Anna Moore has left this conversation.

**WENDY:** I know that's a lie . . .

Thirty minutes later, Anna let herself into her sister's house, carrying four bags of groceries. The cute little cabin that Hayden had inherited from his grandmother wasn't too far from the lake. Close enough to walk on a nice day, far enough that the swarms of summertime tourists seemed a world away. Wendy had the perfect life: the cute home, a husband who loved her, and babies on the way.

Telling herself it was silly to be a little envious, especially since she didn't want any of those things right now, Anna left everything but the pickles in the kitchen and walked down the hall to the main bedroom. There she found her supposedly on-bed-rest sister sitting on the floor of her closet, everything she owned scattered around her, reading a book.

"You came!" Wendy said, and then burst into tears.

Anna grimaced. "The doctor said if you keep crying every five minutes, you're going to get dehydrated."

"I know." Wendy was currently twenty-six weeks pregnant, and the plan was if she didn't go into labor by week thirty-two, her OB-GYN would induce, since carrying triplets for longer than that could get dangerous. She wore a pair of Hayden's sweat bottoms, low-slung beneath her massive belly, and a tank top that was straining to within an inch of its life to hold everything in. There was a stain across the middle because Wendy used her baby bump as her table.

"You're staring at the stain on my shirt, aren't you?"

"Nope. Not me. No way."

"No, I get it." Wendy hiccupped. "I'm falling apart!"

Feeling bad for her lack of patience, Anna dropped to her knees next to her sister. "Listen . . . tacos fall apart, but they're still amazing, right? And so are you."

Wendy's eyes watered again. "You still love me."

"As much as I love tacos." Which unfortunately was a whole lot. Anna took in the mess. "Was there a tornado in here?"

"Ha-ha." Wendy blew her nose. "I was cleaning out my closet and found a baby book Hayden had bought me months ago. Did you know that babies get hot lava poops? Hot lava poops! What does that even mean?"

Horrified, Anna shook her head, unable to even fathom the thought.

Wendy tossed the book aside and made gimme hands at the massive jar of pickles.

Anna held it out of reach. "Not until you get back into bed."

It took the both of them to get her there. Finally, Wendy sat back against the headboard, legs crossed, the pickle jar snugged between as she dove right in. "You know what would make these even better? If they were fried."

"I'm not going anywhere else except back to work," Anna said.

Wendy swallowed a bite of pickle. "You work too hard. You should retire. How long could you live comfortably with what you've saved?"

"Comfortably?" Anna shrugged. "Thirty minutes, give or take."

Wendy sighed. "I know you're upset with me, but I really am sorry for setting you up with my dentist last week. I keep trying because all I want is for you to find a great guy and get married and have babies like me. Is it so wrong to want you happy?"

"First, there are all kinds of happy," Anna said. "But also, that 'great' guy ordered the most expensive thing on the menu, and when I pulled out my credit card to split the bill with him, he smiled and thanked me for buying dinner."

Wendy winced. "I'm—"

"Sorry, I know. But, Wendy, please stop trying to fix me, because I'm not broken. Okay?"

"Okay," Wendy said softly.

Anna nodded, then looked around at the mess again, stilling at the box of her dad's things, the box they'd never been able to get themselves to go through. A sharp jab of grief hit her in her chest like a hot poker. He'd been gone a year and the loss still hurt, proving whoever had come up with the "time heals all wounds" mantra had no idea what they were talking about. Turning away from the box, she found her sister still eating pickles.

"I know what you're thinking," Wendy said, licking her fingers.

"I'm thinking you're going to get heartburn if you eat another one."

"A lot you know. I've had heartburn since five weeks into this five-year-long pregnancy."

Anna snorted.

"Laugh now, but you're the godmother. You get these puppies when they turn into teenagers and send me to the loony bin."

"I love puppies." This from Hayden, who came into the room shrugging out of his suit jacket, moving with a smile toward Wendy. "Hey, babe." He kissed her.

"Hey yourself." Wendy grabbed him by the lapels and sniffed at him. "Wait. Why do you smell like your mom's amazing chicken noodle soup?"

"Because I stopped by her house to pick up a whole big pot of it for you."

"God, I love her."

Hayden went brows up.

Wendy smiled. "Love you too, but let's be honest. I married you for your mom."

Hayden didn't look concerned. He was incredibly laid-back. Anna supposed he had to be to deal with Wendy, plus he used that great energy as CFO of the Moore Foundation, which their dad had started as a way to facilitate getting money and resources to people and places who needed it most.

"I'm going to shower and change," Hayden said, and kissed Wendy's belly. "Hi, babies."

Anna turned away from their cuteness, her gaze once again falling on the box of her dad's things. Kneeling before it, she took a deep breath. After a year, she should be used to missing his laughing eyes, the way he smiled at her like she was his favorite person in the whole world, his warm hugs . . .

Maybe it'd help if she had something of his home at her place. She pulled out a framed picture that sucked the air from her lungs.

"You okay?" Wendy asked.

Unable to answer, she brought the pic to the bed. Wendy let out a soft breath as they both looked at the image of a young Wendy and their pregnant mom at the lake.

"I was almost six here," her sister said softly. "I had a thing about sand, hated it. Mom said I was such a princess that I wouldn't even put my toes in it, so Dad had to carry me the whole time."

A sweet memory, but Anna would give just about anything to also have memories of their mom. Or even one. Shoving the sadness where she shoved all her unwanted emotions—deep, deep down—she distracted herself by taking another dive into the box. Fixating on the flash of something shiny rather than facing any more family photos, she pulled out a small gold coin about half an inch in diameter. "Wow. It's dated 1853."

Wendy's eyes got big. "Let me see!"

Anna dutifully brought it over.

Wendy stared at it. "What if it's worth a ton of money? We could be like those people on that *Antiques Roadshow* who've been sitting on a fortune and don't even know it!"

"It's probably just a reproduction."

"Are there any more?"

Anna went through the box. "No."

Wendy bit the coin. "It tastes like real gold."

"How do you know what gold tastes like?"

"It tastes like this." Wendy held it up to the light. "You know what we need? A coin shop. They'd have an expert there who could help us." She started to push herself to the edge of the bed to get up.

Anna held out a hand. "Stay."

Wendy rolled her eyes, and Anna said, "Yeah, sucks when someone bosses you around and tells you what to do, doesn't it? Now just sit there and eat the pickles in your lap."

"I can't even see my lap. For all I know, I could've finished all the pickles already. And you don't always have to be the keeper of the rules for everyone, you know."

Anna slid her a look. "If this is where you give me the 'live a little' lecture, save your pickled breath."

"Come on. Aren't you the least bit curious about the coin?"

She was trying not to be.

"You could even go now. Come on, you're your own boss."

"Yes, but my caseload is overwhelming right now." Another fib. She was low on jobs. And money. But that was another problem entirely.

"Hayden, make her listen to me," Wendy said as he came back into the room, his hair damp, now wearing basketball shorts and a T-shirt. He took the jar of pickles from Wendy and replaced it with a bowl of soup.

"Like I've ever been able to make either of you listen to me."

"It's not like either of us are rolling in the dough," Wendy said to Anna. "All of Dad's money went to his humanitarian and philanthropy efforts. My teaching salary's on hold for my pregnancy leave, and yeah, Hayden loves his job, but it's not exactly making us rich. An unforeseen windfall could change all of our lives."

Okay, good point. But if their dad had wanted to leave them something other than his reputation, he would have. And call her obstinate—others had used far more derogatory names—but she didn't want anything she hadn't earned.

Unfortunately, Wendy being pregnant threw a wrench in Anna's defiance. This pregnancy was ten years in the making and Wendy's lifelong dream come true. Until her sister safely popped out Things One, Two, and Three, Anna was going to have to suck it up to keep her happy. "Fine. I'll take the coin in tomorrow. Happy?"

"Yes." But then Wendy burst into tears again.

Anna turned to Hayden. "You're up at bat."

Unfazed, he handed Wendy the tissue box from the top of their dresser.

"I'm sorry," Wendy said soggily. "I'm so tired of crying every time someone does something nice for me."

Anna wisely didn't say that she was *also* tired of the crying, mostly because she wanted to keep on breathing.

LATE THE NEXT day, Anna was back at Wendy's, like it or not. All she wanted was a loaded pizza, a shower, and her own bed. Okay, and maybe she also wanted her laundry magically folded and put away, a car that didn't have its "service needed" light on, and she sure wouldn't turn down an orgasm or two. But she'd brought in the coin to check its value, and there'd been a shock.

"I can't believe a news crew was there at the same time as you." Wendy pulled a bag of cheese puffs from Anna's bag.

"Hey, those are mine."

"Finders keepers." Wendy had her laptop open. "I'm searching YouTube for the news segment. They really said the coin was worth over ten grand?"

"Unbelievably, yes." Anna was still stunned. "Apparently it's part of a collection that hasn't been seen in years. The guy asked me if I had the rest of the set."

"Oh my God, do you think we do?"

"Where?" Anna asked.

"Good point."

"Listen . . ." Anna confiscated back her family-size bag of cheese puffs, aka her dinner. "I know the coin's worth a lot, but I think we should keep it until we know why Dad had it—"

"Found it!" Wendy hit play on the video.

A reporter stood in the coin shop next to a very annoyed-looking Anna. "We don't need to see this—"

"Shh! And wow. That sweater you stole from me really makes your eyes pop. But . . . did you even brush your hair?"

Anna ran a hand down her always wild and crazy waves. "Well, it's not like I knew there'd be a camera crew there."

"Yes, but what if you'd run into a cute guy who's into smart-ass, perpetually irritated, brilliant women?" her sister demanded. "And what happened to the emergency lip gloss I put in your purse?"

"You think I'm brilliant?"

"Duh."

The reporter smiled into the camera. "Today we're visiting Sunrise Cove's Rare Coin and Antique Shop, where we came across Anna Moore, who found a rare coin in a box of her deceased father's belongings. Back in the day, Louis Moore made his fortune in real estate wholesaling, flipping before 'flipping' was even a term. Of course he's even more famous for his philanthropy, giving away much of his fortune—"

"Or all of it," Wendy said proudly.

"—and to this very day, Sunrise Cove is grateful to him for donating buildings that became our rec center, the local hospital, and our historic society, among others. Anna, how do you think your dad came to be in possession of the coin? Do you think it's from his rumored cat burglar days?"

Wendy sucked in a breath. "*Cat burglar days?*"

On-screen, Anna said, "He was never a cat burglar."

The reporter turned to the camera, blocking Anna out of the shot. "A modern-day mystery. Makes one wonder what other mysteries might be associated with Louis Moore and if he . . . *cat-burgled* . . . the coin." She smiled. "Back to you, Doug, and the incoming weather system."

Wendy shut her laptop. "You let her defame Dad?"

"Hey, I said he wasn't a cat burglar."

Wendy snatched back the cheese puffs. "What if they take his name off the hospital wing? What if this ruins all the good he did? Ohmigod, what will I tell the babies? They can't grow up with the whole town thinking their grandpa was a thief, they'll get bullied! I mean, you were bullied and look how much it messed you up."

Did all big sisters drive their little sisters bonkers? Or was that just a special skill of Wendy's? "I was bullied because you'd always brush my hair into a squirrel's tail. You're not supposed to brush hair like mine once it's dried! And you never used any product. Do you have any idea how many products I've had to use to keep the frizz at bay?" Anna paused because they both knew in spite of spending a fortune, her hair was still frizzy. "And I'm not messed up. I mean, not terribly."

Her cell phone buzzed with a number she didn't recognize. She wanted to answer with a *Thank you for contacting the abyss, your scream is very important to me, but there are 5,493,823 people ahead of you in line, all of them named Wendy* . . . But she controlled herself. "Anna Moore."

"Anna, this is Suzie McNab, local reporter. We're running a piece on Louis Moore and I'm hoping to get a quote from you."

Anna's stomach sank. "What's the angle?"

"Whether he was the town savior or an infamous cat burglar. What can you tell us?"

"No comment." She disconnected.

Wendy, who'd obviously been able to hear the convo, had gone still, a cheese puff halfway to her mouth. "Why did you do that? You had a chance to clear his name."

"It didn't matter what I would've said—she'd already made up her mind to spin a wild tale."

In a statement of just how upset she was, Wendy shoved the cheese puffs away from her. "'Infamous cat burglar'? Dad couldn't have climbed a building to save his life. His MS made him far too unsteady for that."

"You're remembering how he was in the last few years of his life. Early on, he was an athlete and loved to mountain climb."

"Oh my God. You're right." Wendy closed her eyes. "It's been so long, I'd almost forgotten." Her eyes flew open. "Wait—you don't think he did this, do you? Stole the coin?"

"What I think is that we need a lot more information."

"That's the investigator in you. But you're his daughter. You can't possibly believe— Wait, what am I even saying? You're the job. No emotions, no feelings, nothing too personal."

Hard to be insulted at the truth, but Anna managed it just fine. "It'll blow over."

"Only if we fix it." She leveled Anna with a look of despair. "We have to fix this."

Anna could hear her stress. Not good. "It's just words, Wen. *We* know Dad didn't do this. And anyway, now that he's gone, it doesn't matter what anyone else thinks."

"Of course it matters. What do you think will happen to the foundation if Dad's name is dragged through the mud? Hayden losing his job is the least of it. We do so much good."

"Okay," Anna said carefully. "I hear you. But I still think you're jumping ahead here. Dad didn't steal anything. He'd *never.*"

"We need to prove it," Wendy said softly, hugging her belly.

Anna could withstand a lot of things. Like *a lot* a lot. But

Wendy feeling sick with anxiety right now wasn't one of them. The doctor had been very clear: no stress. "I'll do my best to fix this. But don't get excited," she warned when she could see her sister doing just that. "I'm not even sure where to start, when the only person with any answers is dead— *Why* are you on your phone right now?"

"I'm ordering a GoPro so you can take me along for every step of your investigation. It's got a headband strap and an app that you can download on your phone so if we're connected, I can see everything you see as you see it."

Anna choked out a laugh. "No. Hell no."

"Listen, do you know what it's like to be the same weight as a whale? Or to have to run with your legs crossed to the bathroom so you don't pee on the floor? No, you do not. Also, I've got one alien kicking me in the stomach, another punching me in the lungs, and every time I move, I . . ."

"You what?"

"Toot."

"*Toot?*"

Wendy threw her hands in the air. "Fart. I fart, okay? All the time. And we're not talking little dainty ones that you can hide either. I've been telling Hayden it's him, but I'm pretty sure he's not buying it—" She broke off to narrow her eyes at Anna for laughing her ass off. "Jeez, I haven't seen you laugh in forever, and when you do it's at my expense?"

Anna swiped at the tears of mirth on her cheeks. "I'm not going to wear a GoPro."

"Are you telling me I'm about to push Midnight, Sunshine, and Eclipse out of my hoo-ha and you can't do this one little thing and bring me along?"

"Wen, if you love your babies, you will *not* give them hippy-dippy names. And as for bringing you along, I'll wear earbuds and keep a line open when acceptable, but that's it."

Wendy hugged Anna so hard it hurt, a perfect euphemism for their relationship. But it wasn't until she drove home and entered her condo that she realized once again she'd caved like a cheap suitcase to her sister.

# CHAPTER 2

The building where Anna rented an office was expensive, but in Sunrise Cove, they all were. The pros: safe and well-lit parking, vending machines stocked with saturated fats and sugar, and each floor came with a receptionist.

Anna was on the second level, in the first of six offices, which meant if her door was open, she could hear Candy, the receptionist, chewing gum.

A definite con.

Anna was elbows deep in research for one of the insurance companies she did investigations and analysis for to bring in extra cash. They were facing a civil suit, and the insurance company wanted their ducks in a row.

That was Anna, resident Duck Whisperer Extraordinaire.

Since she had her office door open to draft in fresh air from her window, she heard Candy stop chewing gum to greet someone. Then came a low murmur of an answering male voice, and odd, but she could've sworn he said her name.

"I'm sorry," Candy said. "You're not on her list for today."

"I'm a last-minute add," he said. "Here, I'll just call her." There was a silence while he presumably navigated through his phone, then, "Anna darling . . ."

She stared at her phone, which hadn't rung. But also . . . *Anna darling?*

"You about ready to grab lunch?" he asked, then paused for a beat as if listening to her response. "No worries, I'll be right in."

Anna nearly laughed. No way would that work. Candy might have a sweet-sounding name, but the woman was no pushover. No one got by her, and if they tried, well, the ex–parole officer was working on her black belt in karate and often lamented that she hadn't been able to kick anyone's ass in months.

Anna leaned over her desk, precariously perched, trying to peek out the door, not wanting to miss the ass-kicking.

"She said to come right in," the man said to Candy. "Thanks for your help."

"Anytime, honey."

*What the hell?*

In the next beat, he appeared in Anna's doorway, startling her so that her hands slipped on her desk, making her lose her balance.

The man's face creased in concern. "Are you—"

"Fine!" She straightened, refusing to rub the chin she'd just banged on the wood. "I'm fine."

Appearing to be fighting a smile, he rocked back on his heels. "You sure?"

No, she wasn't sure. For one thing, her pride hurt right along with her chin. "Who are you?"

"Your next appointment." He even looked her right in the eyes as he lied.

Impressive. "I don't have an appointment right now."

"No? Well, don't tell your receptionist." He ambled over to one of the two chairs across from her desk and made himself at home, long legs sprawled out in front of him, comfortable as you please.

She knew "tall, dark, and handsome" was an antiquated saying, but if the shoe fit . . . and this one certainly did. "You lied to her."

He steepled his fingers on his flat belly. "'Lie' is such a strong word."

Leaning against the side of her desk, arms crossed, she gave him her best badass glare.

The corners of his mouth quirked. "My name's Owen Harris, and we need to talk."

"So talk."

"I'd like to know how it is that you're in possession of an 1853 P Liberty Gold coin from the SS *Central America*."

Good thing she'd done some research on the coin and its origins, because she now knew that he was referring to the ship called the SS *Central America*, which had gone down in 1857 during a hurricane off the coast of the Carolinas—with a fortune in gold on board. "Why would I tell you anything?"

"Because you're in possession of a coin that went down with the ship, and I believe it belongs to my great-aunt."

"What makes you believe that?"

He slapped a few pockets before finding and pulling out his phone. While he flipped through his photos, she studied him. He had short, tousled hair in every possible shade of brown, from sun-kissed to dark, which matched the two-day stubble on his jaw. His eyes were an unsettlingly sharp green. Considering that he'd come to her without an appointment, she thought it was damn impolite of him to look as hot as he did.

Leaning forward, he showed her a snap of an old black-and-white picture that held a framed coin collection labeled *1853 P Liberty Gold*. Then he swiped to the next photo—same collection, only the photo was in color now, and all the coins were gone. "They were stolen ten years ago. She filed a report with the police, but it was kept quiet at her request. She no longer enjoys being the center of attention."

She looked up at him, but the man's eyes, in addition to being sharp, were impossible to read. "I fail to see how this proves the coin is your great-aunt's. They're not numbered or anything."

"Any coins that were recovered from the shipwreck ended up in private collections, like the one that belonged to my great-aunt Ruby's family. They purchased the collection legally, then passed them down through the following generations. No one is missing any coins from their collection—except Ruby. So when you popped up with one . . ."

He'd assumed it was his great-aunt's. "Interesting," she said casually while her heart raced. "But still not absolute proof."

He thumbed to another picture. Another old black-and-white, this one of a twentysomething young woman in a wedding dress. Her only jewelry was a stunning necklace.

"That's my great-aunt Ruby on her wedding day," he said. "She's wearing a necklace called the Ruby Red. It'd been given to her by her mother, who'd gotten it from her mother, always passed down on the daughter's wedding day." He swiped to another pic, which was of a painting in an ornate frame. "This was my great-aunt's great-grandma . . . on *her* wedding day."

Anna took in both photos with the same striking necklace. "Very cool," she said genuinely. History fascinated her. "But what does it have to do with the coins?"

"The Ruby Red was stolen on the same day as the coins, and

nothing was ever recovered by the authorities. Have you seen this necklace?"

"Never."

Slipping his phone into his pocket, he shrugged. "Reportedly, you didn't know you had the coin either." He met her gaze, and she realized she *could* read his eyes after all.

He was angry.

"I'm sorry, Mr. Harris," she said. "I truly am. But I don't have the collection or the necklace. Just the one coin, and I still haven't seen proof it belonged to your aunt."

That got her a smile that didn't meet his eyes as he stood and pulled two one-hundred-dollar bills from a pocket and set them on her desk. "Now you really *do* have a client, one who's given you a down payment in good faith. I'm hiring you to find the stolen coins and the Ruby Red. I'm pretty sure the job's going to be easy for you."

Anna stared at him. "Because you think my dad was the thief."

"If the clues fit . . ."

"My dad wouldn't steal a thing."

"Really? Have you checked out his police record?"

Her dad had a police record? Apparently, she'd let emotion cloud her judgment from the moment she'd found the coin four days ago, because if she'd taken this more seriously, researching her dad would've been one of the first things she'd have done.

Her annoying guest let out a low laugh. "And you call yourself an investigator?"

Her spine snapped ramrod straight. "How do you know it's not your aunt frauding you, probably along with her insurance company?" she asked.

"She didn't get a payout."

"Gee, that doesn't sound suspicious at all. Did you know that fifteen percent of all claims are fraudulent?"

"Which means eighty-five percent aren't," he said. "And she didn't get a payout because she wasn't insured. Don't get me started," he muttered at her look of shock. "I had no idea she didn't have any of it covered. She's . . . not well."

Unwanted sympathy for him filled Anna. "I'm sorry. Have you been looking for her things from the beginning?"

"From the beginning, yes. But that didn't last long because the trail went cold."

Until he'd seen her interview . . . She eyed the two hundred bucks on her desk. Starting her own business had been massively expensive. Could she really afford to turn down his business, especially when she knew she could prove her dad's innocence? "You seriously want to hire me?"

He gave her a small smile. "Keep your friends close . . ."

"And your enemies closer." She shook her head at him. "No, thank you. One, working in tandem with a client is dangerous. Two, it'll spook whoever I try to talk to. And three, it's not allowed anyway."

That got her an almost genuine smile. "Are any of those things even true?"

"Sure," she said. "Which one do you like?"

He just shook his head.

"Seriously," she said. "I work alone."

A throat cleared from the doorway. Mari. Anna made a point of looking at the time.

Mari strolled in unapologetically, dropping a bag that smelled like the breakfast burritos she loved so much on Anna's desk, and Anna immediately changed her irritation at Mari's tardiness to gratefulness.

"I assume you forgot to eat again," Mari said, and then eyed their guest. "Hello. I'm Mari, Anna's right hand. And sometimes her left hand too."

Owen smiled at her, flashing white teeth and a dead sexy smile. "Owen Harris. New client."

"Well then . . ." Mari opened a second bag and held it out.

Owen peered in and then removed a cinnamon roll. "Our partnership is off to a good start."

"This is no partnership!" Anna gave Mari a look that had her retreating down the hall to her own office. When the door shut, Anna eyed the man standing before her, casually eating his cinnamon roll. "Before I get started on this . . . *situation*," she said, "is there anything else I should know?"

He studied her a moment while he chewed and swallowed, then licked sugar off his thumb. "You've seen the news and the online stories about your dad being a cat burglar back in the day."

"Baseless rumors."

"Not all of them. I've asked around. The only thing that kept your dad out of jail at the time of the theft was that all the evidence against him was circumstantial."

She drew a deep breath. If there was one thing she hated, it was being a step behind. She currently felt a *mile* behind, which she'd rectify immediately—soon as she got rid of him. "Anything else?"

He shrugged. "Depends on if we're working together or against each other."

"No matter how things go, whatever I find, I'll be honest," she said. "I play by the rules."

That got her a low laugh. "Shame."

She also couldn't be swayed by a good-looking guy, no matter how much her body wanted to be. "I'll be in touch, Mr. Harris."

"Owen. And I realize you're in the position of having something to prove, but don't let that worry you."

She gave a rough laugh. "I don't have to prove anything to you."

"According to everything I've read since you were photographed with the coin, you've got something to prove to a whole bunch of people. And while we're on the subject, I'm going to need the coin back."

"If it turns out that you're right, and the coin we found in my father's belongings is indeed your great-aunt's, that will be no problem."

He looked at her for a long beat. "You expect me to believe you'll be honest, no matter what you find?"

She bristled. "I give every case 110 percent. But I'm telling you right now, my dad was no thief."

He gave a single nod. "I'll expect to hear from you within a few days."

"Or?"

"Or I'll be forced to involve the authorities."

She sent him a glacial stare to cover her unease. "Don't let the door hit you in the ass on your way out, Mr. Harris."

He slid her another smile, and she watched as the man's very fine denim-covered ass walked out the door.

Not ten seconds later, Candy stuck her head in the door. "Holy hot guy," she said. "Good for you."

"It's not like that."

"Girl, you're due. You're past due. Make it 'like that.'"

True story on being past due. She was so far past due, her parts were in danger of expiring. "I hear your phone ringing."

"Shit." Candy vanished.

Anna pulled out her cell phone and called one of her oldest friends, Nikki Hernandez.

"Officer Hernandez."

"Nikki, it's me. Can you look up something?"

"Hey, *chica*. And sure, but it'll cost you. Those drinks you owe me? Top shelf."

"Deal. Can you tell me if Louis Moore has any sort of record?"

There was a beat of silence. "You mean your dad? You want me to look up your dad? Is this about all the articles on the coin?"

"Seriously?" Anna asked. "How many people actually watch the news?"

Nikki didn't answer, but Anna could hear her fingers clicking on a keyboard and tried to be patient. It was nothing, she told herself. Nothing. But then she heard Nikki suck in a breath. A big tell from someone who had the best poker face of anyone Anna knew. "What? What did you find?"

Nikki hesitated. Never a good sign. "Are you *sure* you want to go down this road?"

Of course Anna wasn't sure. "I'm already on this road. Just tell me."

"When he was eighteen, he had a record for petty theft and possession of stolen property. And several times after that, in the following few years, he was suspected of more, but no further convictions."

Anna sank to her chair. "You're positive?"

"I'm looking right at the records. I'm so sorry, *chica*."

"Maybe it was all just wrong place at the wrong time?"

"I mean . . . maybe."

Anna heard the doubt. "But you don't think so."

"Once, yes. But several times?"

*Dad, what the hell?*

"Uh-oh."

Anna stilled. "Uh-oh what?"

"I've accessed the original police report on the coin theft. Looks like your dad was an early suspect then too but was never charged due to lack of evidence."

"Okay." Anna set her forehead to her desk and gulped air. Okay, not being charged was good. "You knew him," she finally said. "Can you see him doing something like this?"

"No. No way."

Anna let out a breath and hoped like hell they were both right, for Wendy's sake. "Thanks." When she disconnected, she looked up, startled to find Owen Harris leaning against her doorjamb, arms crossed. Shit. She mustered a cool expression. "Déjà vu."

"I realized I forgot to leave you my business card," he said.

"*Or* you wanted to overhear what I did next after you left."

"A suspicious thing, aren't you." Pushing off the doorjamb, he set his card on her desk. "I'll talk to you soon."

"Right. Because otherwise you'll call the cops on me."

His gaze met hers. "I don't think I'll have to."

"No? And why is that?"

"Because if you play by the rules, you're also the type to do the right thing. I'll be seeing you, Anna."

*Not if I see you first . . .*

When he was gone, she went back to her desk and sat, then found Mari standing there watching her. "What is this, Annoy Anna Day?"

"Been a long time since I've seen Ms. Cool and Collected get off on the wrong foot with someone. Or be interested in a guy."

"Not my finest moment," Anna admitted. "And I'm *not* interested in him."

"Uh-huh."

"Do you really have nothing better to do right now?"

Mari grinned. "I've got lots to do. But this is way more fun."

Anna picked up Owen's card, which read: *Tahoe Adventures, Owen Harris, co-owner.* So he played for a living. Why did that not surprise her? "Run him, see what you can drum up."

"So is he really a client?"

"For now. Apparently there are a whole bunch more missing coins like the one I found, plus a necklace, all of it worth a fortune, and he seems to believe I have it all hidden somewhere. We need to disabuse him of that notion."

Mari smiled. "And here I thought he was going to just be someone fun to tease you about. But now there's a romantic connection *and* a mystery. Fun day."

Anna shook her head and began searching through her drawers for some Advil. She looked up to find Mari still smiling at her. "You're still standing here why?"

"Right. On it!"

# CHAPTER 3

Owen Harris had long ago learned how to deal with stress and worry—with an adrenaline rush. It was dawn, and today's sunrise stress relief consisted of kitesurfing on five-to-six-foot swells on Tahoe beneath a turbulent sky, courtesy of an incoming summer storm.

Nothing better, in his opinion, and the icing on the cake: he was actually getting paid for this. The clients with him were pro surfers vacationing in the area and had hired him as their guide. Their only requirement had been a high level of difficulty so they'd be challenged.

Owen's specialty.

With the high winds at his back, the sun on his face, the spray of his wake keeping him slightly chilled and on his toes, life didn't get much better. Funny thing about adventuring: concentrating on keeping everyone around him safe usually cleared his head of everything else.

Usually.

But the news report he'd caught three days ago now, the one that showed an auburn-haired, brown-eyed beauty holding a small gold coin while speaking to a reporter, had shocked him.

Yesterday he'd walked into that woman's office with one thing on his mind—getting justice for the only family member he had left, his great-aunt Ruby, who desperately needed a win. If he could just get back what was rightfully hers, maybe she'd smile her smile of old.

Hell, maybe he needed that even more than she did.

But instead of justice, the mystery of his aunt's missing things had deepened, and he'd found an unexpected complication that went by the name Anna Moore. She hadn't been inclined to help him until he'd forced her hand, something he hadn't enjoyed.

But he meant business on this.

His great-aunt had saved his life on more than one level, and he intended to return the favor. A strong gust of wind hit his group just as they all touched down on the water again, followed by a massive swell coming right at them. "Point your board directly at the swell at ninety degrees," he called out, holding back, making sure everyone got over it before he followed.

His clients whooped and hollered their delight, and he relaxed, knowing they could handle themselves. When they made their way back to shore thirty minutes later, he saw them off and turned to his welcome committee.

Turbo, either a seventy-five-pound cotton ball or his ridiculously fluffy Samoyed, stood waiting for him on shore, his tail going so fast it created its own weather system. He was leashed to a picnic table because the last time Owen had left him loose, he'd jumped into another surfer's open vehicle and stolen a burger right out of the guy's hands.

Owen unhooked him, and Turbo took a flying leap. Quickly

spreading his feet, Owen bent his knees for what was incoming, catching the ecstatic wiggle-butt in midair. "Thought we agreed no more jumping."

Unrepentant, his dog licked his face. With a laugh, Owen set him down and Turbo instantly began running in circles, turbo-charged.

Hence his name.

"Okay, okay, you're a good boy. Come on, we gotta get back to work."

White all over except for his coal black eyes, nose, and lips, Turbo had a smile that went from ear to ear and could be seen for miles as he leaned against Owen's legs and stared up at him with his entire doggy heart, which melted Owen's. They'd rescued each other, and he never took that for granted. Pulling on his T-shirt, he patted his thigh. "Seriously. Let's go."

Turbo for sure heard him, but he still chose to bolt toward the water.

"Seriously?" Owen had taken him to doggy training school. Twice. So he knew he wasn't supposed to reward bad behavior, but there was really only one way to Turbo's heart—through his stomach. "If you come right now, I'll give you a treat when we get there."

Turbo stopped so fast he looked like a cartoon cat on a slippery surface as he attempted to turn around. But it was too late. His speed had all four paws coming out from beneath him and he skidded on his butt about ten feet. But in zero-point-five seconds, he'd corrected course and was racing right at Owen, taking him out with a flying tackle.

Owen lay flat on his back, laughing under Turbo's weight. "Sit, you big oaf."

So Turbo sat. Right on top of him.

Shaking his head, Owen pushed him off and stood. "Come on, let's go."

Turbo began trotting in the direction of the building that housed Tahoe Adventures, the business he ran with his best friend, Ky Ortega. At the long set of stairs leading from the beach up to street level, Turbo stopped short and sat abruptly—not out of a sense of obedience, but because he was terrorized by stairs, among other things. "Up you go."

Turbo leapt into his arms, and Owen climbed the stairs for them both. Five minutes later, they walked into their warehouse.

Sami, Owen's office manager, stood waiting for him, arms crossed, eyes narrowed. The first thing she did was offer Turbo a dog biscuit, which the dog swallowed whole. Then he immediately sat, tail wagging, expecting another.

"Not yet. You have to earn another."

Turbo sighed and plopped down for a nap.

Sami turned to Owen. "Glad to see you're not dead. Are you going to pretend you didn't see the wind warning I sent you?"

"Storm swells," he said. "You expect me to pass that up?"

"I expect you to live. I like my paychecks." She shook her head. "You know, for someone so afraid of being helpless or beholden to anyone, dying doesn't seem to bother you."

That she nailed his personal fears with perfection only had him shrugging. He'd exorcized his demons a long time ago. Mostly, anyway. "Don't worry, no plans on dying any time soon."

"Uh-huh. This." Sami waggled a finger between them. "*This* is why we're no longer together. You pretend you're just a simple thrill seeker with no depth, playing life fast and loose. You never let anyone have your important pieces, never promising anything more than the bare minimum. You, Owen Harris, gave me my first gray hair."

"Good thing we're not together anymore then," he said easily. "And it's been four years, you can't possibly still be mad at me. Besides, you work here now, and you get to boss me around. You like that. Much better than dating someone who is—what did you call me back then?—emotionally unavailable."

Sami snorted. "I think I called you a commitment-phobe, but sure, let's go with stupid."

He laughed, and she rolled her eyes before handing him an iPad with a list of his messages. He thumbed through them, stopping at the one from his aunt's caregiver, which read: *We made it to bingo today and she loved it!*

Owen nearly sagged in relief. Back in the day, Ruby had been known as the first lady of Sunrise Cove. She'd been eighteen when she'd become the town's first annual Summer Parade Queen. And then the second. And the third. She'd been known for being vibrant and charismatic.

She'd been those things all her life, until dementia had begun to dull her senses, playing havoc with her memories. It'd been weeks since she'd felt up to her beloved bingo.

Sami smiled. "I thought you'd like that one." She gestured to their conference room. "Staff meeting. The guys are waiting on you."

He headed in. Ky had just entered as well. Braden and Antonio, their employees, were already seated. Owen started their weekly meeting but stopped halfway through going over the upcoming schedule. Braden was totally engrossed in creating a paper airplane. He'd been making them and launching them at Antonio.

Antonio had a small pile of rubber bands in front of him, which he'd been using to steadily shoot down the airplanes.

Ky was the only one paying attention to Owen's spiel, looking relaxed, his hands crossed over his chest in a thoughtful position, his eyes covered with dark shades. Owen was pretty sure his partner was actually sleeping.

By now, Braden had given up on the airplanes and was in a full-out rubber band war with Antonio. No planes or rubber bands had come Owen's way.

Ky still hadn't moved.

Owen sighed. "Gentlemen, if we get through this, breakfast is on me."

A truce was hastily declared and Ky's head swiveled as he pushed his sunglasses to the top of his head. Okay, not asleep. Sometimes it was hard to tell. The rest of the meeting went fast after that, and he sent Braden and Antonio out to pick up breakfast on his dime.

When they were alone, Ky looked at Owen. They considered themselves brothers, if not by blood then by spirit. They were each other's ride-or-dies, so when Ky looked serious, as he did now, Owen knew something was on his mind.

"You see the paper?" Ky asked.

"I didn't know people still read the newspaper, Grandpa."

Ky flipped him the bird, then tossed him the local paper.

Owen looked down at the beautiful Anna Moore staring mutinously into the camera lens. "Is this your version of Tinder? Because I tend to like them sweet and affable."

Ky snorted. "As if."

"I already read this and went to see her."

"And?"

"And she insists her father didn't steal anything. I'm paying her to look into the matter and come up with proof."

"What if she comes up with proof her father is guilty as hell?" Ky asked. "You really think she's going to admit it?"

Owen could still remember Anna's certainty about Louis

Moore's innocence. She'd stood toe to toe with him, clearly believing it with her entire being, and he had to give her credit.
She clearly didn't scare easily.

   *I give every case 110 percent. But I'm telling you right now, my
dad was no thief.*

   Something in her tough-girl, prideful stance and in her sharp
but honest eyes had made him want to believe her. Want to, but
he couldn't. Not when she had his great-aunt's coin in her possession with no explanation.

# CHAPTER 4

To say Wendy felt ready for motherhood would be like saying she was ready to jump off the side of a mountain and hang glide her way down.

Without the hang glider.

On good days, she had her doubts on being able to handle becoming a mom. After all, she'd lost hers at age six. But on the other hand, she'd always dreamed of having her own children.

Just not all of them at the same time.

On the bad days, when her back and legs ached relentlessly and she had to pee every twenty minutes, she knew she was in over her head. Normally when she felt that way, she'd hit up her favorite bakery or coffee shop. But not only couldn't she drive because her belly pressed up against her steering wheel, she also had two watchdogs named Hayden and Anna.

One of the babies kicked her in the ribs. "Behave, Snap," she murmured, rubbing her hands over her belly. Another squirmed its way over to her bladder and sat on it. "Torturing me already, Crackle? And where's Pop—" Before she could even finish the sentence, Pop attempted a somersault and failed because there was only so much room to go around.

Feeling them shift around inside her gave her a sense of peace she'd never known she could have. After a decade, she'd come to terms with the fact that motherhood wasn't going to happen for her, and she'd done her best to be okay with that. She and Hayden had even celebrated it with a drunken night in their hot tub.

A few weeks later she'd gone for her annual at her OB-GYN's and had learned she was pregnant. They'd later checked for a heartbeat.

And had heard three.

*Three.*

She'd looked at Hayden in sheer panic, but here was the thing about having a partner who didn't have anxiety: he'd sat there next to her at the doc's, holding her hand, cool and calm and happy.

Not freaked out at all.

Not even when, a few weeks earlier, thanks to her off-the-charts blood pressure—and the fact that she was carrying an entire litter—her doc had made her go on maternity leave from teaching and put her on a low-fat, low-sodium, low-sugar diet *and* bed rest.

Staying home was the right thing to do, but damn. She missed teaching middle schoolers science. She missed their field excursions to take in all that Tahoe had to offer in the way of adventures and science. She'd been the ski coach too, and she missed all of it so much more than she'd expected.

Unlike ice cream, which she missed *exactly* as much as she'd expected. With a sigh, she stroked Jennifur, her cat. Jennifur's sister was Clawdia, Anna's cat. Clawdia was sweet and chunky and lazy and slept twenty hours a day. Not Jennifur. Nope, her favorite pastimes involved pooping in Wendy's shoes, yakking in the middle of the night, and leaving half-eaten spiders on Wendy's favorite chair.

And she wouldn't change a single strand of fur on her not-sweet head.

"Hey, babe, I'm home!" Hayden yelled as he came through the front door.

"Hey, babe, I'm home too!" Anna yelled, smart-ass as always. It was her sister's love language.

"We brought food!"

*Food!* Since Wendy was allowed to get up to walk a few laps around the house and also to eat, she made her way downstairs and practically attacked her sister for the bags of—she peeked into the bags—yes! Italian.

"Remember that time when we were little?" Anna asked, handing her a plate. "And our cat Blackie got pregnant? She got so hungry she bit you when you were just trying to feed her."

Wendy stopped eating a piece of garlic bread to go brows up. "Are you comparing me to a cat?"

"Well, if the hiss fits . . ."

"Har-har. Give me the update."

"On what?"

"On keeping Dad's name in good standing, what do you mean on what?" This whole asking Anna to look into the coin had started out as a way for Wendy to . . . *encourage* her sister to take on an adventure like she always had in the old days. But it'd shockingly turned into something very real. And now saving their dad's reputation was all she could think about. Well, that and peeing.

Anna waved a breadstick. "I'm still working on it."

"The new library building," Wendy said. "The last thing he donated before he died is finally having its opening ceremony in two weeks, and—"

"And you're worried they'll take Dad's name off the building. Yes, Wendy, I know. Mostly because you've reminded me every single day. I'm on it."

Wendy stared at her. "What aren't you telling me?"

Anna picked up her water bottle and drank. And drank.

"Oh my God, it's that bad?"

Anna finished the entire bottle and set it down. "I'm just going to get another—"

"No more water for you until you tell me whatever it is you're afraid to tell me!"

Anna sighed and looked at Hayden.

He nodded.

Anna met Wendy's gaze. "Dad's got a record."

"Please tell me you're talking about music."

Anna just looked at her, and Wendy's stomach, already sitting low thanks to the babies, sank even further.

"It was petty theft, a very long time ago," Anna said. "Even before he met Mom. He was only eighteen."

"And?"

"And . . . there were several other times he was considered a suspect on a robbery, but nothing stuck."

"And . . . ?"

Anna looked pained. "And apparently the coin he had was part of a set, a really rare set, that was stolen ten years ago along with a necklace called the Ruby Red. Dad was one of five suspects. None of them were ever charged, there wasn't enough evidence."

Wendy's mind raced, and she came to the only conclusion

she could. "There wasn't evidence because he didn't do it. He wouldn't. And my super smart sister's going to prove it."

"I am." Anna reached out and took Wendy's hand, which Wendy thought incredibly sweet until she realized her sister was taking her pulse.

"You're breathless," Anna said.

"Yes, because it's hard work growing babies. Why are you wearing threadbare jeans with holes in the knees and an unflattering gray blazer, which is a terrible color for you?"

"Is it also hard work being nice?"

Wendy stuffed a big bite of spaghetti into her mouth so she wouldn't rise to the bait. Growing up with a single dad who'd worked all the time had been hard. She hadn't always gotten to live the way she'd wanted. So when she'd planned out her adult life, she'd purposely done only things she'd wanted to do. Teach. Ski. Enjoy her husband.

And . . . poke at her sister, because she wanted to see Anna happy too. Was that so bad? "I'm sorry, but—"

Anna pointed her fork at her. "When you add a 'but' onto the back of an apology, you've negated said apology."

Wendy looked at Hayden.

"Both of you need to stop looking at me," he said, eating casual-as-you-please. "I'm not stupid enough to get in the middle of you two."

"You're supposed to side with your wife."

"One would think," he said. "But the last time I did that, you yelled at me for getting in the middle."

"Well, now I'm going to yell at you for not being on my side."

Hayden flashed her a sexy smile. "I'm always on your side."

"Ugh, you two are sickening." Anna stood and stretched. "And for that reason, I'm out."

"What's your hurry?" Wendy looked her over. "I know you don't have a hot date."

"Gee, thanks, Mom."

"Stop waiting for Prince Charming. Get up and find him. The poor idiot might be stuck in a tree or something."

"Trust me, I don't want a Prince Charming. And you need to stay out of my dating life."

Hayden stood up. "You know what? Let's not talk. Let's watch a show."

Anna stopped and narrowed her eyes, because heaven forbid she actually ever *wanted* to stay. "What show?"

"*Survivor*," Wendy said, at the same time Anna said, "*Stranger Things*."

Hayden shook his head. "I'm playing my veto card. I get to pick. It's going to be *Law & Order*, and we'll watch in peace and harmony."

"Only if you're making popcorn," Anna said.

"Done," he said.

Wendy knew the Moore sisters had just both been played, but her husband didn't give her the opportunity to call him out on it. He pulled her out of her chair, and oh how she hated that she needed help, and then sweetly tucked her in on the couch with her favorite throw blanket and hot tea. Decaffeinated, ugh.

Then they all sat through two episodes of *Law & Order*, during which she pretended to fall asleep. Sure enough, ten minutes later, Hayden and Anna sneaked out of the room.

Good thing she knew *exactly* what they were up to, and she wasn't going to ignore it any longer. Extremely pissy, she struggled out of the blanket and off the couch. Sure, she had to roll to her side and onto the floor, then struggle to her feet on her own, but she was motivated because she had two people to yell at. She waddled down the hallway, quietly peered into the nursery, then yelled "aha!" at them from the doorway.

They jumped guiltily.

Wendy crossed her arms to glare at them. It was her new favorite stance because her belly was so big she could rest her arms on it, and she needed all the resting she could get. "Explain yourselves."

Hayden came forward and brushed a kiss to her temple. "We wanted to surprise you."

When Wendy had first gotten pregnant, she'd purchased everything she might need for a baby. But then it turned out she had *three* babies making themselves at home inside her, so they'd had to order two more of everything. The house was now completely overrun with baby stuff.

She truly had zero regrets. What she did have was panic because three! *Three* babies and only *two* boobs! Taking a deep breath, she took in the room. Two of the cribs had been put together, and the third seemed to be about halfway finished. "I wanted to do this."

"I understand." Hayden was gently leading her toward the recliner in the corner, easing her down. Dropping to his knees, he lifted her shirt to kiss her belly and a Cheeto fell out.

He raised a brow.

"I have no idea how that got there," she claimed.

"Uh-huh." He hit the button on the side of the recliner to raise her feet. "You can boss us around from here." He handed her a tall mug he'd clearly had waiting for her.

She eyed it suspiciously. "It's green. Why is my ice cream green?"

"Because it's not ice cream. It's a smoothie. Peach mango."

"Peach mango isn't green."

His eyes were laughing, but he was a very smart man and didn't so much as break a smile. "It's got just a touch of a veggie. For the babies."

Damn, every time he said "for the babies," she melted and he knew it. "It better not be kale."

"Nope. Not kale." He nudged the straw toward her mouth.

She took an obligatory sip and blinked.

"Good, right?"

*More like amazing* . . . "Can you get pregnant while pregnant?" she asked. "Asking for a friend."

He smiled. "You like it."

"I mean, could I have used a little more actual ice cream in my non-ice-cream? Sure. But it's really good." She took another sip and eyed the stack of car seats in a corner, still in their boxes. Did her back seat even fit three car seats? "I think we're going to need a new car," she whispered.

Hayden nodded. "On it. You know how all year you've been making me put five bucks into the 'find jar' every time I ask you where something is that I can't locate?" He smiled. "I've almost got enough to buy you a new car."

Wendy had to laugh. "I owe you."

He smiled. "I like the sound of that."

"Oh my God." Anna covered her ears. "You guys are gross. I gotta go."

"You'll tell me everything as you learn it?" Wendy asked.

"Yep."

Wendy stared at her. "You just blinked twice in a row really fast."

"So?"

"So, that's your tell." Wendy pointed at her. "So tell!"

Anna was heading to the door. "I'm going home to hit the sack. Try not to get too crazy—"

"Anna Michelle Moore, if you don't stop right there, I'm coming with."

"If I tell you, will you stay in that chair?"

"Yes." Well, maybe. But also, maybe not.

"Fine. The Ruby Red belonged to a local woman whose grandnephew came to see me. His name is Owen Harris, and he thinks Dad has the rest of the coins and the necklace. If I don't produce said coins and necklace, he's going to involve the authorities."

The words cleared Wendy's brain of everything except pure shock. "Oh my God."

"I know, right? What an asshole."

"I mean oh my God, you just blinked twice again. You like him!"

"No, I don't."

"Do too."

Anna shook her head. "You couldn't be more wrong. He runs a local adventure company."

Wendy took that in, as well as all that Anna wasn't saying. She knew her sister had been badly burned by two men in her past, men who'd been wild bad boys. Adventure seekers. "Well, you've always been attracted to tall, hot, emotionally unavailable red flags."

"Wendy," Hayden said quietly.

"I'm not trying to rub it in her face!" She looked at Anna. "It's just that sometimes red flags can turn out to be the best thing to ever happen to a person." She winked at her husband, who was evidence of that very fact.

He smiled.

Anna just stared at her. "Okay, you've lost your mind."

"No, it's the universe—"

"If you say the universe has sent me a sign, so help me—"

"Why would I bother?" Wendy asked, tossing up her hands. "Whenever I tell you that, you're like, 'Okay, but I think I'll wait for a signier sign.'"

"I'm going now," Anna said.

"So you'll keep at it? If for no other reason than to stop this Owen Harris from involving the police?"

"Yes, even though Dad wouldn't want us to. He'd hate this, Wen. And anyway, I have no idea where to go with it from here."

"You'll figure it out. You're the investigator."

Anna shook her head. "Why do people keep saying that?"

Wendy was surprised at this question. "Uh, because you're extremely competent and always know what you're doing?"

"I *never* know what I'm doing."

Wendy smiled. "Well, if that's true, then I'll help you."

"No," Hayden said.

She crooked her finger at him.

After a brief pause, he walked warily her way.

"I love you," she whispered, and tugged on him until he leaned over her so she could kiss him. "And I'll sit the whole time."

"Love you too," Hayden said. "But still no."

But Wendy was already trying to stuff her feet back into her laceless tennis shoes, the task made impossible by the fact that she couldn't see her feet. "Can you help me get my shoes on? Wait—" She looked up at Hayden. "Am I wearing pants?"

"Yes." He waggled a brow. "But we can rectify that."

She pointed at him. "That's how I got into this trouble in the first place."

Anna covered her ears. "Stop talking! I'm begging you! Also, it's ten thirty at night, I'm not taking you anywhere."

Wendy pulled out her phone, the screen a little streaked from the popcorn she'd sneaked earlier. Swiping it on her already stained shirt, she got to work.

"What are you doing?" Anna asked suspiciously.

"Adding some more spy gear to the GoPro."

"What are we, MI5?"

"I was thinking more Nancy Drew."

"Nancy Drew didn't have a partner, she was a solo act."

Wendy shrugged. "Then let's go with the Hardy Boys. Also, *I'm* hiring you as well."

"Yeah? Because Owen gave me two hundred bucks as a deposit." Anna held out her hand.

"I'll owe you. And not only that, you need to ignore all your usual rules on this one, A. Go off script, do whatever you have to in order to get us the answers we need. And hey, maybe this Owen might be of some help."

"No, he won't. We're on opposite sides on this. And honestly, he's sharp, Wen. He's going to be a formidable foe."

Wendy hated that Anna still doubted herself. She blamed the asshole exes. After apparently coming to the conclusion that her wild-child impulses had led her down a path she no longer wanted to go, Anna had walled herself off and created some internal Excel sheet, where she kept some known-only-to-herself list of the attributes a guy needed in order to get past her guard.

A list no man could live up to, as if by collecting rules the way other women collected jewelry, she couldn't get hurt again.

The doorbell rang, and Wendy smiled.

"I know that smile," Anna said, eyes narrowed. "It's your I've-done-something-to-interfere-in-Anna's-life smile."

"I don't know what you're talking about."

"You smiled just like that right before you set me up on an online dating site, using an old pic of me paddleboarding as my profile photo, then did a whole bunch of swiping left."

"You mean right," Wendy said. "You swipe right to like."

"Whatever."

"And hey, you got some nice dates out of the deal."

"Except I don't paddleboard anymore, and all those dates expected me to put out because the app was a *hookup* app."

Wendy winced. "Okay, that was my bad. But this is nothing like that. The doorbell was just to announce my package arriving. Or should I say your package. It's the GoPro I ordered the other day. Now you can bring me along on every step of this investigation."

Anna looked at Hayden. "She's out of control."

"I'm hoping it's temporary," Hayden said.

"Wow." Wendy pointed at her husband. "I'm carrying forty-five pounds of Heart, Diamond, and Spade for you."

"No," he said calmly.

"Willow, Maple, and Birch?"

"We aren't naming our girls after trees *or* card suits."

She shrugged, knowing that after she pushed them out of her hoo-ha, he'd undoubtedly give in to whatever names she wanted, and she could tell by the look on his face that he knew it too. Wendy jabbed her finger at her sister. "And you. Don't you judge me until you've flown a mile on my broom."

"Ha-ha," Anna said. "Also, Rachel, Monica, and Phoebe are maybe fifteen pounds total. The rest of the pounds are your contraband foods."

"Well excuse me for needing sustenance."

Anna laughed and kissed her sister on the cheek. "I'm out. Try to relax and rest, okay?"

"No promises." Wendy hugged Anna tight. "And don't you dare forget the package on the doorstep on your way out."

# CHAPTER 5

The next morning after an early client meeting, Anna stood in line at the local coffee shop, desperate for a hit of caffeine, ignoring the steady buzzing of incoming texts from her phone in her pocket. When she finally picked up her order, she inhaled deeply. Damn. No wonder coffee was so confident despite being nothing more than a wet bean, because what other drink whispered in your ear every morning, "I'm worth your last five bucks and you need me, bitch"?

She drank until the caffeine hit before facing her angry phone.

**WENDY:** YOU LEFT THE GOPRO ON MY PORCH LAST NIGHT.

**WENDY:** Hello?

**WENDY:** You can run but you can't hide.

**ANNA:** Actually, I can, because you're as big as a house and can't put on your own shoes.

**WENDY:** Wow. You need more caffeine.

**ANNA:** No, I need to still be asleep. This getting out of bed every day feels excessive.

Shoving her phone away, she drank some more. Only when she felt the anxiety go down a notch did she drive toward the lake. The day was glorious, the sky so blue and pure, the mountains showing off their summer greenery, that it could've been a painting. She parked in front of a large warehouse with a sign that read: TAHOE ADVENTURES.

This wasn't going to go well, but what the hell. She got out of her car for the sole reason that if it was a choice between dealing with Owen or the police, she chose Owen. Last night while staring at her ceiling, she'd come to some conclusions, one of them being that she needed to involve Owen to some degree so he didn't feel the need to bring in the authorities. One disaster at a time.

Letting herself inside the building, she took in the organized chaos that included racks and racks of outdoor adventure equipment, the entire place looking like a grown-up toy box.

A pretty woman in camo capris and a black tank top with the Tahoe Adventures logo over a breast and a name tag that read *Sami* came up to her. "Good morning. How can I help you?"

"I'm looking for Owen Harris."

Sami took in Anna's business clothes. "You're going to have to get in line."

"It's not like that." She'd worn a pencil skirt and a fitted silky top to her meeting. Plus she'd actually put on mascara and had blown the wild waves out of her hair. All of which she'd done for her meeting and *not* for Owen, not even a little bit.

Okay, maybe it had been a little bit for Owen, but only to up her intimidation factor, of course. "This is business."

That got her a smile. "Yeah, that's how it started for me too."

Oh great. So this was Owen's girlfriend. Or wife. Or whatever. It didn't matter. "Don't worry, he's not my type."

"Honey," Sami said on a laugh, "Owen's *everyone's* type." At whatever she saw on Anna's face, she laughed again. "Listen, I keep the man's schedule, so I know you're not on it, which means it isn't business related at all."

Anna opened her mouth just as something hit her in the back of the head. Turning, she found a paper airplane lying at her feet, a poorly constructed one at that. Bending, she scooped it up and made an adjustment.

"Are you serious?" Sami asked someone.

Anna looked up and found a guy across the room smiling at her ruefully. "I'm so sorry," he said, coming closer. "It keeps dipping down too soon. I was aiming for Sami."

"Wow," Sami said.

Ignoring her, the man stuck out his hand to Anna. "Ky Ortega."

"Anna Moore."

"She's here to see Owen," Sami said.

"Ah." Ky nodded. "You're the Anna Moore who found Great-Aunt Ruby's coin."

"No one's proven that to me," she said.

Ky grinned. "You're going to be good for him."

Anna shook her head. "I'm actually pretty sure I'm going to be bad for him."

At this, Ky laughed, at what exactly, Anna had no idea, but Sami was looking amused as well. She handed Ky back the paper airplane. "You're folding the nose wrong. I fixed it."

Ky tossed the plane, and it soared the entire length of the large room. He smiled at her. "Do me a favor."

"I don't do favors for strangers."

"Oh, trust me, we're not going to be strangers. Not if you and Owen are on a case together. I'm hoping you can keep his head out of his own ass."

"Ignore him," Sami said. "Owen's out on the lake with some clients but should be done any minute. If you meet him out on the beach, you'll have a few minutes before his next client shows. The boys are busy today."

Which was how Anna found herself walking down the beach in high heels. She had no idea what Ky had meant about keeping Owen's head out of his own ass, but she really hoped he was kidding. She wasn't the most qualified person to keep someone's head out of their own ass. Hell, she couldn't even do it for herself.

It was warm and sunny, and she found herself taking a deep breath of pine and clean, fresh water, and when she let it out, she realized her shoulders had been up at her ears. The beach was a reminder of happier times, like when her dad had brought her and Wendy here, where they'd run wild and free, completely unaware of his grief and single-parent problems. He'd been so good to them. So kind and gentle and accepting of anything they wanted to do—no matter how crazy. Actually, the crazier the better.

One of those hot poker pangs hit her square in the chest. He wouldn't want her to put herself on the line for him. He wouldn't. She actually started to turn back, but a dog attached by a leash to a picnic table strained to reach her with a whine and a tail wag. It was a big dog, all white fluff with sweet black eyes and a smiling mouth.

"Hey, baby," she said, and hunkered down. A mistake because the big guy came in for a hug and knocked her to her ass.

Laughing, she fought off his kisses. "Aw, you're a good boy, aren't you? Yes, such a good boy. Where's your owner?" She started to look around, her train of thought derailing as five guys walked out of the choppy water carrying paddleboards, looking like they belonged in a remake of *Baywatch*.

They all did some sort of complicated handshake, and then four of them walked off. The lone boarder stacked up the five boards by himself onto a rack with seeming zero effort, still drenched, board shorts molded to a very fit bod, barely clinging to his hips. He locked up the gear with a chain and padlock. Anna still hadn't yet managed to tear her gaze off him when he looked up and she nearly gasped.

Owen Harris.

Good thing this time she had on dark sunglasses so he couldn't see if she accidentally ogled him.

He raised a brow.

"Don't flatter yourself," she said, going for unaffected and not quite making it. "I was looking at the lake. The extremely choppy lake with at least four-foot swells."

"Six in spots," he said.

"So . . . you have a death wish then?"

He gave an almost smile. "Worried about me?"

"Not even a little." Liar, liar, pants on fire. "You seem pretty capable."

That got her a real-deal smile, and damn, it was a doozy. "I am," he said. "And I'm hoping you are too. Did you bring my great-aunt's possessions?"

"As I've said, I only have the one coin, and still no actual proof that it's your great-aunt's." The wind had kicked up, and she shivered. "How did you not freeze out there?"

He shrugged. "I run hot."

No kidding . . . "And your clients?"

"Local pro paddleboarders. I train them. They like the cold water, gives them an edge in competition."

"Your work looks a whole lot like play."

"It is." He looked her over. "You're a tad overdressed, but I'm happy to take you out there if you'd like."

Once upon a time, she might've taken him up on his offer, but she no longer let her impulsive side out to play. Bad things happened whenever she did. "Pass. I don't like to get wet."

He grinned.

"You know what I mean!"

The cutie-pie dog attached to the picnic table perked up when Owen moved toward him and let him loose.

"Yours?" she asked, unable to help but smile as the dog ran in circles around Owen for a minute, grinning from one fluffy ear to the other.

"Turbo," Owen said, "meet Anna."

Turbo never slowed, just widened his circle, getting closer and closer to her and then suddenly taking a flying leap right at her.

Owen moved so fast Anna never saw him coming as he slid between her and Turbo, catching the dog in midair before he could take her out.

"Nice save," she managed.

He set Turbo down. "Not my first rodeo."

Thinking of the woman back at his shop who might or might not be his girlfriend, she tore her gaze off his bare, and still wet, chest, then crouched low to Turbo. "Do you shake?"

Instead, Turbo licked her cheek, making her laugh.

"Interesting," Owen said. "You warm up faster to dogs than people."

She shrugged, petting Turbo, who melted to the ground and exposed his belly for a rubdown. "I'll push a person away until they give up, but I'll kiss a dog I just met right on the mouth."

His lips quirked, but he didn't smile. His eyes looked amused though. And also something else that had her having a few reactions she definitely shouldn't be having. "I've got some intel." Okay, that wasn't an outright lie, but "intel" was definitely a stretch. "You interested or not?"

"Definitely interested." He snatched a towel from the picnic table and began to dry off.

"So . . ." she said, averting her gaze, "I went through the box of my dad's things and came up empty-handed."

"Other than the one coin you already found, you mean."

Right. "Also, I'm going to go visit his ex-girlfriend in hopes that maybe she's still got some of his stuff."

He stilled, then met her gaze, his own serious. Intense, even, as if maybe he was assessing her for honesty. "How do you not know what she has?"

She drew a breath, uncomfortable to have to admit the truth. "Because I haven't seen her since he passed."

He ran the towel over his hair, making it stand up on end, which should've looked ridiculous but instead, somehow, had the opposite effect. "There's something else," she said.

Again he met her gaze.

"Clearly, we're both invested here. And even more clearly, you're determined to prove my dad guilty of this crime."

He said nothing, just watched her. He was a cool, calm one, she'd give him that. But she was also cool and calm. Or trying, anyway. "I'm going to suggest that we share all information."

"Because you'd rather I not publicly accuse your father of this crime."

She ground her back teeth until she could control herself. "Just as I'm assuming you'd rather me not reveal your aunt as one who maybe sold her own treasure and never revealed that fact to the authorities after claiming them stolen. Or maybe she just forgot where she put it."

Now it appeared to be Owen grinding his back teeth. "So . . . what? We're going to be equal partners on this?"

"For a lack of another, less friendly term, yes."

"One condition," he said. "*Honesty.*"

"As long as it goes both ways."

"Deal," he said. "And I'm coming with you to visit the girl-friend."

Normally she could think quickly on her feet, but her mind went blank on how to get out of this unexpected development. She must've made some sort of face, because he said, "Maybe it'll be fun."

"Oh, this will be *anything* other than fun."

He smiled. "We'll see." And then he scooped up Turbo—who had to weigh close to one hundred pounds—and carried his silly, adorable dog up the steep set of stairs to street level.

"He's afraid of stairs," Owen said to her unasked question, not even slightly breathless. "And grates. And cats."

"Cats?"

"Yeah. Before I got him from the humane society, he lived in a home where he was shut up in one room because they had a cat who didn't like dogs. So now, whenever he sees a cat, he cries. Or farts in self-defense."

Anna told her heart not to melt, at both the dog and the man, but unfortunately, her heart didn't take advice from her brain, never had.

# CHAPTER 6

This would no doubt go down as one of Owen's most stupid ideas of all time, teaming up with the daughter of the man who'd stolen valuables from his great-aunt.

*Keep your friends close and your enemies closer . . .*

After changing in his office, he came out to the front to find Ky and Braden in a paper airplane war against Sami and—to his utter shock—Ms. So-Uppity-She-Squeaked-When-She-Walked Anna Moore.

*And* the girls were winning.

Ky grinned at Owen. "She's as badass as you are."

Owen told himself he didn't give a shit what she was. "You about ready?" he asked her dryly.

"What about Turbo?" she asked of the dog sitting obediently—*obediently!*—at her feet.

"Sami can watch him."

Anna raised a brow. "Isn't your girlfriend going to mind dog-sitting?"

"Oh, I'm not his girlfriend," Sami said. "Not anymore anyway.

We didn't work. Mostly because he's a terrible boyfriend, but the good news is that he's a really great boss."

Anna didn't appear to know what to say to that. She was slightly taller than average, with a slender body that had enough curves to get Owen's full attention. The first time he'd seen her, her hair had been wavy and uncontrolled, giving her a just-rolled-out-of-bed look that was sexy as hell.

Today her hair was silky smooth and shiny, giving her a polished, elegant look—until she threw the paper airplane in her hands. It flew with such perfectly aimed speed and accuracy toward Braden's head that he had to hit the floor to avoid it.

"You should marry her," Ky said in a stage whisper.

Owen held the front door open for Anna, flipping off Ky behind her back. As they headed through the parking lot, her phone buzzed, which it'd been doing on and off since she'd first found him on the beach, a fact she appeared to be studiously ignoring.

When he caught her glancing at him, he nudged his chin toward the phone lighting up her pocket. "Do you need to get that?"

"Nope." She stopped beside a rather beat-up-looking Honda.

"If you'd rather," he said, "I could drive."

"I'm not getting into your car."

"You're right. Because it's not a car. It's a truck."

She rolled her eyes so hard he was surprised they didn't fall right out of their sockets. "You know what I mean," she said. "You could be an ax murderer for all I know. After all, you sneaked into my office and yelled at me."

"I never yell."

"It was a tone."

He could admit she had a point there. "Okay, how about

this. You send your wingman my license plate and phone number."

"Wing*woman*. And I will." She pulled out her phone and typed a text, glancing over at him, then typed some more. "Giving a description," she said. "Short, chunky, with a comb-over."

He laughed.

"Poor oral hygiene," she added.

"Do you want to know how I'd describe you?"

"Definitely not."

He was still smiling. "Sharp-tongued. Smart. Hot. Grumpy."

"Well, the last one is true anyway," she muttered.

It was *all* true and more, since he suspected that grumpiness hid a tender, soft heart that bled for the people she cared about. Since he liked breathing, he kept it to himself as he drove them out of the lot and toward the address she'd reluctantly given him.

And he thought *he* had trust issues. *Nothing* about this uptight woman in the tight skirt that was killing him slowly was his type, and yet . . . he found himself enjoying her. She went toe to toe with him and gave as good as she got. No one called him out on his shit—and yet she did, challenging him as well, something that hadn't happened in far too long. "What can you tell me about the girlfriend?" he asked.

"Sonya? They dated for ten years, up until he died."

He glanced over at her. She had the prettiest eyes he'd ever seen. Good thing he'd been deceived by pretty eyes before and could remain unmoved. "So how did you end up with the coin instead of her?"

"At the time he died, he lived with me."

That surprised him. "Not with Sonya?"

"He had MS, and her town house is two stories. My condo

is too, but he stayed in the downstairs bedroom. They dated for five years before his diagnosis. After, she visited him a lot, but I took care of him."

"By yourself? No siblings?"

"I've got an older sister," she said. "But Wendy was going through a rough patch at the time." She shrugged.

And damn. He tangled with the fast judgment he'd made about her and lost. "I'm sorry about your dad," he said quietly. "I know what it's like to take care of someone you love and watch them fade away."

He felt the weight of her stare. "Your dad too?" she finally asked.

"My mom. She died when I was a teenager. My great-aunt Ruby took me in. She's got dementia now, which is why I need to get the necklace back for her, before I lose her entirely. My hope is that it will bring her back some good memories."

She had her hand to her chest now, like she felt this to her core. "I'm so sorry about your aunt." She was quiet a moment. "I'm guessing that you can understand why this is so important to me and my sister as well. Family is everything, and my dad really was a good guy."

He knew she believed that, but she was either forgetting or ignoring that the guy had a record, not to mention the coin. Instead of reminding her and renewing their feud, he said, "Everyone makes mistakes. But that doesn't mean my great-aunt has to suffer for those mistakes."

She didn't say anything to this, but the line of her mouth tightened as he parked in front of the town house she'd directed him to.

"I'll be quick," she said, and got out of the truck.

Oh hell no. When he got out with her, she shot him a glare

that probably worked on most people, but not on him. He matched her brisk pace, impressed and a little turned on by how she could seriously move in those heels.

She said nothing, but it was crystal clear their momentary truce, if it'd ever been that, was over.

ANNA SLOWED HER pace the closer they got to Sonya's front door, knowing just how hard this was going to be. In fact, it had all the makings of a disaster.

Her phone rang. Shocker, it was her "wingwoman" Wendy.

"You refuse to use the GoPro," her sister said, "so at least put in your AirPods and slip the phone in your pocket so I can hear you. If you don't, I'll take a cab over there right now."

"Shit. *Fine.*" She pulled her AirPods from her purse and put them into her ears, then pocketed her phone. That was when she realized she had an audience of two to this nightmare—her sister, and the guy who appeared to never have met Anna's fun, old friend named Anxiety.

Even more annoying, Owen, who'd changed from those sexy board shorts and nothing else into faded jeans and a long-sleeved black shirt, looked like her own personal kryptonite. Shaking that off, she jogged up the three steps to the front porch and stared at the door, nerves hitting hard. She hadn't seen Sonya in a long time.

Her own doing. She'd never resented her dad getting a second chance at love, that had nothing to do with it. Neither did her deep-down secret wish to get a *first* chance for herself.

Someday.

Maybe . . .

"You going to knock?" Owen asked at her side.

*Okay, maybe not . . .*

"Omigod," Wendy said in her ear. "He's got a great voice, doesn't he?"

Anna sucked in a breath. Yes. Yes, he did. "No talking."

When Wendy didn't respond, she took that as a good sign and reached out to rap on the door—but it opened before she could.

"Anna, darling!" Sonya cried, arms already open.

Anna melted into the hug as all the memories she'd buried deep bombarded her. "I'm sorry it's been so long—"

"Shh, it's okay." Sonya gave her another warm squeeze, her scent bringing Anna back to being in the kitchen and burning cookies with her, the two of them laughing at Sonya's inability to bake, playing games, shopping, spending time long after it was cool to hang out at home.

"I've missed you," Sonya whispered.

Anna closed her eyes. "Same." She couldn't have said why she hadn't come sooner, except that in her experience, memories tended to be painful. "Thanks for seeing me."

"Don't start with that. I was so excited when you called, I made your favorite cookies."

Anna smiled. "Burned?"

"Ha! Okay, so I lied about making them." She eyed Anna's new sidekick. "Who's this?"

"Owen Harris. Owen, this is Sonya. Sonya, Owen."

"I hope you like store-bought cookies," Sonya said, shaking Owen's hand.

He gave an easy smile. "I like any cookies."

Sonya beamed at him, charmed. "And now I also hope that you're dating him, A."

Anna slid her gaze to Owen, who was looking pretty damned pleased with himself. "I'm not."

"She never did have good taste in men," Sonya said.

Owen lifted his hands, like *What are you gonna do, ya know?*

Sonya grinned at Anna. "You two have a vibe."

"Like we want to smother each other with a pillow?" Anna asked.

"Like you should get married." Sonya laughed at whatever look of horror Anna's face had creased into. "Okay, okay, I'm getting the feeling this isn't a social visit. What can I do for you two?"

Anna pulled out the coin and held it up.

Sonya's smile faded. "You better come inside."

Anna and Owen exchanged glances, and for the first time in her life, she dreaded stepping over the threshold. But step over it she did. Owen followed, respectfully quiet, though he did come up behind her with a light hand at her back, leaning in to whisper, "You okay?"

Her sarcastic "Like you care" was rude and uncalled for, but that was what she did when she was out of her comfort zone— sadly, not a rare occurrence. She used her razor-sharp tongue to keep people at a distance. It was her superpower.

His gaze held hers, and his warm hand at her back gave her a gentle pat, making her feel like a first-class jerk. They walked down a hallway that had pictures of her dad over the years lining the walls. She was there too. And Wendy. Lots of good memories, most of which caused a lump in her throat she couldn't swallow away.

She and Owen sat on the couch in the living room. Sonya took the chair on the other side of the coffee table. Leaning in, she held out her hand. Anna dropped the coin into her palm, watching as Sonya drew a deep breath and stared at it. "You're looking for information."

"No," Anna said, her mouth speaking without permission from her brain.

"Yes," Owen said. He looked at Anna with a calm, almost gentle expression. "We need information."

"I'm not sure I can help, but I'll try." Sonya looked at Anna. "I just need to know . . . are you sure?"

She knew Sonya would do only what Anna wanted, no matter how charming Owen might be. "Yes," she said softly. "I'm sure."

Sonya nodded. "First of all, your dad once told me that if you came asking, I should tell you everything I know."

Oh boy.

"Which admittedly isn't much," Sonya warned. "But he was a troubled youth, and he made mistakes."

"Illegal ones?" Anna asked.

"Second," Sonya said, ignoring the question, "he did what he had to in order to take care of you girls. He always said he'd do anything to keep you from suffering poverty the way he did."

Anna realized she was holding her breath and dragged in some desperately needed air. She wondered what Wendy was thinking, but for once her sister appeared to be listening to her directive and remained silent.

"When your mom died," Sonya said, "he took on every menial job he could to take care of you both. But those jobs didn't pay enough to cover medical insurance, keep a roof over your heads, and put food in your bellies. This was way before me, of course, but apparently you were on the verge of eviction when one of you ended up in the hospital with pneumonia."

"Me," Anna whispered, feeling the weight of Owen's gaze but unable to look at him. "I'm the one who got pneumonia." She'd been a sickly thing, and had never, not once, considered what that might've cost her dad.

Sonya nodded. "You have to understand, he needed to make sure you had your basic needs covered, that you were never left wanting for anything. Well, except maybe his time, since out of necessity, he was always working."

Anna pressed a hand to her belly, which had begun to hurt. "Did he support us with . . . questionable jobs?" She could only imagine how Wendy would feel if he had. It'd destroy her, and she was already so vulnerable.

"No." Sonya shook her head. "Take that worry off your plate right now, okay? He walked away from that life before you girls came along. After that, he needed to be legit, for the two of you. More than anything, he wanted that. The only thing he was guilty of after losing your mom was investing in some high-risk endeavors. He lost some, but then some other things paid off. Big. Once that happened, what you think of as his philanthropy? He thought of as restitution. In fact, he'd secretly managed to pay back everything he'd gotten in not so legal ways. He was incredibly proud of that, of parlaying his skills into one hundred percent legitimacy in order to make up for any bad choices he'd made when he'd been young."

As hard as this all was to hear, Anna understood it. "What can you tell me about the time before he went legit?"

"Not too much, really. I do know that early on, he hung with some pretty unsavory people. He hooked up with a partner he shouldn't have. They did a few . . . jobs together and were successful mostly because Louis was the brains of the operation and made sure any jobs were victimless." She gave a small smile. "He had a code of honor that meant a lot to him. I don't know who the partner was though, other than Louis always said the big difference between him and this guy was that while he'd done bad things to give you a better life, this partner had done bad things for a good time."

"He never said a word about any of this," Anna breathed. And her bigger worry—if once upon a time he'd done "bad stuff," wasn't it possible that ten years ago he'd stolen the coins and the Ruby Red, even if he'd supposedly been legit by then? "You recognized the coin I showed you. Did he do that job?"

"Sweetie, I believe he declined the job. But again, even back when he was doing things he shouldn't have, he was Robin Hood. He'd never have taken from an innocent. Never." She sat back. "As for why I recognized the coin, I've seen the news."

Anna nodded, grateful to Owen and Wendy for remaining silent. "So you don't know how he got the coin or how it is that it was in his things at Wendy's?"

Sonya shook her head. "I don't."

"You mentioned some unsavory people that Dad had been acquainted with, including a possible partner. Did you ever see or meet any of them?"

"No. Honey, you've got to understand, he'd left that life behind long before I came into the picture. He wanted to be the kind of man you girls could respect and look up to. He'd honestly hoped and prayed none of this would ever come to light. I can't imagine how he ended up with one of the coins. I suppose it's possible he was still in contact with someone from his past, someone who did the job, but I never met them."

"Even if you had, the coin was in his belongings, which wouldn't connect any of those people to the theft," Anna said quietly, more to herself than anyone else. *But it attaches the theft to Dad . . .* That lump still sat in her throat, as big as a regulation football. She'd always looked up to her dad and respected him. So, so much. But could she still do that now?

Sonya was watching her think and gently shaking her head

back and forth. "He was still the amazing man you loved, Anna. No matter what."

"No matter what," Wendy whispered in her ear.

Anna wanted to believe that, she really did. And while Wendy and her dad had always been able to see all the colors of life, for Anna, life was black and white, right and wrong . . .

A little while later, as they were leaving, Sonya gave Anna a tight hug. "Please don't wait another year to come by. You're always welcome here, you know that, right?"

Anna squeezed her back, nodding.

Back inside his truck, Owen pulled on his seat belt but didn't start the engine. She rested her head back and closed her eyes.

"You still okay?" he asked quietly.

"Yeah."

"Liar."

True story. She might be acting like she was okay, but deep down she needed a tub of ice cream all to herself. "If you could give me a moment for a badly needed breakdown, that'd be great."

"Anna—"

Keeping her eyes closed, she held up a hand in his direction. "Listen, everything we just heard pretty much shattered the image I had of my dad. I need a second."

He didn't speak, and she concentrated on breathing. When she could talk without bursting into tears, she drew one last deep breath and opened her eyes to find Owen not on his phone, not playing with the radio, just quietly sitting, watching her with concern. "I'm better now," she said.

He nodded. "Good."

"And in case you didn't notice, there's still no real proof that my dad is your bad guy."

"Maybe not yet," he said. "But Robin Hood was still a thief. You know that, right?"

"He's right," Wendy said in her ear. "Don't shoot the messenger."

"There's a reasonable explanation," Anna said to them both. "And I'm going to find it."

"*We're* going to find it," Owen said.

She turned in her seat to look at him. His eyes were steely with resolve but also still soft with that concern. He was worried about her. She really didn't want to be moved by that, or by the respect he'd shown both her and Sonya inside, but she was.

"We're in this together, Anna."

"We are. You've got as much skin in the game as me and Wendy. But when it's over, it's over. This . . ." She gestured between them. "This *ends*."

"Well, that sounds hasty," Wendy said.

Anna ignored her while Owen gave her a half smile. "I didn't know there was a this."

She grimaced with embarrassment and annoyance at her loose tongue, and he laughed. "No take-backs. It's out there now. There's a this."

She glared at him. "Just because I said it doesn't mean I'm going to act on it. You're as wrong for me as wrong can get."

"Then why do you keep staring at my mouth all hungry-like?"

She really needed to teach her facial expressions how to use their inside voices. "Because it never stops moving?"

In her ear Wendy gasped. "You're staring at his mouth? Introduce me!"

Anna sighed. "My sister wants me to introduce you. Wendy, Owen. Owen, Wendy, my very pregnant, nosy, interfering older sister."

Owen leaned in close to Anna, his mouth near her ear, and without permission, her body disconnected from her brain, tilting her head to give him better access—

"Nice to meet you, Wendy," he murmured, and, eyes laughing, sat back.

Anna was still waiting for her brain to reboot when Wendy said, "Now see, if you were using the GoPro, I'd be able to see him. Is he as big a thirst trap as he sounds?"

Yes. Yes, he was, dammit. "You're married," she grated out. "And please never say 'thirst trap' again."

Owen grinned.

"Hey, being married doesn't mean I can't look," Wendy said. "Does he have a six-pack? You know I love me a six-pack."

"Eight," she said, and when Owen laughed out loud, she realized he could actually hear everything her sister said. And *that* was why there'd be no *this*. He couldn't take a damn thing seriously.

"So, what's the next step?" he asked.

Okay, so maybe he could take *some* things seriously. "I want to hunt down the guy Sonya referred to as my dad's partner."

"Okay. How are we going to do that?"

She slid him a look at the "we."

His return look dared to not even try to keep him out of the loop. A sigh escaped her. "I don't know yet. But when I do, I'll get in touch."

"Looking forward to it."

She was glad one of them was.

# CHAPTER 7

Over the next few days, Owen thought about what he and Anna had learned from Sonya. He thought about it while rafting clients down the Yuba River. He thought about it while hanging off the side of a mountain on Donner Summit with Ky, trying out a new adventure to add to their menu. He thought about it while walking into the memory care facility to check in on his great-aunt Ruby.

Entering her two-room apartment, he found her pacing while Nan, one of her caregivers, tried to get her to sit.

"I don't want to sit!" Ruby snapped.

"I've got her," Owen said quietly to Nan. "Why don't you take your lunch break? I'll stay until you get back."

When Nan smiled gratefully at him and left, Owen took Ruby's hand and looked into her eyes. They'd always been sky blue, but they had faded in the past few years. Now there were whole days and weeks when the sparkle in her gaze was also gone, replaced by a dull lifelessness that terrified him. Today she wasn't lifeless, she was agitated. "You okay?" he asked.

"Why wouldn't I be?"

She'd gotten dressed today, which was good to see. She'd even gone to bingo again—which was why he was here. He'd gotten a call from the front desk that they'd had to boot her out of the room. Not for the first time either. Since she didn't want to stop walking, he tried to loop her arm in his to keep her steady on her feet, but she kept swatting his hand away.

"Boy, I'm not a damn invalid."

"Well, given that you just got kicked out of bingo, I'd definitely agree with you."

She snorted. "They're an old, fussy, self-righteous gaggle of geese. Janice, Mabel, Sarah Jane, Thelma, Opal, Phyllis, Judith . . . none of them can take a joke, not a single one."

She'd been ejected for heckling, and he absolutely believed it because he'd been on the wrong end of her sassiness for . . . well, all his life. But that she was even aware of her surroundings today—and could name every single person in that bingo room—was such a huge relief, he couldn't bring himself to ask her to stop being so unruly, as the manager of the place had asked him to do.

"And I know it was Judith who got me kicked out." Ruby shook her head. "She's been complaining about my apple tree shedding in her yard—like I can control that! And anyway, she lets her dogs poop on my front lawn!"

Ruby hadn't lived in her house for a year now. And she didn't have an apple tree, which Owen knew because he took care of her house and yard himself. He tried to get her to settle on the couch while he unpacked the two bags of groceries he'd brought her, but she didn't want to sit. She wanted to tail along after him, complaining about everything he unloaded.

"I hate tomato soup," she said. Which, for the record, was her absolute favorite lunch and had been for decades. "Just go away," she said. "I don't need anyone coming around here stealing from me. You took that twenty from my purse. I know it was you."

He scrubbed a hand down his face, feeling emotionally and mentally exhausted. "How about a nap?"

"I'm not tired. Do I look tired? You just want me to go lay down so you can rifle through my things and steal something else."

He hated this part, where she vanished into her agitation and fear. "Are you hungry? I'll make you lunch."

"*No.*"

"A TV show then? I could put on one of your favorites."

She hesitated. "Not the news. I hate the news."

"I know." He took her hand and helped her into her recliner. Then he remoted the TV on and navigated to one of the *Real Housewives* shows, which, for reasons he didn't understand, she loved.

Ten minutes into an episode, he got a call from Sami. Anna had stopped by the warehouse, looking for him.

Interesting. He texted Anna, letting her know she could come by and giving her the address, then called the front desk to approve her.

After his and Anna's visit with Sonya the other day, she'd been nearly silent when he'd driven her back to her car. It'd been then that she'd met his gaze, and for a single heartbeat, there'd been an energy between them that had nothing to do with the mystery and everything to do with good old-fashioned chemistry.

Immediately afterward, Anna had exited the truck with a speed that suggested her ass had caught fire. When two days had gone with no word from her, he'd tried calling. She hadn't answered. He could take a hint, but she'd agreed to be partners, and he intended to hold her to that. He'd told himself if she didn't get in touch with him in the next day or so, he'd track her down.

Seemed he wouldn't have to do that after all.

When a soft knock came at the door, he turned up the volume on the TV so Ruby would be distracted, but he needn't have bothered: she'd fallen asleep.

Moving to the door, he pulled it open. He really didn't want it to, but the sight of her somehow made his day. She was in jeans, beat-up sneaks, and a white tee that showed off her toned body in a way that made his blood hum. She also had a GoPro on a chain around her neck and an earpiece in her ear, and he had to admit, at least to himself, that seeing her gave him his first smile in hours. "Heading to work in the mines, or are you Secret Service?" he asked.

"Don't start. And don't ask." She paused. *"And please*, for the love of God, stop talking."

He went brows up.

"Not you," she said. "Wendy."

Owen bent down and looked into the camera. "Hey, Wendy. How you doing today?"

Anna put a finger to her ear. "She says she's good, which is ridiculous because she called me at three a.m. to drive over and make her pancakes because her husband's on an overnight business trip and the *babies* were hungry."

"Babies?" he asked. "Plural?"

"She's having triplets."

He let out a low whistle. "Well then clearly, pancakes were in order."

Anna listened to something from Wendy, then said, "No."

As an only child, Owen found himself utterly fascinated by this sibling relationship. "What did she say?"

"No," Anna said again. "Hell no." She listened to something more from her sister and sighed. "You're seriously going to blackmail me about the Disneyland thing? Fine, but remember, paybacks are a bitch." She looked at Owen. "Wendy would like you to know that you have the kind of voice that should be narrating sexy romance novels."

He grinned. "Thanks. And now I need the Disneyland story."

She grimaced. "Trust me, you don't. I'll just say it involved the Pirates of the Caribbean ride, a swim, and being locked away in the Disneyland jail for a few hours."

"Wow. You go all in."

"Yeah, that's me. All in for just about anything."

"Except mixing business with pleasure," he said.

Anna put a finger to her twitching eye.

"Are you having a seizure?" he asked. "Blink twice if you need help."

"How many times do I have to blink in order to vanish? Wendy, I'm disconnecting now. Your feet better be up or I'm telling Hayden you put a gallon of chocolate syrup on your pancakes." She pulled out her phone and cut the call, then met Owen's gaze. "I'm sorry for the imposition. I thought we should talk."

"You could've saved yourself a trip and just answered the phone when I called. Or better yet, asked me out when I saw you last."

"I'm not here to ask you out."

"Too bad. I'm good at dates."

"Why does that not surprise me?" She sighed. "And I'm sorry, I was working when you called. And as for the last time you saw me, after the visit with Sonya . . ." She hesitated. "I wasn't at my best. Not that it mattered, because as we've discussed, this is strictly a professional relationship."

He smiled. "You said relationship."

A sense of satisfaction filled him at the genuine irritation in her gaze. They were nearly on even ground then, as she definitely invoked massive amounts of irritation within him as well. Except . . . he was fooling himself. Irritation fell to a distant second place behind a near-blinding animal attraction to her.

"To review," she said, "this is work only."

"Understood." He cocked his head. "But just out of curiosity . . . why?"

She hesitated, and he got even more curious.

"Fine," she finally said. "If you must know . . ." Her gaze shifted from his. "People don't tend to attach to me."

Moved both by the words and the soft way she'd let them escape, he thought he might enjoy even five minutes with anyone who'd hurt her. "So you hold yourself back."

She shrugged. "It's worked out pretty good for me."

He was good at reading people. Real good. He tended to go with body language and eyes over the words coming out of a person's mouth. And at Anna's slightly hunched shoulders and hooded eyes, an unwanted emotion tugged on his heart, hard. "Well, while we're being honest," he said, his voice a little husky, "then you should know I'm a leaver."

She met his gaze, unable to hide her initial response of surprise. "Perfect," she said a beat later. "So we can never be."

She looked relieved enough that he felt a little insulted.

"Do you think I could talk to your great-aunt?"

"No."

"No?" she asked. "I know you want to solve this thing as

much as I do, and she's the only person still alive who might have answers, like *real* answers."

"I get that, but she's having a bad day—" He broke off when Anna's eyes shifted from him to something over his shoulder.

Owen turned just as his aunt came up at his side. In the five minutes since he'd left her sleeping in her chair, she'd gotten up, put on her pj's, had curlers askance in the front of her hair, and had applied a face mask as if it was bedtime and not one in the afternoon. She looked small, fragile, and older than he'd ever seen her. Worse, the once strong, once incredibly resilient woman would hate knowing someone was seeing her in such a weak moment.

But to his shock, Ruby took one look at Anna and her face lit up. "Cami! Oh, honey, I was hoping you'd stop by today."

Cami had been Owen's mom, and she'd been gone for years. But the one surefire way to turn his aunt into a shrieking banshee was to correct her when she forgot something—such as Cami's passing. He met Anna's gaze and tried to figure out how to avoid the bad situation barreling down on them at the speed of light.

But Anna smiled warmly at his aunt. "Of course I stopped by."

Ruby beamed, and it was so surprising, Owen found himself choked up as his great-aunt took Anna's hand in hers. "You look beautiful today. How's your mom, honey?"

Owen's maternal grandma had been gone for a long time, but that wasn't what caught his attention. It was the quick flash of pain on Anna's face. Her voice was rough with emotion when she spoke. "My mom's doing good."

"Oh, that's lovely. You know she promised me her recipe for her famous rum balls, but I think she's holding out on me."

Anna's lips quirked. "She holds out on everyone."

Ruby surprised Owen by laughing and then hugging Anna, her curlers quivering. Anna didn't hesitate, just wrapped her arms around Ruby right back.

Owen honestly hadn't known he was into sharp, cynical, feisty firecrackers with a side of sweet, but apparently there was a first time for everything.

ANNA LOOKED AT Owen, not sure how he wanted to play this.

"Come in, come in," Ruby said. "I'll rustle up some snacks."

Anna had always been told that she'd been impulsive from the womb—*Always in a hurry*—and nothing had changed. But now that she was here, she knew it'd been wrong to surprise Owen like this.

He met her gaze, his own hooded. Was he annoyed? He wouldn't be the first to be exasperated by her and certainly wouldn't be the last . . . Before he could remove her from the apartment, she started to follow Ruby to the kitchen, but Owen caught her by the hand.

She braced herself to be kicked out, something else she would understand, but she really wanted to know what Ruby remembered, if anything, about the coins and the necklace. "Owen, I—"

"Thank you," he said. "For playing along."

She froze, surprised. "Um . . . no problem. And for the record, I know I should've called you first."

"Agreed," Wendy said in her ear.

Anna turned off the GoPro and removed her earpiece. Then she pulled her hand from Owen's. Mostly because she liked the feel of his warm, callused palm against hers far too much. "I've got a question." She hesitated, already knowing the answer but hoping all the same. "You still think my dad did it."

"That wasn't a question."

She gave him a long look.

He didn't smile, but she was pretty sure he wanted to. "It's all circumstantial at best," he said, "but I don't think he can be ruled out."

She drew a deep breath. Let it out. Last night she'd had drinks with Nikki. Anna had asked for details on the other suspects in the theft of the coins and the necklace. And this morning, Nikki had sent her a quick text with shocking information.

Information she had to share since she'd promised him they were partners on this. "After your aunt reported the theft, the investigation yielded four other possible suspects in the theft."

His eyes sharpened. "I researched the case extensively. That's not public knowledge."

"No," she agreed.

He waited a beat. "And . . . ?"

"I'm not revealing my source, but I will tell you that the intel is good. No arrests were made."

He opened his mouth, but before he could speak, a woman came up behind them. She wore a name tag that read: *Hi, I'm Nan Alcott, and I'm your caregiver today.* "I'm back," she said to Owen. "And I brought sandwiches to share with Ruby." She lowered her voice. "Sometimes a meal she isn't used to can nudge her out of her own head."

"Thank you. She said she was going to make snacks."

"She always says that when she needs a moment. I'll go look after her."

Owen nodded, and Anna took in the solemn look in his eyes. She could only imagine what he went through with Ruby on a daily basis, but she figured he wouldn't appreciate sympathy. "I'm still planning on proving you wrong about my dad."

He gave a very small smile. "Just out of curiosity, do you always have to be right?"

She grimaced. "Yes."

"Only at work?" he asked, clearly teasing. "Or at home too? Wait, let me guess. At work, at home, and also in bed."

That jerked a startled laugh out of her. "Wouldn't you like to know." She shook her head. "Can we go back to being serious?"

"Sure." He leaned against the doorjamb, arms crossed over his chest. "By all means, let's go back to serious. What's the plan?"

She took a beat, because how many guys did she know who could've let her be in charge on this? Other than Hayden, zero—a fact she appreciated more than she could say, given what the stakes were for her.

And him.

"I'm waiting for a detailed email with info on the other suspects to hit," she said. "Should happen today. In the meantime, I was hoping to see if Ruby remembered anything. Were the necklace and coins taken from here?"

He shook his head. "From her house, which is in the area. Immediately after the theft, I searched the place up and down to make sure she hadn't just misplaced them, but they're not there. As for talking to her about it, unfortunately, that wasn't going to happen today. Not in her current state."

"Who was Cami?" she asked quietly.

"My mom."

She took in his careful calm. She was starting to get that it was his default, and that he held a lot in far beneath the surface. Even so, because she sensed that his grief, well-hidden as it was, felt a whole bunch like her own grief, she had to look away. "I understand," she said quietly. "I lost my mom too."

His gaze was back on hers. "How long ago?"

"When I was born."

A rough sound of pain escaped him, and that, along with his quiet but heartfelt oath, reached her more than any "I'm sorry" would have.

"It's especially hard to lose the good ones," he murmured, and maybe because she was standing there feeling far too choked up to speak, he filled the silence for her. "We were in Santa Barbara when I was a kid, so we didn't see much of Ruby in those days. Didn't matter, my mom gave me everything of herself. We were poor as could be, but she made life an adventure."

She smiled at that. "Did you guys travel?"

"No, we could barely scrounge up enough to eat, but I never even realized how much she must've struggled. She'd bury pennies in our small, un-landscaped backyard, leave huge boot prints in the dirt, and hand me a treasure map. She'd tell me pirates had come in the night to bury their treasure." His mouth curved. "I'd stay out there for hours, while she got quiet time to herself for the price of a handful of pennies." He shook his head. "I was always kinda skeptical about Santa, the Easter Bunny, and the Tooth Fairy, because visiting every kid in the world over one night never seemed plausible. But the pirates only visited me, so they had to be real."

She laughed. "That's how you ended up adventuring for a living. You were bit early by the bug."

"Definitely how it started," he agreed. "My mom and I ended up here in Tahoe when I was in fifth grade. When she died, I waited time out until I graduated high school, then walked away from a college scholarship and left town. I just needed out. Ky and I did the whole backpacking-through-Europe thing. And then Africa. And then South America. Asia."

"Next-level adventuring."

A small smile came into his eyes. "All thanks to my mom, really."

She looked away, unable to shake her own upbringing and how much she realized she hadn't known her dad at all.

"Anna."

She closed her eyes. She felt him tip her face up to his and met his gaze.

"What you've learned about your dad doesn't have to change how you feel about him," he said.

"But how can it not? I mean, it's starting to feel like I never knew him at all, and now . . ." She said the rest on a whisper: "I don't know who I am either."

"You're the woman who cares about . . . well, everything. Deeply. But . . ."

She narrowed her eyes at the "but."

He smiled, probably at her attitude. "You see things in black and white," he said. "Your dad breaking the law hurts you, but you need to put yourself in his shoes. A single dad with two little girls to take care of and no one to help him out. You heard my story. I've been destitute. At rock bottom, with no light at the end of the tunnel and no way out. Your dad knew what that was like and simply did what he had to in order to protect his own."

She stared at him. "You can say that because it's not *your* dad."

"True." A muscle bunched in his jaw. "My dad was never part of my life. His choice, not mine." He shook his head. "My mom brought herself and me here to Tahoe, to Ruby, who took us in. She never made us feel unwanted, and supported us without question, even though she hadn't even had a family of her own, by choice." He paused. "Life isn't black and white, Anna. You like your control and living by a set of rules because of the way your dad lived his life. It makes you feel safe. But you're not responsible for what he did. And that's not the only thing you are, the daughter of a man who walked a line you wouldn't have. You're *you*. Fierce. Passionate. Protective. And once you get your mind set on something, you don't let go."

She took a deep breath at all the truths he'd flung at her. And more than that, he'd said it all in a tone that said he admired her. Well, except maybe for that last part. "The not-letting-go thing didn't sound like a compliment."

"To me, it is."

"Because you're Mr. Easy, Mr. Nothing Bothers You?" she asked.

His eyes were steady on hers, maybe a little amused now. "Not always."

She wanted to hear more, but just then her phone lit up with a text from Wendy, and all it said was 911.

# CHAPTER 8

Wendy tossed her phone aside after texting Anna their longtime 911 emergency code, which meant "bring French fries, pronto."

She then peed for the fifth time in an hour and lumbered back to bed, swearing as she attempted to get the pillows behind her just right while her babies—Anna, Elsa, and Olaf?—tap-danced inside of her, pushing all of her guts up into her lungs. Growing an entire litter of puppies had given her a whole new level of gratitude toward her mom.

Wendy had gotten the email from Nikki with the details of the five suspects in the Ruby Red case. Okay, so she'd hacked into Anna's email, and she was terribly sorry about it. Or at least that would be the story she'd tell her sister.

She looked through the supplies she'd just had delivered: a dry-erase board, dry-erase pens, magnets, and, oops, a soda. She was sipping it when her stomach rumbled, squished as it was. "Soon," she promised the babies. "I sent up the bat signal. Your auntie Anna will be here with food soon."

Getting as cozy as possible—she already had to pee again—she got to work, pulling the large board into her lap. Thanks to her belly, she could only see the top half. Having printed off the photos of their suspects—minus her dad, because she couldn't bring herself to consider him a suspect—she began to put her "murder" board together—all while keeping an eye on the Find My app and the moving dot of her sister making her way there.

Wendy had finished getting all the suspects on the board just as Anna burst into her bedroom, skidding to a stop at Wendy's bedside, making Jennifur leap straight up in the air and hiss before jumping off the bed.

"Are you okay?" Anna demanded of Wendy. "What happened?" She looked around. "Where's the emergency?"

Wendy looked at her sister's empty hands. "The emergency's that I don't see a Happy Meal in your hands."

A tall, leanly muscled man came in behind Anna, and wow. Owen Harris was even better-looking in person than he'd been on camera. Wendy beamed at him. "Hello."

"No. No casual hellos," Anna said. "You texted me 911! I've been imagining the worst, guilty as hell because I knew you were here all alone. And yet here you are, happy as a cat that got the cream."

"Not true," Wendy said. "I'm not happy at all without fries."

Anna looked at Owen. "She's going to be the death of me, I swear."

"Hey," Wendy said, "911's *always* been our code for *bring your sister a Happy Meal pronto*."

"Not while one of us is growing babies it isn't! 911's for actual emergencies, Wendy."

"Okay, fine. Noted. And it's no biggie, I've got enough leftovers to feed the entire town, courtesy of Hayden. He got tired of having to go out at two in the morning when I woke up hungry and keeps the fridge fully stocked now." She paused to suck in a breath as someone tap-danced on her bladder.

"What was that?" Anna asked, frustration gone, replaced by concern. "You just winced."

"Yes, because Willow, Maple, and Birch are doing Zumba on my stomach."

"I mean, sure," Anna said casually. "If you want them to be mercilessly mocked. Charlotte, Emily, and Anne—or An*na*, *get it?*—sound much better."

"You just want a baby named after you."

"Well, duh."

Owen laughed, and when both women looked at him, he smiled at Wendy, nodding to the belly she was rubbing. "They kicking?"

"Mercilessly. Here." She shifted the board off her lap and grabbed his hand to put his palm on her belly. "Feel for yourself."

Anna looked horrified. "You do remember that Hayden asked you to stop taking strangers to second base, right?"

Wendy shrugged. "In just a few short weeks, an entire team of strangers will be up close and personal with *all* my lady bits."

Owen smiled at her as the babies punted against his hand. "Does it hurt?"

She couldn't have held back her goofy grin if she'd tried. "No. Not at all. I mean my organs are feeling the squeeze, but the babies moving around is the best thing I've ever felt." After years and years of trying, everything about being pregnant was even better than she'd thought it would be. Sure, she had gas that could take down an elephant and acne for the first time in her life and taking a deep breath was a thing of the past, but she wouldn't change a thing. Well, okay, so she'd change the gassy part. "It's kind of magical, actually. So what's my sister been like? Is she being mean? Because I can take her off Santa's list."

Owen looked at Anna. "Not mean."

"You sure?" Wendy asked. "Because Anna can be like"—she searched for the right words to describe her mercurial, tough, wonderful sister—"a set of Christmas lights: complicated and an absolute mess half the time, but once you figure her out, she's festive and can be quite pleasant."

"Ignore her." Anna climbed onto the bed and sat at Wendy's other side, pressing her cheek against Wendy's belly. When the babies nudged against her face, Anna nudged them back. "Hi, our babies, how we doing?"

Wendy melted a little bit. Or a lot. Anna had been through so much. Too much. It'd made her far too serious, jaded, and unreachable a lot of the time, but right now, she was none of those things, just her sweet baby sis. Wendy stroked her hair, as she'd been doing since Anna had been a toddler. "Did you really not get me a Happy Meal?"

Anna choked on a rough laugh. "No, and you know why. Your doctor wants you watching your shit-food intake. And don't think I don't see that soda you've got hiding behind the lamp on your nightstand."

Wendy sighed and looked at Owen. "She's got some dramatic tendencies."

Owen smiled and held up his pointer finger and thumb about an inch apart.

Wendy laughed.

"Hey," Anna said. "Don't encourage him. He's not funny."

"Oh, I'm funny," Owen said.

Wendy was grinning. "This is better than bacon, and I miss bacon a lot."

"Whatever," Anna said. "And you've got the drama thing all wrong. It's you who loves drama."

"Wow." Wendy rethought this and smiled. "Okay, maybe it's true. But when I say I love drama, I don't mean my own drama. I mean I love *other* people's drama."

Owen laughed, and Wendy beamed at him. Oh yes, he would do nicely. "Just FYI, I'm the sister who's into emotions and feels. Anna, as you might've noticed, is all 'evidence' and 'proof,' blah blah."

Anna turned to Owen with an I-dare-you-to-comment look.

He wisely did not. And Wendy loved that, how well he already knew her. "She wasn't always so controlled and careful," she said. "In fact, as a kid she was feral."

Owen looked at Anna. "Now that I'd have liked to see."

"Standing right here," Anna muttered.

Wendy looked at her sister. "She's got a knack for connecting with others while giving very little of herself away. I think she stopped trusting herself after getting hurt a few times. She also automatically assumes others don't trust her either."

"Gee, thanks, Dr. Wendy," Anna said dryly, and homed in on the murder board for the first time. "What's this?"

"Nice subject change, but I'll allow it because . . . ta-da!" Wendy gestured to the board. "I made us a murder board! Although, in this case, 'murder' is a euphemism for the missing necklace and gold coins. Now, I've listed out the suspects we got from Nikki. Minus Dad, of course." She looked at Owen. "Nikki is a good friend of Anna's, and lucky for us, she's a cop."

"She gave you the list of suspects on file?" he asked.

"No, she didn't give Wendy anything." Anna's eyes were narrowed. "You accessed my email again, didn't you? What have I told you about invading my privacy?"

"I know, I know, and I'm sorry. But look, I've saved you a lot of time here."

Anna, able to focus on what really mattered at any given moment, something Wendy admired and could admit she lacked, stared at the board, taking it all in. Not easy, the way it kept jumping from the triplets' swim practice.

Wendy batted her lashes at Owen. "Do you think you could use a few of your muscles to set the board on top of my dresser so we can all see it?"

"Wendy!" Anna turned to Owen. "Feel free to ignore that, both the bossiness and the sexual harassment. She has no boundaries."

Hard to argue the truth, but Wendy couldn't stop smiling because she was delighted beyond words at seeing that spark of life in her sister's eyes. "My sister's just grumpy because she hasn't . . . dated in a while."

Anna pointed at her. "Stop it. Stop it right now."

"Stop what?" Wendy asked innocently.

"You know what. Stop matchmaking. This is work. Owen and I have discussed this—we aren't each other's type."

"Not that it seems to matter," Owen murmured.

Wendy grinned at him.

Ignoring them both, Anna picked up the board and walked it to the wall herself. Owen came up behind her, caging her in to help steady the board against the wall.

A quick flash of something crossed Anna's face. Confusion. Pleasure. Confusion at the pleasure . . . Just watching someone go toe to toe with her closed-off sister made Wendy's tummy feel all soft and squishy inside, or it would have if she had any room left inside her.

Anna and Owen stood in front of the dresser, studying the

murder board. Owen's eyes were unreadable, his hands in his pockets, his thoughts his own. Unlike Hayden, who Wendy could read like the back of her hand, this man was good at hiding himself when he wanted to.

But so was Anna.

"You really should be resting," Anna said without turning to look at Wendy. "For Rachel, Monica, and Phoebe."

"Oh, you mean Faith, Hope, and Joy?" Wendy asked. "And yeah, okay, you might have a point." She *was* pretty tired. And she definitely needed a nap before Hayden got home. He'd promised retribution if he found her taxing herself. Now, granted, his idea of "retribution" was always of the sexy variety. In fact, just a few nights ago it'd involved her promising to lie very still while he had his merry way with her. This had been much harder than she'd expected, not moving while Hayden kissed, nibbled, and licked his way over her entire body, stopping to linger at all the places that he knew made her squirm—

"Earth to Wendy . . ."

She looked up and found Anna staring at her with concern.

"I'm fine. Just having a hot flash—pregnancy-related, of course." Anna wasn't the only liar in the family. She fanned her face. "Okay, so if you look at the board, you'll see I also printed our suspects' potential motives and possible connections." She'd also given them labels: Bank Robber Dude, Master Safe Cracker Guy, B&E Specialist, and Extortionist."

Anna took in the face of the man labeled Bank Robber Dude. "Joe Shade robbed a bank? And he was one of the suspects in the Ruby Red theft?"

"Yes," Wendy said softly. "And he's earned a nickname since we knew him—Shady Joe."

"Who is he?" Owen asked.

"A long-ago friend of my dad's," Anna said. "His son, Will, went to middle school with me. But then one day, Dad and Joe had a falling-out, and we never saw either of them again." She turned to Wendy. "You think Joe was Dad's early partner."

"It's possible, right?"

"Yeah, it's possible." Anna was on her phone. "Huh. Joe's a convicted felon, currently serving twenty years for grand larceny and burglary."

"Maybe Will would tell you if Joe ever talked about the theft," Owen said. "Or saw the necklace and coins. Or, even better, left something behind."

Anna nodded thoughtfully. "People talk, it's in our nature. Will might not even realize he knows something until I jog his memory."

"How will you locate him?" Wendy asked.

"If you have his number, I can get his cell phone hacked to get a location," Owen said casually.

Wendy and Anna stared at him.

He shrugged. "Got a friend who could do it in less than five minutes."

"Illegally," Anna said. "And illegal anything is against my rules."

Which, as Wendy knew, was the knell of death as far as Anna was concerned. "My sister loves her rules. They make her feel safe and secure."

"Please stop talking," Anna said, and turned to Owen. "And you. You can't just hack someone's phone."

"But you can ask a cop to get you information on a burglary?"

"Yes, because asking for that information isn't illegal."

Owen remained cool, calm, and unruffled. "Rules are great, Anna, but what about *people*? Justice trumps rules."

"Hey, I care about people too," she said. "But rules are critical. They create order, and who doesn't like order?"

Both Wendy and Owen looked at her blandly.

She rolled her eyes. "Oh, forget it. And anyway, I can find him—legally—in five minutes too." She pulled her phone back out. "Your internet connection is unstable," she complained to Wendy.

"Yes, well, my internet connection can join my club."

"Got him," Anna said, head still bent over her phone.

"Wow," Wendy said, marveled and proud. "That was fast, even for you."

"It's his socials. People really have no idea how easy it is to stalk them. He works at the View bussing tables."

"I know the restaurant, it's on West Shore," Owen said. "But if Joe and your dad were . . . associates at one time, and they're both known suspects, one of whom had a coin, a case could be made that they might have worked together on this heist."

Wendy didn't like the implication, but she could see how he got there. She slid a look to Anna to see how she was taking it. Her sister's face was predictably blank. Well, except for the storm in her eyes. Not an angry storm, but an emotional one. Even as a child, Anna could internalize her feelings, making it hard to reach her. Wendy had always figured it came from not knowing their mom. Their dad had always said it came from stubbornness.

Probably both were accurate.

"It's a stretch at best," Anna said.

Owen shrugged. "Maybe."

"One thing I've learned in the field," Anna said quietly, "is to never get locked into an opinion too early. It puts blinders on you, and you could miss the truth."

Owen nodded. He was leaning against the dresser, hands in

his pockets as he continued to study the murder board, cool as a cucumber. But something came into his eyes whenever they slid to her sister, something hungry, something . . . achy.

And oh how Anna deserved *this*, a man who both was hungry for her and yet also ached for her. Wendy very nearly chortled in glee and rubbed her hands together. Only her own phone ringing could distract her because the call was Hayden. "Hello?" she whispered.

"Hello," Hayden whispered back. "Why are we whispering?"

"Because I'm spying on Anna and Owen."

"Babe—"

"Shh!" She watched Anna and Owen at the board, heads together, then moving in tandem to look down at something on Owen's phone. There was an obvious ease between them, in the way they stood close to each other, but more than that was Anna's sweet, soft expression, which she hadn't seen in a long time.

Her sister asked Owen a question. He pointed at something on his phone, and as he spoke, Anna listened intently, eyes on his.

She didn't listen to many people this way. Maybe to Wendy, and a few other people she respected. And, apparently, also to Owen.

Anna appeared to sort through her thoughts before speaking, her voice too quiet for Wendy to catch. But Owen took in her every word, giving back the same respect that she'd given him.

"They're so good together," she whispered.

"No interfering," Hayden said. "You remember what happened the last time you interfered in her love life."

Yes. Yes, she did, and her stomach hurt thinking about it. "Okay, well, I love you, gotta go—"

"Wen—"

Her finger disconnected the call. Whoops.

"So what now?" Owen asked Anna.

"We figure this case out so my sister can butt out of my life and go back to concentrating on growing Piper, Prue, and Phoebe."

The corner of Owen's mouth twitched. "Piper, Prue, and Phoebe weren't triplets."

Anna gaped at him. "You know *Charmed*?"

"Doesn't everyone?"

Her eyes narrowed suspiciously.

He turned to Wendy. "You mentioned you've got leftovers? Because I think we have a hangry situation going on."

"Standing right here," Anna said, then sighed. "And also maybe a little true."

Wendy smiled. "I've got Mexican and Italian, whichever you want."

Owen looked at Anna.

Anna rolled her eyes at them. "Mexican." She paused. "No, wait. Italian."

Wendy snorted.

"Oh, I'm sorry," Anna said. "Did I roll my eyes too loud?"

"So all the food then," Owen said. "Got it."

When he was gone, Wendy looked at Anna, who was watching the empty doorway Owen had vanished from. Her mood already looked improved, possibly by just the thought of food, although Wendy would bet it was actually Owen himself. Not many made it to Anna's inner circle enough to understand that she wasn't nearly as tough as she wanted people to believe. Sure, she had a hard-coated shell, but on the inside she was a big softie. And it would appear her guard was taking a beating by Owen's easy energy. He was a calm kind of guy, with an air of quiet authority about him that seemed oddly soothing. He felt . . . safe and secure.

And her sister would never admit it, but she craved safety and security.

It broke Wendy's heart. "You like him."

"Actually, he's the most infuriating human I've ever met."

Wendy laughed. "Have you looked in the mirror?"

"Whatever," Anna said, and looked away.

A huge tell.

"Look, I can see you're in matchmaking mode, but he's the opposite of what I'd be looking for. If I was looking, that is."

Wendy shrugged. "Maybe him being off-brand for you is a good thing. Ever since you got hurt, you always date the same guy—uptight and boring. And even you know it, because you end up dumping them quickly. And what about William, the guy you went out with before the dentist? What happened to him?"

"If you must know, he wore too much cologne."

Owen walked into the room with a stack of takeout boxes. "Good reason to dump someone."

Wendy grinned at him. "Thank you so much. Would you mind going back for some bottled waters? Top shelf in the fridge? I'm feeling parched."

Looking amused, Owen set down the food and left again.

Anna's eyes were narrowed. "What are you up to?"

"Just wondering why you're lying to yourself."

"About what?"

"You know what?" Wendy said. "Let's move on. What about the guy before William? What was his name? John Thomas?"

"He went by JT," Anna said. "In fact, he used acronyms for *everything*. He even spoke in acronyms. He'd say 'BTW, we got to leave ASAP BAE gets there.'"

"BAE?"

"Before Anyone Else . . ."

Wendy laughed. "You realize you're just proving my point, right?"

Anna crossed her arms, the picture of irritation. "Look, not everyone dreams of being with someone long term."

"So you don't want to be loved." All amusement had fled from Wendy as they got down to the real issue.

"And it's not like I don't believe in love and marriage," Anna said. "I've seen it work with you and Hayden. I just don't think it's for me. I've tried and failed."

"Honey," Wendy said softly. "If you mean Michael and what happened last year, that wasn't your fault. It was mine."

"What are you talking about?"

"I'm the one who set you up with him, and he hurt you—"

Anna let out a breath and then took Wendy's hand. "Listen to me very carefully. You didn't make me fall for him. Or make him do what he did. That was on him, not you. So please, I'm begging you, consider yourself completely forgiven and know I never want to talk about him again, ever. *And*, for the love of God, stop thinking you have to fix me."

"I would, if you'd just give love another try. Why can't you do that?"

"Because I'm dumb?"

Wendy rolled her eyes.

"Fine. Because I'm scared, okay?" Anna got really quiet. "What if I fall in love, and once again it isn't returned?"

Wendy fought tears because she knew Anna would hate them. She'd think Wendy felt sorry for her. "You need to refer to your previous answer of being dumb. Because you, Anna Michelle Moore, are the most lovable person I know." All she had to do was make her sister believe it.

# CHAPTER 9

It was several hours later, when Hayden got home from work, before Anna felt she could leave Wendy. She'd told Owen he didn't have to stay, but he had. And then Hayden had shown up with a tray of his mom's famous taquitos and it would've been plain old rude to leave without eating a few. Or a dozen . . .

When Hayden and Owen carried all the dishes down to the kitchen, Anna turned to Wendy and brought up something Hayden had mentioned while they'd been eating. "Why does your husband think you have ghosts in this house?"

Wendy bit her lower lip.

Anna laughed. "I knew it. You did something. Spill."

"A few days ago, he annoyed me by suggesting I might want to tone down my sarcasm when he's just trying to help. I mean, first of all, being sarcastic on a regular basis can add up to three years to a person's life."

"Which means you're going to live forever then."

Wendy thought about it and shrugged at the truth. "Anyway, then he went downstairs to the living room to watch TV in peace, whatever. But also, eff that. I downloaded the LG remote app and turned off the TV from up here . . . twice." She bit her lower lip again. "Okay, five times. When I heard him coming upstairs, I pretended I was asleep. So yeah. Now he thinks we have ghosts."

"Wow," Anna said.

"Right? Brilliant."

"I was thinking evil."

A few minutes later, Hayden and Owen finished cleaning up, and she and Owen said their goodbyes and got into his truck in companionable silence. Up until then, there'd always been a sense of . . . not competition, that was the wrong word, but she'd always been aware that they were on very different sides, even with the undeniable attraction and chemistry between them.

That hadn't gone away.

In fact, if anything, the sexual pull had intensified. But something new had happened as well. They worked shockingly well as a team. Like, it was . . . easy. Which made no sense to her. "I hope you won't hold anything that happened in there against me," she said. "I've never brought a guy to Wendy's house before, and I think I blew some of her brain cells."

He smiled. "I like her. I like watching you two banter. You're close."

"We're something," she said on a rough laugh. "I think our relationship is like . . . you know how when you go to reheat something in the microwave and forget to cover it?"

He snorted, but she held up a hand. "Wait, I've got one more. I have no doubt she'd give me a kidney if I needed one, but I'm not allowed to touch her charger."

He outright laughed as he parked behind her car at his aunt's. "What's next, Anna?"

Gah, the way he said her name . . . Her mind raced, dropping images of all the things they could do to alleviate their sexual pull. "I don't think I'm ready to sleep with you," she burst out with.

At the flash of surprise on his face, she winced. "Aaaaaand . . . that's not what you were asking."

"No, but . . ." His smile was way too confident. "You're thinking about sleeping with me."

If he only knew the things she'd imagined them doing, none of which involved sleeping. Just thinking about it made her cheeks hot.

His smile faded and his eyes darkened. "When you're ready, just tell me when and where."

She closed her eyes and very nearly put a hand over her mouth before it could say *NOW!* "Back to the topic of our investigation," she said desperately. "You were asking me what's next in the investigation."

"Yes, and you seemed surprised that I would ask."

"Most men would have their own agenda."

He studied her for a minute. "I'm not most men. Plus, you're smart and good at your job. I trust your instincts."

That was kind, but she knew it went deeper. Unlike her, he didn't need a plan. He could go off script and was open to . . . well, anything.

Her virtual opposite.

He was still watching her. "One of these days we should have a talk about the men who've been in your life. The ones who hurt you."

Dammit, Wendy had a big mouth. "It isn't necessarily them. I can be cold and aloof and hard to understand."

He shook his head. "We're going to have to agree to disagree there. The Anna Moore I know is fierce, wildly passionate, and deeply caring." He looked into her eyes with an intensity that not only surprised her but made her heart beat a little too fast. "Not cold or aloof or hard to understand at all."

"The plan is to go visit Will at work," she said, in desperate need of a subject change.

He looked at the time. "Under the guise of a nightcap?"

She nodded. "Sounds good to me."

"Still okay in the truck, or do you want to drive?"

The way he offered her choices and really cared about her agenda as well as his was . . . way too attractive. "We're already in the truck, so let's just go."

He turned over the engine and pulled back out into the street. "Feels like a date."

"You'd have to work a lot harder to get that lucky."

He looked amused, like he knew she was lying. "Tell me something about you," he said.

"You did just hear me say this *isn't* a date, right?"

He smiled. "You like people to think you're all work."

"Yep, and no play. Ask anyone."

"I'm asking you."

Turning in her seat, she studied his profile. "Because you're curious about me."

He glanced over at her. "Is that hard to believe?"

"Yes," she said frankly, and was surprised when he laughed low in his throat, a very sexy sound. Dammit.

"I don't believe you're all work and no play," he said. "What are your hobbies?"

"Work." She had no idea why she was being so stubborn. Or maybe she did know. He was tempting, far too tempting.

He sent her a knowing look, and she sighed. "Fine." She thought about it. "I like switching between the same three apps for hours, not speaking to anyone for days at a time, and listening to the same songs I've been listening to for years."

"You're a daydreamer."

She stared at him in shock, because no one, *no one*, had ever guessed that about her, that when she was using social media for brain rest or listening to music, she was usually imagining herself in situations that would literally never happen—such as having a family of her own, like Wendy was.

Owen flashed her a smile, and she shook her head at him. "Show-off."

"But I'm right."

She wasn't going to admit it. "Your turn."

"My entire life is a hobby."

She shook her head. "That's a cop-out so you don't have to tell the truth. You forget, I run my own business too. I know damn well that even when you love the work so much it doesn't feel like work, there's a lot more to it than people see. It's hard. It's stressful. It's not all fun and games, no matter what you want people to believe."

He nodded but didn't say anything, and she thought that was it. He wasn't going to open up.

But then he spoke, quietly there in the dark, intimate interior of his truck. "I like to fish. It's quiet and relaxing and calms my brain. Also, if I've had a long week or month, I'm the happiest on a couch with a remote for an entire day."

"Sounds like we both like to be alone to de-stress."

"Or we haven't met the right person to de-stress with."

Or that . . .

Before she knew it, he'd parked at the restaurant. He looked over and flashed a grin that had a whole lot of bad boy in it.

*Remember: You're done with bad boys!*

"We've all got our secrets," he said. "I respect that. But I think one of yours is that you like me a little bit."

She sucked in a breath because he was wrong. She liked him more than a little bit.

Unbothered by her silence, he just smiled. "Don't worry. I'll grow on you."

That was what she was afraid of. "Not going to happen. We live entirely different lives. And you put yours on the line to entertain people."

He shook his head. "I don't ever put my life on the line, not for fun. I know what I'm doing, and a lot of prep and planning and research goes into every adventure that Ky and I provide." He paused, his gaze holding hers prisoner. "You should let me prove it to you. I could take you out sometime. Do something new. Maybe camping."

Her stomach bottomed out. "Been there, done that," she said grimly as memories swamped her, none good.

His eyes were warm, curious . . . caring. "Think I lost you there for a minute."

"Bad experiences is all," she said as lightly as she could. "Adventuring, like dating, isn't for me. Something always goes wrong with either."

"Like . . . ?"

She went with the easiest story to tell. "My dad took me and Wendy camping once. I was a brat, complaining the whole hike in, then fell asleep instead of helping set up. When I woke up, I was alone. They'd jokingly left me on my own, thinking they were being funny."

His smile had faded. "How old were you?"

"Ten. I should've just stayed put, but I freaked out and ran off and took things from a bad joke to dangerous when I slipped off the trail into a ravine and broke my ankle." She shook her head. "They felt horrible, and I should've known better, that they wouldn't have really left me."

"Not at ten." He reached across the console for her hand. "You said experiences," Owen said. "Plural. As in there are other instances where you got hurt."

"Yes, but it's probably not what you think."

"Well, I'm thinking some bad shit," he said. "How many experiences are we talking?"

"Just a couple of others."

His hand was warm against hers, his palm a little rough with calluses. She turned her head away from the sight of their entwined fingers to look out her passenger-side window. "The second time was around five years ago now, out in Desolation Wilderness with a college boyfriend. He'd talked me into hiking in to camp for a few days. On night one, we got in a huge fight and Adam . . . left. I actually thought he was kidding at first, like my sister and my dad had been all those years before, but . . ." She shook her head. "I stayed up the whole night, expecting him to show back up. At dawn, I started walking back on my own and ran into a bear."

He drew a deep inhale, then let it out, like he needed the calm. "Were you hurt?"

"No." She actually found a rough laugh. "The bear and I took one look at each other and both squeaked, falling to our asses. He was quicker to get up and took off. I did the same, in the opposite direction. Thankfully, before I got too lost, a nice couple took pity on me and led me out."

He was quiet a moment, looking at his thumb as he stroked it over hers. "And the other time?"

She shook her head. She wasn't ready to go there. Might not ever be. "Tell me one of yours."

She felt the weight of his gaze, but he didn't push. Instead, he said, "I got my heart stomped on by someone I thought I loved." He paused. "I wasn't enough for her. We'd been together since high school, but she thought of me as a fixer-upper. Only, I didn't want to be fixed. She wanted a guy who made more money, someone who didn't put good living ahead of a big fat paycheck."

"I'm sorry, Owen."

"Don't be." He lifted a shoulder. "It was lesson learned for me. I ran into her a few years ago. Ky and I had made a success of ourselves, and she admitted she'd made a mistake."

"Don't tell me you forgave her."

"I do forgive her." He smiled. "Which isn't the same thing as forgetting."

She smiled too. "You deserve better anyway."

"Right back at you."

Somehow she was leaning into him, so close she could feel the warmth of his body and his breath against her lips.

"Anna?"

She tore her gaze off his far-too-sexy mouth. "Hmm?"

"I want to kiss you."

Only he didn't. "Is there a 'but' coming?" she asked. "Because I sense a but."

"But . . ." His eyes were both heated and amused. "I'm going to need you to say you want that too before I pull you in close, put my mouth on yours, and make us both wish we were somewhere far more private than a parking lot."

Her body had some interesting reactions to that, all of them pretty shocking given that she'd abused her shower massager that very morning. "Yes."

He arched a brow. "Yes?"

"Yes! Yes, I want you to kiss me, dammit."

She caught a quick grin from him, and then he closed the distance and all annoyance vanished. *Everything* vanished, because his lips were warm and somehow both soft and firm and then his tongue touched hers and the next thing she knew, she was climbing over the console—with an assist from a pair of strong, determined arms—to straddle him.

"God, you taste sweet," he murmured, one hand wrapped up in her hair, the other on her ass, when she heard her own soft moan. She'd be embarrassed if she didn't *know*, if she couldn't *feel*, that Owen was right there with her. After all, she was rocking on the evidence, and all she could think was *yes please*—

A phone rang.

Hers.

They froze, eyes locked on each other as her phone continued to ring. She slowly pulled back, frustrated and yet also relieved because whew, no time for bad decisions today.

OWEN FELT ANNA pulling away, felt also her walls starting to close herself off from him. "Stay with me," he whispered.

And she did, for another deliciously long moment, but then her phone immediately started ringing again, and she looked at the screen. "I'm sorry." She rested her forehead to his for a single heartbeat. "It's work."

She pulled away, a visceral reminder that he wasn't, and probably never would be, a priority in her life. He'd definitely seen this movie and hadn't liked the ending. It was all a little hard to accept since she still had her free hand in his hair. He was no better, currently still holding two palmfuls of a very sweet ass.

"Yes," she said into her phone. "It's being handled." Her hand dropped away, and then she was no longer even looking at him.

The sweetly eager Anna, the one who'd melted for him at his touch, had disappeared, and in her place was the stubborn, uptight woman he'd first met in her office.

He'd spooked her.

To make matters even worse, she wasn't just ignoring him, but had straightened and was sitting on his lap like he was a damn chair. Then she opened the driver's door, slid off him, and walked away without so much as a backward glance.

He drew a deep breath, feeling dismissed and not liking it much. He didn't need this, he really didn't. His current single lifestyle suited him, casual encounters only, both on the job and off. And nothing about Anna would be casual—

A tap at the window had him looking up into her face. When he powered down the window, she put a hand over her phone. "Just got a text from Wendy, who found out Will isn't working again until tomorrow, evening shift, starting at five. I plan to be here at four thirty to get the lay of the land, if you want to meet back here. But for now, I have to go, I'm needed back at my office."

"This late?"

"My cases are often a twenty-four seven endeavor."

"Get in, I'll take you to your car."

Adding insult to injury, she shook her head, barely meeting his gaze. "Don't worry about it. I've already ordered an Uber."

Yep. He'd most definitely spooked her. And maybe himself as well. He spent the rest of the evening telling himself it was absolutely for the best.

# CHAPTER 10

The next afternoon, Anna was at her computer in her office, Mari at her side. They were staring at footage from a client's front door camera. In this particular case, the client had won the house in her divorce, but her ex, in order to avoid paying childcare, had vanished.

Anna had been hired to find him, and she'd done just that.

"It's so freaky." Mari shook her head as they both watched the missing husband sneak in the front door at two in the morning. Thanks to interior cameras that Anna had asked her client if she could place inside, they stared as the guy went upstairs and then from there climbed into the attic access.

"I'm shook," Mari said in disbelief. "He's phrogging her. Living right beneath her nose."

"More accurately, above her nose."

Mari sat back. "Love stinks."

"Couldn't agree with you more."

"But also," Mari said, "I hate being alone."

Anna shrugged. "The next time you feel alone, you could

remember there are fifteen billion antibodies flowing through your veins who'd die in order to protect you."

"You read too much."

"Is that even a thing?" Anna asked.

"Hey, I can't help it that I love too easily. And it's not like I don't know that I'm infamous for falling in love with someone made entirely of red flags, try to fix them, get hurt, and then go on a three-month bender to get over him."

"It wasn't three months," Anna said. "It was three days, which I know because I tracked you down in Mexico and brought you home."

Mari set her head on Anna's shoulder. "Did I thank you?"

"Profusely. In tequila."

"Right." Mari smiled. "Good times.

Anna glanced at the time and stood. "I've gotta run. Lock up?"

"Of course." Mari's smile went sly. "I'll want details in the morning of this non-date date you're going on with Sexy Coin Guy."

"You mean Owen Harris?"

Mari grinned. "So you *do* think he's sexy."

Anna ignored this and headed to the door.

"Don't do anything I wouldn't do!"

She ignored that too, because there was nothing Mari wouldn't do. By four thirty she'd parked at the restaurant and put Wendy in her ear and her phone in her pocket because her sister had insisted on coming along.

In return, Anna had extracted the promise that Wendy wouldn't talk because she couldn't deal with Owen, Will, *and* Wendy at the same time.

Walking through the lot, she looked around. She didn't see

Owen's truck. Probably for the best after yesterday, when she'd stupidly lost herself in his kiss. She wanted to believe it made no sense, that they had zero in common. But even she knew that didn't matter.

"I hope you're wearing mascara this time," Wendy whispered as Anna entered the restaurant and took a seat at the bar.

Yeah, she was wearing mascara, and even worse, she'd lost her mind and had actually put on a dress. "Shh." She eyed the time again, and her palms began to sweat just as her phone buzzed an incoming text.

**OWEN:** I'm on my way. Please don't leave.

A waitress came by and asked if she wanted a drink.

"Yes," Wendy said.

Anna had no idea why she asked for a glass of wine. No problem, she decided. She'd use it as a cover. Only when the drink came, a few sips jumped right into her mouth.

The good news was that by the time Owen arrived ten minutes later, she was feeling much more relaxed. And damn, he looked edible in jeans and a white button-down, which she decided was the wine's fault.

"You okay?" Wendy asked in her ear. "You just moaned."

Ignoring that, she held Owen's gaze. "You, um— You . . ."

He grinned. "Have I made you speechless?"

"Ohmigod, what is he wearing? Details!" Wendy demanded.

"Nope," she said to both Owen and her sister.

Owen smiled. "You're drinking wine. There's a linen tablecloth. You're wearing a sexy-as-hell dress, and your hair's down again. Is this a date, babe?"

Shit. She knew she'd gone one step too far with the hair. "Absolutely not. Although, nice touch on the button-down shirt. You didn't have to dress up for me. *Babe.*"

He looked amused, both by the "babe" and possibly by how hard she was working at not being attracted to him.

"So." She drew a deep breath. "I owe you an apology for yesterday."

"Huh." He sat next to her. "I've never had anyone apologize to me about a kiss before. So you didn't like it."

If she'd liked it any more than she had, she'd have self-combusted on the spot. "It was . . . fine." She was just about to add that while they were talking about said kiss, it could never, ever happen again, when he leaned in.

"If it was only fine," he said, voice husky, "then clearly I have something to work on."

Anna snorted because he didn't have to work on shit. He was magic, and he knew it.

In her ear, Wendy had gasped. "You didn't tell me you kissed! *When?*"

Possibly misinterpreting her silence, Owen let his smile fade. "And I'm sorry I'm late. I was afraid you'd think I was standing you up."

She shrugged and pretended to look around for Will, whom she'd honestly forgotten about.

"Was there tongue?" Wendy asked.

"Anna," Owen said. "Look at me?"

She turned back to find him watching her with a mix of rueful regret and earnestness.

"I'd never stand you up," he said.

Her chest tightened. Because while she'd definitely been

stood up before, and had let it bead off her back, she realized that being stood up by Owen would really hurt. And that in itself was ten times scarier than the kiss.

His hand covered hers where it rested on the table. "Anna—"

Her drink server stopped on her way past their bar table and went brows up at the sight of Owen, looking him over appreciatively. Anna got it, he was extremely nice to look at, but there was a familiarity in the woman's gaze, an intimacy that couldn't be ignored.

"Well, look who the cat dragged in," the server said.

Owen smiled. "Hey, Caitlin."

"Hey yourself. Looking good. Which is annoying as shit. How do you never age?"

"Good genes?"

Caitlin snorted at him and looked at Anna. "You with this guy?"

"Is she an ex?" Wendy asked in her ear. "Is she pretty? Can you take her?"

Caitlin playfully nudged Anna. "Hon, let me give you some advice on Owen Harris."

"Quick, lean in closer so I don't miss anything," Wendy said. "This just got interesting."

"He knows how to make a woman melt," Caitlin said. "I'll give him that." She lowered her voice to a stage whisper. "Just don't give him your heart."

"Ouch," Owen murmured.

"Don't worry," Wendy said. "Exes are always bitter."

"*No* worries," Anna said. A lie, of course. She was made up of approximately 99 percent worry. "My heart's locked up tight."

"Another ouch," Owen said.

"Smart girl." Caitlin smiled at Owen. "How you doing, honey?"

"Can't complain." He smiled, the very picture of "no worries." "You about done trying to scare off my date?"

"You're on a date?" Wendy again. "*Yay!* Tell me you shaved all the way up. Like to the North Pole—"

"This isn't a date," Anna said to everyone within hearing.

Caitlin smiled at her. "I like you. Your wine's on me."

When she was gone, Anna just looked at Owen.

"It was a long time ago," he said. "Like . . . five years ago?" His phone rang, and when he looked at the screen, he winced. "I'm sorry, it's my aunt's caregiver. I've got to get this."

"No worries," she repeated, mostly for herself. She needed the reminder.

With a grateful smile, Owen stood up to take the call in presumably a quieter place. While he was gone, Caitlin came back with menus. "Your waiter should be here any minute. So have you known Owen long?"

Anna had to think about that. Had it only been a week? It seemed like she'd known him forever, and that startled her. "Long enough," she said, not sure why she answered like that. She wasn't . . . jealous? Damn. She was *totally* jealous of the obvious friendship that lingered between Caitlin and Owen.

"Sorry, had to pee," Wendy said in her ear. "I left you on the bed. What did I miss?"

"Look," Caitlin said, "you seem really nice. Can I be honest with you?"

"Ohhh," Wendy said. "Say yes!"

"Uh—"

"Listen, us girls have to stick together, right? Owen's a great guy, truly. Just . . . be careful with your heart, because he won't be."

"Everyone's got exes," Wendy said. "It doesn't mean anything."

"I thought we were doing great," Caitlin said. "I was wrong." She paused. "I figured it out when every week he'd visit his mom's grave site and never take me. Not one time. He had invisible barriers protecting him that kept me on the outside looking in. Fact is, I wanted more and he couldn't give it to me. He can't give it to anyone."

Anna blinked, unsure what to do with that. "Uh . . ." Wow, wasn't she eloquent today.

Caitlin patted her hand. "That all said, I still think he's a great guy, just not the forever guy." And then she was gone, and that amazing, warm, caring guy was heading back toward the table, slipping his phone in his pocket.

# CHAPTER 11

"Your aunt okay?" Anna asked as Owen sat back down.

"As okay as she gets."

Anna knew loss, but she'd never lost someone who was still alive. That had to be hard. Then she caught sight of Caitlin across the restaurant. *Don't ask.* "Do you miss her?" Damn, her mouth had a big mouth.

Owen followed her gaze. "Caitlin? No, because we're still friends."

She nodded like she understood. But she didn't, not really. "And it didn't work out because . . . ?"

Owen lifted a shoulder.

"You don't know?"

He met her gaze, a wry humor there. "Oh, I know. It's just not very flattering to me."

Okay, that made her smile. "This I have to hear."

He grimaced. "You want to feel better about yourself through my own idiocy?"

"Yes."

He tipped his head back and laughed, and frankly, she was

dazzled. Which was really annoying. "Hey, I told you my stories."

"Not all of them."

True.

His eyes held hers, letting her in. "Caitlin and I broke up because she said she couldn't reach me. Said that when it came to the deep stuff, I was an island of one. I was everything she wanted in a man except for that."

"I love him so much," Wendy said. "Please let's keep him."

Anna gave Owen a small smile. "We're quite the pair."

"This is all I'm saying!" Wendy said.

"Yes." Owen's eyes were still intense. "We are. And again, I'm really sorry I was late. We had an emergency on the water. A family was out kayaking and one flipped over. Of course it was the teenager, who'd taken off her life vest."

"Oh my God. Is she okay?"

"She's fine," he said. "I got to her in time, but she scared the shit out of me. I hate it when people don't follow the guidelines, which are in place for a reason."

She stared at him.

"What?"

She shook her head. "That's the sexiest thing you've ever said."

"Really? I thought maybe it would've been when I said you tasted sweet."

Wendy choked, and Anna reached into her pocket and turned down the volume.

"Is Wendy in your ear?" Owen asked. "Hi, Wendy."

"Tell him hi!"

Anna ignored her. She fanned her hot face and searched for Will. No sighting yet. Then she searched for something else—a safe topic. "I also wanted to say something about yesterday.

Sometimes I get so caught up in the job, I forget myself. I didn't mean to just dismiss you like that."

In her ear, Wendy snorted. "*Sometimes?*"

Anna kept her gaze on Owen. "It was rude. And I'm sorry for that."

He studied her for a beat. "Anything else?"

She swallowed hard and hoped her sudden nerves weren't showing. "What else would there be?"

"I don't know. Maybe you're freaked out because you have burgeoning feelings for me."

Wendy cackled.

Anna did her best to keep her expression even because of course he could tell she had feelings for him. Not that she had any intention of admitting them out loud.

He was smiling, but not a mocking smile. It was gentle, almost . . . tender. "It's not the worst thing that could happen," he said. "Us liking each other."

It was for her. She was done with heartache. Done. Done. Done. "We said this wasn't happening. We're wrong for each other." She didn't like the desperation in her voice. "And that's still true."

"Is there a reason we couldn't explore this to make sure? Or, if you need an expiration date, we could say we try until the case is over."

Her heart skipped a beat.

"Ohmigod, say yes," Wendy said. "Hey, Owen! She says yes!"

Owen smiled. "I could kiss you again if that would help."

"Not necessary," Anna said quickly, then paused at the odd crunching in her ear. "Are you eating popcorn?"

Owen didn't even blink. He was clearly getting used to Wendy being their third wheel.

"Are you kidding?" Wendy asked. "This is better than when I used to watch *Days of Our Lives*. Yes, I'm eating popcorn. And why are you talking to me instead of answering him? Say yes, you're going to explore this!"

Did she want to? Her body was begging *yes, please*. But her brain was flashing warning signals, all while Owen sat there calm, sure.

"Do you need a murder board to work this out?" he asked.

She pointed at him and opened her mouth to answer, but out of the corner of her eye she saw Will coming onto the floor from the back. Thank God. No time to make a bad decision. "Showtime."

Will headed their way, head down, tying on his apron. As he got closer, Anna said his name and he looked up. Blinked. "Anna? Wow, talk about a blast from my past. You look great." His gaze ran over her. "Really great. Like smoking-hot great."

Owen cleared his throat, and Anna turned to him. "Owen, this is Will. Will, Owen."

Will absently shook Owen's hand while still smiling at Anna. "It's sure been a long time." He crouched at her side. "How's Wendy? How's your dad?"

Her throat closed. Even though she'd told this story a thousand times, whenever anyone asked about her dad, it was still like a fresh stab to the heart. "I guess you haven't heard. He passed away a year ago."

Will made a pained sound. "I just moved back to town." He squeezed her hand. "I'm sorry. I know how hard it is to lose someone."

She'd done research on Joe now and knew he'd gone to jail once before, back when she'd been in middle school. At the time, Will had been in school with her one day and gone the next. When she'd asked her dad about it, he hadn't known where they'd gone. Or so he'd said. But she knew from her deep dive on Joe that Will had ended up in foster care.

When Anna's mom died, she'd had her dad to raise her. Will hadn't had anyone.

Will glanced at Owen before redirecting back to Anna. "Am I interrupting a date?"

"No," she said.

"Yes," Owen said.

Wendy snorted in Anna's ear. "They're checking to see who's got the bigger dick. Might want to give them a minute."

Anna disconnected her, then looked at Will. "Actually, I came here looking for you."

Will seemed surprised. "Really?"

"Yes. I wanted to ask you some questions about your dad."

Will's smile vanished. "I haven't talked to that son of a bitch in three years. What do you want with him anyway?"

"We're investigating a missing necklace called the Ruby Red and a very rare coin collection."

"The *stolen* Ruby Red and coin collection," Owen said, showing Will pictures from his phone, watching his face as he studied the pics.

Will shook his head. "Never seen either or heard my dad talk about them. And he's a bragger—which is why he's serving time. He boasted about a big job he did and got caught."

Anna felt Owen's gaze on her, and she knew he was wondering why her dad, by all accounts an upstanding guy, would be associated with someone like Joe.

And the truth was, she didn't know.

"Will, you knew my dad," she said. "Do you think he could've had anything to do with this?"

Will thought about it. "I couldn't really say, but I do know that he pulled off at least one heist with my dad back in the day."

Anna sucked in a breath. It'd been bad enough to find out her dad had a police record. Worse to then have Sonya acknowledge he also had a dark past. But this. This was her biggest nightmare coming true, and it would absolutely kill Wendy. "This . . . this can't be true."

Will looked confused and possibly hurt. "Why would I lie to you? We've been friends since we were kids."

True story.

Owen was still watching Will. "And you're sure your dad never mentioned this particular job?"

Will shook his head. "Nope." He rose to his feet, looking around at his section. "I need to get to work."

"And you've got no intel or insight on any of this," Owen said.

"Owen," Anna said quietly, but he didn't break eye contact with Will.

Will was staring right back at him. "You accusing me of something?"

"I'm sorry," she said to Will, trying to break up the over-whelming testosterone overload. "We didn't come here to accuse you of anything."

Will dropped the stare down with Owen and looked at her. "Don't worry about it. I'm sorry I can't help, but I've really got to get a move on. Do you want to order something?"

"Sure. I'd love some apps. Maybe the sliders and fries." She looked at Owen. "Want to share?"

When he nodded but didn't speak, she gave an inward eye roll—*men*—then stood and gave Will a hug. "Thank you for the time." She watched him walk off before turning to Owen.

"He was lying about not knowing if Joe was involved," he said.

"And you know this how?"

"His body language. And how can you *not* know?"

Normally on a job, she had some mental distance and could judge a person's behavior, including body language. But with this job, she had zero mental distance. It was embarrassing, as she'd never been anything less than professional. She remembered how the day before she'd straddled him in his truck. Yep, professionalism had gone out the window. "Will never got along with his dad. I don't think he'd lie to me about him."

Owen shook his head. "I feel like I'm missing some pieces of this puzzle. Were you two a thing?"

"No." She sighed. "I feel sorry for him, okay? He's had a pretty rough life."

"Everyone's had troubles at some point. It doesn't excuse hurting other people."

She knew Owen had been hurt when his dad had chosen not to be a part of his life, and also when he'd lost his mom and hadn't had anyone else in his life except his great-aunt. Then hurt again when he'd been walked away from by a woman he'd loved. Abandonment issues, she understood. Holding his gaze, she took his hand in hers. "I hate how you were hurt."

Turning his hand over to entwine their fingers, he shrugged. "I'm good now, and this isn't about me. But for the record, I hate how you've been hurt too. Will you tell me about the one you kept to yourself?"

She took another sip of her wine but was pretty sure it wouldn't be enough. "It wasn't physically or anything like that." Why was she doing this? But she knew why. He'd been honest with her about his heartbreaks, and she wanted to do the same. "About a year and a half ago, I was dating this guy. Michael was wildly exciting and a big risk taker, and I . . . wasn't. After growing up with a free-spirit dad with few to no rules . . ." She broke off. Grimaced. "I don't mean to give you the wrong idea of my dad. I loved him, so much, but I didn't love the loose and fancy-free household with no guidelines, no expectations, no rules."

"And those are the things that make you feel safe."

However much she hated that that was true, she couldn't argue with it. And when she couldn't get those things from the people in her life, she'd gone without, burying herself in her work, the only place where she could control her world. But still, she'd struggled to find herself, had felt adrift, alone, feeling unable to connect with anyone, even with her sister at times. "Somehow Michael got past my barriers anyway." She'd tried to forget, but apparently no one could forget how dumb being in love could make them. "It was the first time I'd ever really fallen for a guy, even though he couldn't have been more different than me. He was a trust fund baby, and . . ." Fun. Sexy. But also . . . wild and reckless, always playing hard and fast with the rules of life. "When it came right down to it, we wanted different things from life."

"Because he was wealthy?"

"Because he thought he was above pesky little things like the law. He ended up in jail, nailed for tax evasion."

He winced. "Oh shit."

She shrugged, like no big deal, when it had been a *really* big deal at the time. It'd been a complete shock, and she'd been devastated.

Beyond devastated.

Even worse, as attracted to Owen as she was, he was every bit the free spirit Michael was. Minus the being a criminal part, of course, but it was a good reminder of why she couldn't fall for him. No way, no how, because Owen, out of anyone she'd ever met, he could detonate her careful control without even trying. And that careful control was the only thing that kept her from getting hurt.

She realized she was holding her breath and forced herself to let it go. Also, normally whenever she thought of Michael, she felt a sharp pain in her chest. But at the moment, all she felt was . . . nothing. Over herself, she shook her head. "You know way too much about me."

He smiled. "If it helps, I like what I know."

"Give it some time," she quipped.

He didn't smile. Instead, his eyes were dark and serious. "More time is just going to increase my problem."

"Oh yeah? And what problem is that?"

"Falling. For you." His gaze dropped to her mouth, and she felt her body react predictably, but the real surprise was how her heart skipped a beat.

"I can't fall for you, Owen," she whispered.

"Does that mean you are? Falling?"

Hard and fast. "Did you not just hear me?" she asked, hearing her own frustration and, dammit, sadness in her voice. She didn't want to give herself away, didn't want to let him know she already felt far too much for him as it was. Owen Harris, no matter what he believed about himself, *was* a true keeper.

She was not. "We're a terrible idea. You should be running for the hills."

"I don't run." His voice was thoughtful, his eyes focused on only her. "But also, as long as we're honest with each other, what could go wrong?"

"Are you kidding? Only *everything*!"

He stared at her, then shook his head. "You don't trust me."

"Well, to be fair, I don't trust anyone."

"Anna, I've been honest with you from the start. That won't change."

"Okay," she said slowly. "But if you want to be honest, then let's be honest. Guys like you aren't into girls like me."

Clearly stunned, he sat back in his chair. "What are you talking about, 'guys like me'?"

Why did the question make her defensive and angry? "I'm just asking you to be straightforward with me about intentions. You're playing nice because of your aunt. You're here because of what happened to her, but also because of who my dad was—which means you don't trust me to tell you everything I learn regarding this case. So please do me a favor and don't pretend we're on the same page, much less the same side." And then with that, she dropped some money on the table and walked away.

Because that was what she did when the going got tough. She got going. She just wished she'd gotten a slider first.

# CHAPTER 12

Wendy was bored out of her mind. She'd read, watched TV, and played a few games on her phone. Maybe after she worked her way through the contraband bag of cookies she was munching on, she'd nap. Yeah, a nap sounded perfect. Contrary to popular belief, it didn't take much to thrill her. Some food. Good sleep, the kind where you woke up with drool making your cheek stick to the pillow. A soft pair of yoga pants that would *never* see a yoga class. No social obligations whatsoever . . .

And now she could add being pregnant. Because even though she was currently little more than a vessel for Rose, Ivy, and Daisy—maybe?—people were treating her like a pampered princess.

Perking up when she heard someone enter the house, she quickly shoved the bag of cookies behind her pillow. "If you're a robber," she yelled, "take whatever you want, but please bring me a Popsicle first! Chocolate. No, wait! Vanilla! Strawberry!"

A few seconds later, Anna appeared in the doorway with a

Popsicle. "Strawberry," she said, and handed it over. "What are you doing?"

"Nothing. Just growing babies. Nothing to see here." She smiled as a distraction. "Hey, so what do you think of Rose, Ivy, and Daisy?"

"Cute, especially if you're a gardener."

Wendy sighed because they both knew she had the blackest thumb on the planet.

"Maybe you should go with Aurora, Belle, and Jasmin." Anna stilled, dramatically sniffing the air. "You've been eating something."

"Nope." Wendy shook her head. "Not me."

"Uh-huh." Anna picked something off Wendy's T-shirt. "And I suppose these cookie crumbs all over you fell from the sky?"

Shit. "These? They're, um, crumbs from the toast I ate earlier."

Quick as lightning, Anna reached behind Wendy's pillow and came up with the family-size bag of cookies. "Wow."

"Hey, the doctor said in an emergency, I could eat whatever I need."

"Do tell."

"I felt cranky," Wendy said. "Sugar's good for cranky. Don't you dare eat those."

Anna shook her head, clearly unimpressed with the ridiculous lie.

And she was right. Wendy could've done better. "They're dark chocolate chip," she said in her defense. "Which everyone knows is healthy. Plus, the babies *love* it when I eat healthy. *And* they taste like heaven."

"Did they also taste like shame?"

Wendy sighed. "Maybe a little."

Anna perched a hip on her bed. "How are you really?"

"How am I?" Wendy gestured to herself. "Look at me. I'm wider than a house. I can't see them, but my toes feel like sausages. My nipples hurt. And my va-jay-jay is having a *lot* of feels."

Anna grimaced.

"Hey, you asked."

"My mistake. Are you getting up every hour to take a lap?"

"I can't get out of bed. My blankets have accepted me as one of their own, and if I leave now I'll lose their trust. Do you have any popcorn?"

Anna pulled an apple from her bag and handed it over.

Wendy stared at it. "This is the oddest-looking popcorn I've ever seen."

"Hayden told me not to feed you salty stuff unless you were out of control."

"Hello!" Wendy raised a hand. "*Out of control!* Can't you tell?"

"With you?" Anna shrugged. "I gauge it off how much of the whites of your eyes I can see."

"Whatever." Prepregnancy, she'd have pounced on her sister and they'd have wrestled until one of them tapped out, but pouncing was a thing of the past. Just like cookies, wild gorilla sex, and being able to see if she was wearing pants.

"Your bedroom's a war room," Anna said, looking around.

Wendy tried to see it through her sister's eyes and admitted she might have a point. She had a map of the entire area up on one wall, two whiteboards on another, one being their murder board. The other was filled with color-coded sticky notes on what research they had on their suspects so far. Organization wasn't her strong suit, but she'd channeled her inner Anna and was quite proud of herself.

Or at least she had been until her sister moved around cleaning and straightening up, then reorganized the way Wendy had her notes posted. By the time she was done, everything was lined up and perfectly placed. "You're a freak, you know that, right?"

Anna snorted. "I do, because you tell me all the time."

"And I still can't believe you wouldn't wear the GoPro to talk to Will."

"Really? You can't believe I wouldn't wear a camera on my forehead into a restaurant where I was trying to be discreet and get information out of a witness?"

Okay, so Wendy supposed she could admit she saw the problem.

"And I called you beforehand, left the line open, and wore an earbud so you could still hear me. It's not my fault you couldn't behave."

"We could get a small camera in a brooch," Wendy said, eyeing them on Amazon from her phone.

"And maybe if I was ninety, I'd go along with that." Anna was pacing now. She made yet another pass, then pivoted on a foot to pace the length of Wendy's bedroom again.

"You're going to wear out my new Costco runner."

Another pass.

"At least walk through the kitchen and get me something to eat," Wendy said.

"You've eaten the entire kitchen."

"Damn. You're mean when you do that thing you do."

"What thing?"

"You know what thing. You know *exactly* what thing. Something good comes along in your life and you sabotage it. Your self-care is zero out of ten."

"Hey, I exercised this morning. Even did a face mask." Anna paused. "And okay, so I also had ten thousand milligrams of caffeine and ate eighty pizza rolls." She sighed. "Sometimes the line between self-care and self-destruction is a fine one."

"Face it," Wendy said. "You're afraid to be loved."

"Well, that's just ridiculous."

"Really? 'Guys like you aren't into girls like me'? What was that? Anna, you're the best person I know." Dammit, her throat got tight. "The best," she whispered.

"Wait." Anna stopped pacing to stare at her. "How did you hear that? I disconnected you before I said that."

"Well, you missed or something," Wendy said. "I heard everything until my phone battery died when you got into an Uber." She sniffed.

Anna froze. "What are you doing?"

"Nothing. I got something in my eye is all."

Anna sighed. "*Please* don't cry."

"I'll stop crying when you start believing in yourself."

"Not this again." Anna tossed up her hands. "I believe in myself! Jeez."

Wendy knew this was only a partial truth. Anna did believe in her worth as it related to her job, friends, and life in general. But when it came to opening her heart, she was 100 percent full of mistrust and closed up tighter than a drum.

"Look," Anna said, "I said what I did because . . . well, he pisses me off."

"Pisses you off, or . . ."

Anna's eyes narrowed. "Don't say it."

". . . makes you all soft and mushy inside?"

"*Definitely* pissed off."

Wendy snorted. "Do you want to know what I think?"

"Not even a little bit."

"I think you're still nursing a broken heart, and you're mad about it. You loved Dad and he died, and you're mad. Michael broke your heart, and you're mad at that too—"

"We are so not talking about this."

"Oh, you don't have to," Wendy said. "I already know. It's why you dump everyone who wants to be in your life. You leave before they can."

Anna crossed her arms. "For the record, I didn't leave Michael. He went to jail."

"He was an asshole. So was Adam. And for that matter, so am I for pushing you to find someone when you're not ready. I'll back off."

"Can I get that in writing?"

"Most definitely not."

With a rough laugh, Anna kicked off her shoes and crawled onto the bed next to Wendy.

Jennifur, who'd been sleeping on Hayden's pillow, lifted a sleepy head. Anna kissed her snout, then settled, and just like when they'd been little, whenever Anna had needed love, she set her head on Wendy's shoulder and cuddled in.

Heart melted, Wendy wrapped her arms around her and hugged her tight. For days and weeks and months she'd been stressing that she wouldn't know how to mom. But right now, right here, with maternal feelings swamping her for her sister and best friend and only blood family, she felt a sense of relief and love so strong it brought tears to her eyes. "I'm going to be okay," she whispered, not meaning to say it out loud.

"I'm so glad," Anna said, sounding amused. "And me? Am I going to be okay?"

"TBD."

They both laughed, and then the babies squirmed in unison against Anna, who let out a little sound of pure love and gently rubbed Wendy's belly. "We're going to be outnumbered soon."

"I know."

"You scared?"

"Only if you're planning on running away from me."

Anna lifted her head and met Wendy's gaze. "Are you going to make me change disgusting lava poops?"

"No."

Anna laughed. "Liar."

Wendy smiled. "I used to change your diapers. Seems only fair you pay me back."

"Oh sure, play that card." Anna sat up. "I'm hungry. Going to go raid your kitchen. Need anything?"

"Yes. I need to know why you're so hard on yourself."

"For that, we'd need copious amounts of alcohol, but since you're knocked up, let's stick to snacks. Hold, please." She vanished.

Five minutes later, Anna appeared in the doorway with a baking pan.

Jennifur lifted her head again.

"What did you cook that fast?" Wendy asked.

"Cheese, crackers, grapes, flavored freeze-dried snap peas—both barbecue and pickle flavored—olives, just because you have the black jumbo ones, which you know I can't resist—and oh! You had some sliced deli turkey, which I slathered with cream cheese and rolled up. You are welcome."

"There's only two of us—you know that, right?"

"Five," Anna said on a smirk, gently patting Wendy's belly.

"And the reason for the huge pan?"

"Couldn't find a big enough plate." She climbed back onto the bed, and they dug in. "I should've known you'd caught the whole convo. You didn't ask me about Will after the meeting. *And* you've added him to the suspects."

"You disagree?"

"No." Anna looked at her. "You heard what he said about Dad."

"I did. I just don't happen to believe him." Wendy took a faux barbecue chip and sighed in pleasure, as though there weren't enough salt and trans fats for her system. "Did you know a serving size of regular chips is ten? Ten chips. *Total.*"

Anna snorted. "I ate at least ten while standing in your pantry, trying to decide what I wanted to eat."

Wendy laughed. "A serving size should be 'until you feel better.'"

"Yeah, and then the nutritional information wouldn't matter because it's medicinal."

"Fudging A." Wendy picked up a turkey-and-cream-cheese roll-up. "You make good snacks. Sometimes I go looking and can't find anything that I wouldn't have to actually do work for, so then I lower my snackspectations and eat something I didn't really want because I was lazy. But you're never lazy."

"I feel lazy right now."

Wendy looked at her. "You deserve to be lazy once in a while." She waved the roll-up in one hand and a chip in the other. "Okay, let's hear it. Why you said what you said to Owen."

"It's a long story."

Wendy gestured to her belly. "I've got a few weeks. Is it a longer story than a few weeks?"

Anna rolled her eyes.

"You're better than this," Wendy said. "Now tell me. I'll help you start." Wendy licked remnant cream cheese off her thumb and reached for a stack of crackers. "Your first sentence should begin with the word 'Owen.'"

"Are you seriously going to touch everything after you just licked your fingers?"

"Yes. *Speak*."

"Fine. Let's look at Owen's life. He runs an adventure company. He windsurfs in six-foot waves. He climbs mountains. For fun. In comparison, I go to work and shuffle papers."

"What about the time you busted open an insurance fraud case on a yacht where the owners shot at you when you got caught snooping?"

"That was just unlucky on my part," Anna said. "I hardly ever get shot at."

"No, sometimes you're threatened with a knife."

Anna shrugged. "My point is that I don't go seeking excitement, sometimes I just run into it by accident."

"Are you hearing yourself? That makes it all the more exciting and wild!"

"But that's the thing, Wen. I don't *want* exciting and wild. Adam was exciting and wild, and I tried to keep up with him, but he scared me. And then Michael was a wash-and-repeat. I didn't learn a thing."

"They were reckless," Wendy said. "You were right to be scared. That's just common sense." She paused. "And I know what you're not saying, that Dad was more of the same."

Anna set down her turkey roll-up. "I couldn't have loved him more," she said quietly. "But yeah, he also took a lot of risks, like when we lost our place and had to move. That was . . ."

"Terrifying," Wendy agreed, chest tight. "You were only three, and after we moved, you had nightmares for a long time." She could remember her own nightmares after a few visits from CPS. They could've been taken away, but thankfully they weren't. "He got it together after that though. Got steady work, and things were never that bad again."

And what neither of them said was maybe that was thanks to a possible whole other source of income they hadn't known about. "You're afraid Owen is reckless."

"What I'm saying is that it doesn't really matter because I'm not looking for a long-haul sort of guy. This time, whatever happens is *just* for now, nothing more. I've decided I'm going to take all the fun I can get because, well, you've seen him. He's hot, and he makes me feel alive like nobody else has, so I'm just going to savor that for a second, maybe two."

"Did you forget you walked out on him?" She laughed at the look on Anna's face. "You did."

"I'm going to apologize."

Wendy was quiet for a moment, but she couldn't hold her tongue. "I feel like you're settling."

"And I feel like I'm being smart."

They ate in comfortable silence for a few moments. Or at least Wendy did, but then she realized Anna was watching her. "What?"

"You've been hiding it well, but something's off. What's wrong?"

She shrugged. As the big sister, she didn't want to be weak. "Other than being as big as a house, I'm fine."

"Now who's hiding the truth?" Anna asked. "Spill or I'll take the snacks away. And I could do it too—you can't run fast enough to catch me." She eyed Wendy's massive pregnancy boobs. "At least not without getting a black eye."

Wendy pushed around the snap peas, wishing they were real chips. "A group of my friends came over yesterday—none of whom have babies yet—and I could tell they were surprised by how big I was, my limitations, and how easily I tired." She tried to shrug it off.

"You've always been the glue that keeps everyone together, and right now you're probably just too tired."

"Yeah." She sighed. "Do you know how hard it is to be the extroverted, people-pleasing, everyone's-best-friend? It doesn't matter if I'm having a bad day, I always feel like I've gotta be upbeat and chipper."

"Oh, is it hard being so universally beloved?" Anna asked on a laugh. "Listen, it's because your energy is infectious. You can make or break anyone's day with just a look. Luckily, you tend to use your powers for good."

Wendy took that as a compliment, but it was also a burden. When their mom had died, leaving their dad so incredibly heartbroken, she'd made it her own personal mission to be the bright light in the family. But lately, she'd felt like that light had dimmed. The responsibility of keeping her babies healthy and inside her until it was safe for them to come out was really starting to weigh on her. "I feel like I'm letting everyone down."

"Not me." Anna was quiet a moment. "Wait. Do *I* make you feel that way?"

"Sometimes."

Anna flinched, and Wendy took her hand. "No, listen. I've always wanted to be more like you. Focused. Organized. Driven. I mean, yes, I used to be a teacher, but with the prices of daycare, I doubt I'll get to go back to it for a while, which means now I'm not even that. I'm just a walking, talking baby carrier."

Anna smiled. "Did you know I used to try to be more interesting and exciting for you and Dad, so I'd fit in?"

At that, Wendy burst into messy crocodile tears. "I'm so sorry! But you fit. Always. Forever!"

Anna handed her a box of tissues.

Wendy blew her nose. "Just FYI, I agree with Owen. I think Will was lying to you. Dad didn't do this. No way, no how, and the fact that Will tried to make you think otherwise tells me he knows more than he's letting on."

"But what if Dad did do it?"

"How can you ever say that? Dad would never—"

"Wen, the evidence is pointing right at him."

Wendy shook her head, a cracker stuck in her throat. "But what about Shady Joe? Seems to me, *that's* where the evidence is really pointing."

"Except Dad's the only one who has been caught with a coin in his possession," Anna pointed out.

As ANNA WAS leaving Wendy's, she saw Hayden coming down the street. She waved, then called her sister. "Hey," she said through her earbuds. "Your hubby's coming down your street right now." Reaching over to disconnect without looking, she drove the mile to her place. Stepping out of the car, she checked her phone for messages, then blinked at the realization that once again she hadn't disconnected from Wendy. Nope, instead, she'd inadvertently hit the hold button.

"Dumb," she told herself, and took the call off hold. She then went to disconnect the call but froze because . . . Wendy was talking, presumably to Hayden.

"You mean four," her sister was saying. "Once I give birth, I'll have four kids."

Anna blinked in confusion. Apparently, Hayden did too, because Wendy clarified.

"The triplets and Anna."

Anna froze. *What the—*

"Well, you did always want an entire litter," Hayden said.

Wendy laughed. "True enough." Then the laughter left her voice. "I worry about her, Hayden."

"Blanche, Rose, or Dorothy?"

"Not the triplets! And hard no on the Golden Girls."

Hayden chuckled. "Okay, fine. And why are you worried about Anna?"

Anna knew she should hang up, that Wendy had no idea their phones were still connected, but she couldn't move.

"I'm worried that with the babies, I won't have time to take care of Anna too, worried that she won't be okay. That she'll spiral again."

*Again . . .*

"Babe, Anna's a big girl. And you've meddled enough."

"If you're talking about how I set this whole thing in motion by asking her to figure out the coin's worth—"

"Which you did to force her on an adventure so she'd get out of her own head—"

"*Encourage*, not force," Wendy corrected. "And yes, I do realize how big it all backfired. It's my own fault that now Dad's name could be dragged through the mud publicly, destroying his legacy."

"Yet another reason to stop meddling," Hayden said, his tone soft and gentle.

Anna had turned to stone, her hand to her heart. Because what. The. Hell.

"I only meant to give her an excuse to have some fun," Wendy said.

"How's that working out for you?"

Wendy huffed out a sigh.

"You need to come clean," Hayden said. "Tell her the truth.

That you never meant to put her in a position where she'd have to prove your dad's innocence."

"Hello, did you not hear my worry about making her spiral again?"

Hayden murmured something that Anna missed. She didn't care, because betrayal had hit her square in the chest, stealing her breath, speeding up her heartbeat so that all she could hear was it pounding in her ears. Somehow she managed to disconnect the call and drop her forehead to her front door, which she hadn't even realized she'd walked to.

. . . *she'll spiral again* . . .

She gave herself a single moment of pity, then found her spine, straightened it, and went inside.

Clawdia sat in the entryway, her mismatched blue and green eyes narrowed up at her. Probably, she smelled Jennifur on her. The sisters hated each other. The cat sisters, not her and Wendy. Although, there were days . . .

"I'm late. I'm sorry." She scooped her up and cuddled her in close, getting a headbutt in the face—Clawdia's form of affection. "I'm glad *you* don't have a cell phone."

Clawdia began a rumbling purr that sounded like an old muscle car in need of a tune-up. She sat in the bathroom while Anna stripped down and climbed into the favorite part of her condo—her bathtub. The hot, steamy water rose up to her neck, and she leaned her head back with a heavyhearted sigh.

The thing was, she couldn't decide if she was embarrassed, sad, or mad, though she was making a good play for all three. She'd nearly fallen asleep when a knock came at her door. Nope, there was no one she wanted to see. Not a single soul.

Okay, well, maybe Owen.

When the knock came again, she tried to remember if she

had any packages coming. Probably Wendy with new spy gear. With a sigh, she hoisted herself out of the tub, wrapped up in a towel, and padded to the door. Going up on tiptoe, she peered out the peephole and froze.

Not Owen.

Will.

This was turning into a helluva day.

"I can hear you breathing," Will said.

That was a lie, because she wasn't breathing at all.

"Can we talk?" he asked through the wood.

"Now's not a great time. Why don't we meet at my office—"

"Please, Anna? We were friends once. I'm hoping that means as much to you as it means to me."

Shit. She turned to her coat closet on her right. It was the height of summer and the night was a warm one, but the only thing she had to cover up with was her full-length down jacket. She pulled it on and zipped it up to her chin. Then she drew a deep breath and opened the front door.

Will took in the hair piled on top of her head, the wisps wet from steam. Then her undoubtedly rosy face and the jacket with her bare feet poking out the bottom. He arched his brows.

"I was in the tub," she said. And was that alcohol she smelled on him? "What can I do for you?"

He tried to peer past her. "You alone?"

"What's going on, Will?"

He smiled, and for a beat she saw the vulnerable kid she'd once known. "Not letting me in, huh?"

"Not tonight, sorry."

He nodded, his smile fading, and that quick blink of the long-ago kid was gone, replaced by a man on the edge.

"Just get to the point, is that it?" he asked. "Fine. I want to see the coin."

With his smile gone, he looked . . . well, a whole lot like how she remembered Shady Joe looking. Rough around the edges. Closed off. She didn't like the way it made her feel vulnerable. "I can't show it to you."

"Why?"

"Because it's not here," she said.

"Where is it?"

"With the authorities." She tried to look completely at ease while naked beneath the coat and feeling far too exposed. "After all, it's not mine."

He lost the last vestige of his earlier friendliness. "I don't believe you."

"Believe what you want. This conversation's over." She started to shut the door, but he shoved his boot inside, stopping the door from shutting all the way.

Anna drew a deep, steady breath. "I'm not playing games, Will."

"You sure about that? Because it feels a whole bunch like you're playing with me. Let me in, Anna. We need to talk."

"Back up or I'll call the cops."

He held her gaze for a long beat, then must've decided she was serious because he pulled his foot free.

She didn't wait to see what he intended to do next. She shut the door, hit the lock and bolt, and then stood there, watching out the peephole long after Will was gone.

Whelp. No way was sleep going to happen now. She quickly stripped out of the down jacket that had her overheating, then went to her bedroom closet and pulled on a sundress before going to her second-favorite spot to think.

Her roof.

# CHAPTER 13

Midnight found Owen in bed, staring at the ceiling. He needed to be sleeping, he was beyond exhausted, but . . . he couldn't. Not when all he could think about was the look on Anna's face that evening just before she walked away from him.

*Guys like you aren't into girls like me . . .*

He wasn't even sure what she'd meant by that, but his heart ached that she'd even think such a thing about herself. "Nope," he said, and got out of bed.

Turbo lifted his big head, blinking sleepily at him. Turbo did not have trouble falling asleep because of stress. His dog didn't know the meaning of stress. "Go back to sleep."

When he pulled on jeans, Turbo sighed and stretched, hopping off the bed, tail wagging. Whatever the adventure was, he was in.

"No," Owen said, searching for his shoes. He found one under the bed—complete with Turbo-size teeth marks. He shot a dirty look at his dog, and Turbo's tail wagged even harder—doggy denial.

Owen found his other shoe near the door. He shoved his foot

in and met a web glob of Turbo saliva. Awesome. "You're still not coming."

Turbo trotted to the door.

"Like, at all."

Turbo nudged his nose to the door handle as if he could open it by his sheer level of enthusiasm.

"I'm serious."

Five minutes later, Owen was wrapping a seat belt around his ridiculous dog. "You're going to behave. No crotch sniffing. No eating anything. I mean it. Not like the time I brought you to Ruby's and you stuffed your nose in everyone's crotch and ate a couch."

Turbo did his best to look repentant. A complete lie.

Owen drove them through the dark, still night, thoughts forming that he hadn't let settle before now. Anna being so sure of her dad's innocence. His being so certain Ruby had been a victim . . .

But there was a truth he hadn't allowed to surface until now. What if Ruby had lost or misplaced the necklace and coins herself?

When he parked on Anna's street, he studied her two-story condo. It was dark, but everything inside him told him that she wasn't sleeping either. And then he realized the roof was lit up with fairy lights.

She was up there.

"Do you think she's okay?" he asked Turbo.

Turbo didn't know.

He eyed the fire escape, which he couldn't possibly reach unless he climbed the fence, but he didn't want to scare her to death. Plus, Turbo would have to stay in the car. He glanced at his dog. Probably best that he do that anyway. He pulled out his cell phone and stared at it. How to text her without looking like he was there for a booty call? Then his phone buzzed in his hand.

ANNA: I believe it's customary when you show up at someone's place for a booty call that you send a "you up?" text.

OWEN: Not a booty call. Can I see you? Just to talk?

ANNA: See, yep. Talk, hard pass.

Turbo yawned.

Owen looked at Turbo. "She's not okay. I'm going up. You're going to wait here with patience and self-control."

Turbo lay down and closed his eyes.

Owen got out and studied the fence. It would probably hold his weight. He scaled it quickly, then reached up for the fire escape. Once he pulled it down, the rest of the climb was a cinch.

He dropped onto the roof and straightened. It was small but clean, and completely private thanks to the outdoor privacy screen wrapping around all four sides, serving as a protection from neighboring condos. There was a green velour couch, an overturned pallet box for a makeshift coffee table, and a small portable fridge as an end table. Fairy lights were strung from corner to corner and also crisscrossed overhead.

And on the green velour couch, legs stretched out on the pallet box, sat the woman he couldn't stop thinking about.

She had a big bag of Doritos on her lap, a six-pack of beer minus one next to her bare, crossed feet. He couldn't see her face, but he didn't have to in order to know something was wrong. Really wrong. There was a stillness to her that he wasn't used to, all her usual vibrant, feisty energy at rest, a sadness settling around her as dark as the night.

He came around to the front of the couch. She wore a simple blue sundress, and her hair was piled on top of her head, which was tipped back as she stared up at the stars. "You've seen me, so feel free to go now."

He moved closer. Not wanting to crowd her, he didn't take a seat next to her. Instead, he crouched at her side and studied her face.

Definitely sad.

Definitely had been crying.

"What's wrong?" he asked quietly.

"Did you miss my no-talking decree?"

He looked her over. She wasn't hurt, at least not on the outside. One of the spaghetti straps of her sundress had slipped off a shoulder. With her feet on the box, the hem had slipped up her thighs, making her legs look a mile long. At any other moment, he'd be fantasizing about her wrapping them around him. "Anna."

"Fine." She shrugged. "It's been a shitty day that ended with an annoying visit from Will when I was in the tub."

He tensed. He hadn't liked the guy from the moment he'd laid eyes on him, and it had nothing to do with his feelings for the woman before him. "Annoying how?"

Something in his voice must've alerted her because she turned her head and met his gaze. "You know I can handle myself, right?"

"I do know. I think you're the most capable woman I've ever met."

That seemed to mollify her. "He wanted to see the coin," she said. "I lied, told him I didn't have it, that I'd given it to the authorities."

"Good thinking."

"He didn't believe me."

He felt his inner caveman stir. "So he . . . what? Left quietly?"

"He'd been drinking." She lifted a shoulder. "It took a little encouragement."

Anger churned in his gut as he ran his gaze over her, looking for any obvious signs of injury. "What kind of encouragement?"

"You want to know if you need to beat the shit out of him."

"Yes."

She shook her head. "I used words, not fists, and he left."

He wanted to press for more information, but he also wanted her to know he trusted her to handle herself. "And the rest of your shitty day?" he asked with what he thought was a cool calm.

For a long moment, she didn't speak, and he thought that was it. She didn't intend to tell him anything else, which was killing him because *what else had happened*?

"I had a fight with my sister." She paused. "Well, actually, she doesn't know we're in a fight this time." Her eyes filled but didn't spill, and he realized there was nothing as humbling as being witness to the strongest woman he'd ever met allowing him to see her vulnerable.

"It was my stupid phone," she said softly. "She didn't know I still had my earbuds in or that I'd hit hold instead of disconnecting our call." She closed her eyes. "She was telling Hayden how in the beginning, she'd tried to send me on a wild goose chase about the coin so I'd"—she used air quotes—"'have an excuse to have some fun.'" She shook her head. "Because with Wendy moving on with her life and having babies and all, she won't have the same amount of time to take care of me."

He didn't say anything, and she turned her head and looked at him, her brilliant eyes swimming with hurt and betrayal.

He rose and gestured to the spot next to her. "May I?"

She nodded, and he sat at her side. "I'm sorry, Anna."

She leaned into him and very slowly set her head on his shoulder. He wrapped his arm around her, holding her close, and she sighed softly.

"I shouldn't care what she thinks. I should be pissed off she's always trying to manipulate me. Also, why do you always smell good?" She turned her face into his chest and inhaled deeply. "And why, when you touch me, does everything else sort of fade away?"

Very gently, he stroked a loose auburn wave from her temple, tucking it behind her ear. "Right back at you."

She closed her eyes, but he didn't have to be able to see them to know she was miserable. "If it helps, I think you're the most capable, strong, resilient, fascinating, and smartest woman I've ever met."

Her lips curved slightly. "Yes, but that's only because you want to sleep with me."

"Well, yeah. I mean, have you seen yourself?" he teased with a smile, which he let fade as he held her gaze. He also held his tongue because she seemed incline to talk even though she'd said she didn't want to, and he wanted to give her the space to do that without his getting in her way.

She'd cracked a small smile at his quip but looked away. "She told Hayden she didn't want me to spiral again."

He winced for her inwardly. Because spiral . . . *again*?

"Do you want to know the worst part?"

He reached for her hand and gave it a light squeeze. "Yes."

"I can't even be mad. Because I *have* spiraled in the past. Twice. Once when I was sixteen, when I found out my mom died in childbirth with me. Up until then, I'd thought she died in a car accident. That's what my dad had told me, but I had to write an essay in my English class about our biggest trauma, and I googled my mom's name to get some more information on her."

"Oh, Anna," he breathed, hurting for her.

"I get why he lied. He didn't want me to blame myself for her death. Unfortunately, that's exactly what happened." When he opened his mouth, she said, "It's okay. I got to a better place."

"And the again part?" he asked quietly.

She looked away. "For a hot minute, when Michael went to jail, I came under some suspicion for claiming not to know anything and being unable to help in the investigation against him."

He hated that the men in her life had screwed with her so badly. Cupping one side of her jaw in his hand, he gently turned her face back to him. "I hope you were able to convince the authorities you were innocent."

"How do you know I was innocent?"

"I just know."

That won him a small smile. "I have the feeling that also circles back to the whole you-want-to-sleep-with-me thing."

He laughed softly. "Don't think I don't know you're trying to change the subject."

"Fine. I honestly knew nothing and managed to convince the police of that. But the doubts, the whispers, the rumors . . ." She shook her head. "I don't know, I let it get inside me and eat me up. I . . . fell apart. Not as badly as I did when I found out about my mom and the fact that even Wendy had kept that secret from me, but I climbed into bed and didn't want to leave. I got some counseling and meds. If it wasn't for Wendy, along with good friends like Mari and Nikki, I'd probably still be in bed. They showed up every day, refusing to let me wallow alone."

He entangled their fingers and brought their joined hands to his heart, which ached for her. "I'm sorry you went through that," he said, instead of what he *wanted* to say, which was that he'd like to hunt down her ex and give him a piece of his mind and possibly a fist to the face.

"And then there's my secret freakout . . . I'm afraid Wendy's going to . . ." She swallowed hard. "Die in childbirth."

Pulling her in, he hugged her tight, rocking them both a little for comfort, having no idea what to say. *It's going to be all right?* No one knew that. *Don't worry?* He'd never patronize her that way.

"The thing is," she said, keeping her face buried against his chest, "about Wendy being worried: I get it. I do. Except . . ." She shook her head. "I don't know if it's because I've grown up, or if I've slowly come into my own, but I've never felt stronger. Inside and out. And Wendy knows that, or she should, I'm with her all the damn time. So she has no business doubting me."

"Maybe she's scared too."

She lifted her face. "Of what?"

"Of her own life getting so crazy that she might lose a bit of you."

"It won't be her own life to cause that, but the fact that she can't stop trying to direct mine."

He had to really work on that holding-his-tongue thing, because he didn't want to stem the flow. Learning more about her, the real her, fascinated him. She was captivating. Complicated. Beautiful.

She gave him a long look and the "gimme" gesture. "Let's hear it."

"Hear what?"

"You've got a contrasting opinion about something I just said."

"This is your life, Anna. I'll never be the person in it who tries to direct it for you."

"Tell me anyway."

"She's your only blood family. If you have a problem with what she's doing, you should tell her rather than letting your resentment build inside you until it ruptures your relationship." He paused. "I don't have any siblings, but I had my mom, and we pretty much raised each other. She's gone now, but I'd give anything, *anything*, to have her back, even if it was just to argue with her one more time."

"You think I should tell Wendy that I heard what she said about me?"

"I think you should do what feels right for you."

She stared at him, then shook her head. "I can't confront her. She has too much stress and worry as it is, I won't add to it."

He hated that she was scared for Wendy and had kept that fact as her own burden this whole time. He was attracted to so many things about her, but this might be his very favorite thing: how much she cared.

"I mean, am I angry she tried to manipulate me into an adventure with this coin thing, which turned out to be something very real?" she asked. "Yes. I'm furious. But the truth is, she's been the self-proclaimed boss of me since birth. It doesn't make it okay, but I should've said something a long time ago."

"Anna." He slid a callus-roughened palm up her back to the nape of her neck, his fingers threading into her hair. She shivered, which made him want to do it again, but first, because he wasn't as good as she at burying feelings: "Promise me something."

Her expression turned a little wary. "No promises."

Right. "Just this one: Don't bury this deep. It'll only eat at you."

She put a hand to his chest. "You care about me."

"Far more than I meant to. And while we're here talking about feelings, I'd like to know what you meant when you said guys like me aren't into girls like you."

She drew a deep breath. "I've told you my relationship history. I've given my heart away, and I wasn't exciting enough to keep."

He cupped her face. "That's their loss, because you're the most exciting, fascinating woman I've ever met."

ANNA FELT HER gaze drop from his eyes to his mouth, which she really wanted on hers again. She wanted that far more than she wanted to hear herself talk. Frankly, she was quite tired of herself and *really* tired of being on an emotional roller coaster. When she was with Owen, all her emotions settled. Calmed. She'd never experienced anything like it. She'd never been addicted to anything, ever—well, maybe ice cream—but she could feel herself willing to fall into an addiction to one Owen Harris. She opened her mouth to say his name at the exact moment he whispered hers.

Their gazes locked and held, his revealing a rare hesitation that maybe she should heed. She'd worked long and hard to rein herself in. Nothing good had ever come of her letting loose, giving up control. Those days of following her every impulse were long gone.

Long.

Gone.

Nope. No way would she give in to them, no matter how sexy Owen was. And good Lord, he was as sexy as they came. But he was also a man who lived a dangerous lifestyle, plus she doubted he'd ever corral his adventurous side. And why would he? He'd made it work for him.

But it didn't work for Anna.

And yet somehow this made him even more desirable. Fisting her hands in his shirt, she tried to pull him into her.

Only he held firm, his lips hovering over hers until she couldn't stand it any longer. "Dammit," she whispered against them. "I like you so much more than I should." Sliding her hands into his hair, she closed the millimeter of space between them and kissed him. By the time he lifted his head, she was shaking and breathing heavily.

"I like you so much more than I should too," he said quietly. "But I won't take advantage of you when you're feeling vulnerable. I need to go before something happens tonight that you'll regret."

"What makes you think I'll regret it?" She was both overheating at the thought of the "it" in question and somehow wanting, needing, to lighten the mood. "Are you . . . bad at *it*?"

She expected a smile. Instead, his eyes heated. "Under any other circumstances, I'd say *try me*. But this isn't the right time. You've had a difficult day, you're going through a lot. You need—"

"You're not really going to try to tell me what I need, are you?"

A wry smile came and went in his eyes. "No."

She smiled back while pressing herself fully against him, getting a thrill from the hitch in his breathing. He cupped her face in his hands, eyes on hers as the rough pads of his fingers slid along her jawline. "I want you, Anna. So much, but—"

"No buts," she breathed, kissing one corner of his mouth, then the other, fisting her hand in his shirt to keep him from moving away. "Stay tonight," she said. "*Please—*"

Thankfully he shut her up by crushing his mouth to hers—she hadn't wanted to talk anymore. She didn't want to feel hurt and betrayed anymore. All she wanted was this. Pulling back, she got up on her knees, turning to face Owen.

"You have a plan," he said.

She did. But at the moment, she was into show-not-tell, so she climbed into his lap. She hadn't expected to tell him about what had happened with Wendy, any more than she'd expected him to show up when, as it turned out, she'd needed someone more than she'd known.

Him. She'd needed him.

She'd asked him to not talk, and he hadn't. He'd just listened, making her want to give him some of what he'd given her.

So she did.

She'd barely leaned over him when his hands went to her hips, guiding her so that she was straddling him, the insides of her thighs snugged to the outside of his.

"Tell me more about this plan," he murmured huskily, his fingers tracing their way up and down her back, palming her ass.

With a smile, she slid her hands beneath his shirt to get at his warm skin. "Finally. I thought you were going to play hard to get forever."

He laughed.

"My plan," she said, grinning back at him, "involves driving us both out of our minds so that we can't think. I'm tired of thinking."

He opened his mouth to say something, but just in case, she kissed him. Kissed him until whatever words he'd intended to let loose turned into a rough, thrillingly masculine groan. When she broke it off to breathe and try to tug off his shirt, his lips curved into a sinful smile.

"Don't tease me," she said. She needed his clothes off. Needed him inside her.

Yesterday.

"Here, Anna?"

*Yes. A thousand times yes, please. Right here, right now.*

He captured her busy hands in his, making her whimper in frustration as his mouth then bypassed hers to skim along her jaw to her ear. He whispered her name in a way that had her eyes fluttering closed, because just the dark velvet sound of his voice reverberated through her like sinful seduction. Trying to facilitate things along, she tugged her hands free and worked to get his shirt off him.

"There are a lot of things I'd do for you," he said. "But rushing this isn't one of them." He held her close, 175 pounds of lean muscle and highly motivated and determined male testosterone surrounding her. With a wicked smile that sent a shiver of the very best kind through her, he kissed down her throat, eliciting a sound of pleasure from her.

"Love that sound," he murmured.

She had her hands inside his clothes, trying to get him naked. "Owen."

"Right here." His fingers nudged down the other strap of her sundress and with a little encouragement, the material slipped to her waist and she was bared to him and the night. "Mmm, and the way you taste . . ." Lowering his head, he kissed everything he'd uncovered. "And I especially love the way you look like this."

"At your mercy, you mean."

"You've got that entirely backward." He pulled off his shirt, which left her momentarily stunned as she stared at him in appreciation. She'd seen him shirtless before, at the beach, but that didn't lessen the impact any. Wrapping her arms around his neck, she pressed herself as close as possible to the hard planes of his body, but she needed still more, so she reached between them to open his jeans.

Suddenly he stilled, eyes apologetic. "Anna, I don't have anything on me."

It took her sex-addled brain a moment to understand what he'd said. "Oh. I, um . . . I'm on the pill. And as for . . . other concerns, I haven't done this in a while. Like, a really long while."

He cupped her face, his own serious. "Same."

"Yeah, right." She poked him. "You forget, I've met two of your conquests already."

He smiled. "This might be hard to believe, but it's been a long time for me too."

"How long?"

"Six months, maybe more."

He was a man of few words, but he knew how to make those few words count. She took a deep breath and concentrated on the way his fingertips were tracing up and down her spine, leaving a fire in their wake that she felt all the way to her toes. She opened her eyes and looked into his, her heart clenching as she saw something that she hadn't expected to find.

Emotion.

It was raw and unspoken, but as apparent as the beat of her heart. When he brushed his lips across hers, she laced her fingers in his hair, holding him close. "Can we get to the 'here, now' portion of the evening?"

With a low, sexy laugh, he urged her dress up her thighs, giving a heartfelt groan at the sight of her little black undies. She gasped as his fingers teased her over the silky material until she was panting. They wriggled to get into a good position, bumping into each other, laughing and swearing as they tried to line things up. Finally, he let her sink over him until he was in as deep as he could go. When she rolled her hips to his, his head fell back, eyes closed, a look of raw pleasure on his face.

"Slow," his voice rumbled.

She tried. She really did. But she couldn't hold back, and apparently he couldn't either. They took each other, hard and fast, until they both lost their minds.

After, when he opened his eyes and looked deep into hers, he gave her a crooked smile. "For the record, I'm at *your* mercy, Anna. Always."

*Same* . . . Even more shocking, she'd let her true nature out. What they'd just done had been spontaneous and more than a little wild, and she'd instigated it. Hi. Hello. It was her. *She* was the bad influence. *She'd* been the one unable to keep her hands to herself.

And yet, as promised, she had zero regrets.

They were still cuddled up on the couch in the afterglow when a loud horn sounded from the street and made her jump.

The horn went off again, another short blast, and then another.

"Oh shit," Owen muttered.

"What?"

"Turbo hits the horn when he feels he's waited too long. He used to just eat a seat, but he got tired of being in trouble. The horn is his new favorite thing."

While Anna laughed, Owen threw his clothes back on. The view was pretty awesome, and when she heard a soft chuckle, she tore her eyes off his bod and met his amused gaze.

"What?" she said. "I like to look."

He grinned. "Good to know—"

Another horn beep, longer this time.

Owen swore again and shoved his feet into his beat-up running shoes before heading to the edge of the roof where the fire escape began. "Oh, and, Anna? I like to look at you too."

And then he was gone.

# CHAPTER 14

Wendy lay sleepless in bed, her mind revved up like it knew something that the rest of her didn't. She'd long ago learned not to ignore her sometimes odd sense of unease, as it meant something was off or wrong.

But she didn't know what. Sage, Rosemary, and Thyme—hmm, probably not—were all present and accounted for and having a grand old time inside her. Her pulse was normal.

What could be wrong? Hayden had gotten a call from work about a systems crash and had gone in. He probably wouldn't be back for a while. And Anna . . . huh. It was midnight, and Wendy realized her sister hadn't called or texted her today.

Her sister radar was humming.

Rolling out of her cocoon, she reached for her phone and texted Anna, *You okay?* When she didn't get an immediate response—weird in its own right because one thing she could always count on Anna for was to always be there—she texted a question mark. She distracted herself by wondering if her toenail polish was chipped, but when she still didn't hear back from Anna, she called.

And got her voicemail.

She then checked the Find My app and was relieved to see Anna's dot at home, probably asleep.

Except . . . she still had a feeling of impending doom. This meant sleep would be all but impossible. Food would probably help. So she climbed out of bed and hit up the kitchen for a quick snack, then migrated back to the bedroom. It took a lot of nest building and pillow twisting, but after a few minutes, she was cradled like a boat docked on dry land and finally ready to sleep.

Almost.

Ugh. Stupid bladder.

After a trip to the bathroom and a second rebuilding of the nest, she finally managed to drift off and didn't wake up until she felt the telltale change in air pressure that meant she wasn't alone.

Hayden hardly made a sound crossing the room. He pulled back the blankets to kiss her belly in greeting. "Did you kiddos wear Mommy out again?"

The babies nudged and squirmed in answer. "Victoria, Ginger, and Mel missed you," she murmured.

"We're not naming our babies after the Spice Girls."

She gasped in surprise. "You know the Spice Girls' names? Who are you, and what have you done with my husband?"

He grimaced. "You're going to tell Anna, aren't you?"

"Of course I am. In fact, I'm going to call her right now—" She stopped short because one, she still hadn't gotten a response from Anna, and two, she also suddenly remembered something.

Last night, when Anna had left at the same time that Hayden had come home, she'd been distracted. Hayden had come inside, and they'd been talking when she'd heard something from her phone lying on her bed. Three short beeps, the kind you heard when a call had just been disconnected. At the time, she'd been too addled by exhaustion to think anything of it.

But now her brain was racing. Because Anna had called her briefly as she drove away, letting her know Hayden was pulling in. Anna had disconnected the call. But . . . what if she hadn't? What if she'd accidentally put her on hold again? Wendy tried to remember what she'd been talking to Hayden about . . .

Oh shit.

She'd been talking to Hayden about *Anna*.

Oh, God. She'd said how worried she was and how she'd set this whole nightmare in motion by trying to keep Anna busy so she wouldn't spiral again.

What if Anna had heard her? Calm down, because really, what were the chances? But given the way her heart was racing, she had to think the chances were high. "Uh-oh."

Hayden went brows up. "That's your I've-done-something-bad 'uh-oh.' What did you do?"

"Me?" She made a grand gesture to her belly. "Do I look like I'm capable of doing anything? It's a misunderstanding!" A misunderstanding of the highest magnitude that was all her own fault, but no need to admit guilt. Yet. "Gimme your phone for a sec."

He handed it over, then watched curiously as Wendy hit her sister's number and waited. And sure enough, Anna answered, voice low and husky, like maybe she'd woken her up. "When you're alive," she snapped, "you answer your phone!"

Disconnect.

Wendy pulled Hayden's phone from her ear and stared at it. "Wow."

"What?"

"She hung up on me!"

Hayden's phone began to ring. He wriggled his fingers in a hand-it-over gesture, so Wendy did. "Hey," he said, obviously to Anna. He listened for a beat. "Uh-huh," he said, his eyes tracking to Wendy.

Ruh-roh.

"Uh-huh," he said again.

Yep, this was bad. Very, very bad.

Hayden sighed. "These days people frown on men attempting to control their wives, but if you could give me more details, I'll see what I can do." He listened some more. His mouth was grim. "Understood." He disconnected and looked at Wendy.

"Well?" she asked.

"Do you want to revise your earlier statement, the one where you said you didn't do anything?"

"What did she tell you?"

"She wouldn't give me any details. All she'd say was that she wasn't ready to talk to you unless it was about the babies, your health, or the babies' health. Those are the only reasons you're to call or text her until otherwise notified. She needs a little space." He pulled her into him. "Why does she need space, Wen?"

Wendy sniffed. "She overheard our conversation last night."

He was quiet a moment, clearly running said conversation through his head. He grimaced. "So . . . you're going to give her the space, right?"

"How much space does she need, do you think?"

"Wendy."

"Just kidding. I'll give her space." Probably. Maybe. Hopefully . . . "Obviously, I wish she hadn't heard us saying all that about her—"

"*Us?*"

She sucked in a breath and felt her eyes fill again. Because, dammit, he was right. It'd been all her.

"And how could she have heard?" Hayden asked. "She was already gone. Did she come back inside for something?"

"No, she called me as she was leaving to let me know you were pulling up. My phone had slipped off my pillow and I couldn't easily reach it, so I let her disconnect the call. Only I'm guessing she didn't actually disconnect, that she accidentally hit hold by mistake, which she's done before. I assume when she realized her mistake, she took the call off hold and I was, you know, saying stuff about her."

"I mean, you've done worse." He brushed a kiss to her temple. "But I'm sure an apology would help."

"Do you remember exactly what I said?"

"You mentioned sending her on a goose chase about the coin and how you hope she doesn't spiral again."

She deflated. "Did I really say 'spiral'?"

"Yes."

Okay, this was bad. Really bad.

"Wen, just own up to it. Talk it through with her, tell her you worry, but you would never hurt her on purpose."

She sighed. "I hate when you use sound logic and reasoning or whatever, when I'm really just looking for someone to be as overdramatic about this situation as I am."

"Babe." He leaned over her and brushed his mouth to hers. "Listen, there's nothing you can do about this right now. Think about something else. What did you do today?"

"I don't know. Breathed a lot. Sighed a lot. Peed a lot. The list goes on."

He smiled sympathetically. "I brought you something you're going to like." He vanished for a moment and came back with a pound cake that had a mountain of strawberries glued to the top with whipped cream.

"I've never loved you more," she whispered reverently.

"I hope you'll still feel that way when I tell you it's sugar-free."

"Fork."

He pulled a plastic fork from his back pocket, and she found a laugh. "You know me well."

"I do." He stripped out of his shirt, and she paused, fork halfway up to her mouth, to enjoy the sight as he headed into the bathroom for a shower.

"Oh and hey," she yelled at his retreating and very sexy back. "What have I done that's worse?"

He poked his head back out. "Is that one of those rhetorical questions?"

"No, I really want to know."

"Okay, how about that time you signed her up on what you thought was a dating site but was really a hookup site."

"That was an accident!"

He nodded. "And setting her up with a guy you knew would be bad for her? Michael?"

"I didn't know he'd be bad for her, I thought he'd be fun. And I feel like shit for how it went down. Anything else?"

"That time you yelled at her for taking your phone charger, but then a week later you found it in the bottom of your purse and you never told her."

Gah. Note to self: don't ask for any more examples of her being a bad sister.

WENDY WOKE UP to wiggling babies and a gurgling stomach. She reached for her husband, but he wasn't there. The sheets were warm though, and she realized she could hear the shower going. This meant he'd gone running without waking her up—a first. The man was hot, but he couldn't be quiet to save his own life.

His being up and getting ready for the day meant that he hopefully had plans to feed her pronto. While she was fantasizing about pancakes and sausage, he came out of the bathroom, steam swirling all around him. Naked, he strolled toward his dresser, completely natural, as comfortable out of clothes as he was in them. And why shouldn't he be? He played basketball with his buddies several times a week, was also on a hockey team, and on the days he hadn't done anything active, he ran.

By choice.

Boggling. But it sure gave her something nice to look at, and even nicer to touch whenever she wanted.

He looked at her and laughed. "You're thinking about sex or food."

"How do you know?"

"Because you're drooling." He grinned when she swiped her chin just in case he was being serious. "Which is it? Sex or food?"

"Guess."

"Don't worry. I know where I stack up against pancakes and sausage."

"Does that upset you?" she asked, suddenly worried.

He gave a soft laugh. "Babe, I'll be second fiddle to food any day, as long as I'm your number one man."

Her heart melted. "Always."

"Good thing then that I ordered takeout from the diner. Pancakes and sausage." He leaned over the bed and kissed her belly, then her mouth. "You hear from Anna?"

"No, and I'm working my way up to groveling. Still planning the speech."

"She doesn't want a speech. Go with your first instinct and grovel." He kissed the top of her head. "Later."

When he'd left the bedroom, she flopped back and muttered to herself, "No 'I love you, Wendy.' No 'Be safe, Wendy.'" Maturely, she stuck her tongue out at her bedroom door. "I know you find me entertaining, but a little romance wouldn't kill you." She knew this was completely and totally unfair. He was romantic. He was just more a man of action than words. But sometimes, a girl needed the words . . .

The bedroom door opened, and she was pulled into a set of warm, strong arms. Hayden kissed her until her knees buckled. "I love you, be safe," he said in a low voice. Then he flashed a grin, tugged playfully on her ponytail, and strode out again.

She grinned and reached for her phone to call Anna, but hesitated instead of dialing. Sagging back, she stared up at the ceiling. For most of their growing-up years, Wendy had been the babysitter, mom, dad, teacher, parole officer, and authority on all things involving Anna. And somehow, when she hadn't been looking, Anna had grown up to be 100 percent independent from everyone.

Including Wendy.

She wanted to talk to Anna about that, and so many other things, wanted to hug her tight and make promises and apologies and clear the air, but Anna, who never asked for anything, had asked for some space.

And Wendy, if she wanted any shot at getting her sister back, was going to have to oblige.

# CHAPTER 15

O wen was yanked from an erotic dream involving a moonlit night on the lake and a naked Anna when his phone began buzzing its way across his nightstand. It was 6:00 a.m., and the caller was the woman in his dream.

"Sorry if I woke you," Anna said.

He scrubbed a hand down his face, trying to shrug off the sensual fog. Turbo helped by climbing up his body to lick his face. "You okay?" he asked Anna, not the dog, who he gently pushed away.

"I've . . . got a question," she said.

In his dream she'd had a question too, involving kissing her way down his body and asking him after each brush of her lips if he liked what she was doing . . .

"So?" she asked.

He'd missed her question and did his best to shove the dream away.

"I'm not sure you understand how this phone thing works," she said. "You have to actually use words."

"Maybe I'd rather use my words on other things."

"Ah, so you *do* have an allocated number of words per day. I knew it." There was amusement in her voice now. "What is it? One hundred? Two hundred?"

He smiled. "Anna."

"One."

He laughed.

"Oh, crap," she said. "I gotta go, my other line's going off."

"Your question—"

But she was gone.

He was still thinking about her a few hours later at work out on the lake, when a hard gust of wind came out of nowhere, knocking him right off his paddleboard and face-first into the water.

When he surfaced, Ky was laughing so hard he nearly fell off his own board. "You okay, princess? Need a hand?"

He offered Ky his middle finger and climbed back on his board, eyeing the wild whitecaps that had appeared across the water as far as the eye could see. Had to be fifteen knots, which certainly hadn't been in his daily weather memo. But that was Tahoe for you—in regards to the weather, the only thing you could predict was that it would be unpredictable.

They'd given a kayaking class that had ended an hour ago and were now trying out some new boards. "Someone wasn't thinking about what he was doing," Ky said. "Someone's mind was far away. Probably on the woman who's turned him upside down and inside out—just like that last gust of wind."

Owen rolled his eyes. "I was thinking about how I'm going to kick my partner's ass back to shore so that he has to buy lunch."

"You're on. Three, two . . ." And Ky took off.

"Cheater!" Owen yelled.

As they'd done a thousand times, they raced for the beach,

dogging the crazy swells the best they could. When Ky, ahead of Owen by one length of a board, turned to look back and eye him smugly, Owen grinned. Ky's smug smile faded as he whipped back around, but it was too late.

He took a huge swell right in the face and was launched.

Owen laughed so hard, he had to drop to his knees to hold on.

Ky surfaced, sputtering. "I meant to do that," he said as Owen stood back up and passed right on by him.

"Hey, what about the bro code!" Ky yelled at his back. "You stop when your bro is down!"

"Not if your 'bro' is a cheater!" He was grinning as he got closer to shore. Lunch always tasted better when Ky had to buy—

Ky came up alongside him and launched off his board to take Owen out in a flying tackle. They then spent a good ten minutes trying to drown each other, made all the easier by their laughter because they each kept getting caught under a swell with their mouth open. Luckily, Owen was a slightly better swimmer and was able to shove clear and get back on his board just as the winds . . .

Died.

"*Seriously?*"

Ky grinned as he came up on him, and Owen started paddling like his life depended on it. He hit the beach half a second before Ky. They lay there huffing and puffing beneath a gorgeous summer sun.

"Sheer luck," Ky claimed.

"Keep telling yourself that."

They dried off and locked up the boards, then sat on the beach a moment to catch their breath. "With a bottle of something sparkly, this could be a date," Ky said.

"You're not my type."

"Because I don't have auburn hair and pretty brown eyes?" Ky asked with a smirk.

"Because you're a dumbass." But now he was thinking about Anna, remembering of all things the look on her face when she'd told him about Will's visit. Her voice had been calm, though her body language had been anything but. Will had spooked her. "I'm thinking about dropping this whole thing with the missing coins and necklace," he said. "It's starting to feel dangerous for Anna."

Ky looked surprised. "I don't know her like you do, but I do know she'd hate that, man." He studied Owen. "And maybe it's not so much for her sake as it is for yours?"

"What the hell does that mean?"

"It means," Ky said in such a reasonable tone that Owen wanted to punch him, "that I think you'd feel safer backing off because then you don't have to decide whether or not to keep her in your life. Which we both know you want to."

"*You* know nothing."

Ky smiled, but it faded quick. "Look, we've both been alone a long time. We're used to having no one care. She's good for you."

Owen shook his head. That wasn't the point. The point was that he'd pushed her to solve this case—for his and his aunt's sake. And now she had psycho Will on her ass. He'd let his emotions get in the way, and now she was in danger, he could feel it in his bones. "Do you love Sami?"

Ky's head whipped around, and he stared at Owen like he'd grown a second head. With horns. "What?"

"I know you have feelings for her, and it's okay. She has feelings for you too."

Ky had gone deer in the headlights. "But you two—"

"Weren't good for each other, and our feelings never went deeper than friends," Owen said. "It's okay. You're good for her. Do you care about her?"

Ky blinked once, slow as an owl. "Are we seriously going to talk about this?"

"Yes."

Ky sighed. "Fine. Yeah. I care about her."

"And you'd protect her, right? Even if it meant walking away? Because you love her."

"Are you saying you're falling in love with Anna— Shit." Ky ran his hands over his face, swearing beneath his breath. "Look, man, next time you decide to have an emotional meltdown, text me so I can call in sick."

"It wasn't a meltdown," Owen said, but he was talking to himself because Ky had pushed to his feet and was walking away.

And hell, maybe it was a meltdown. Or as close to one as a man like him could get. He caught up with Ky just as they walked into the front door of headquarters. Turbo leapt off his bed in the entryway and ran toward Owen, his entire hind end wriggling, his tail whipping the air. Once he'd wagged his tail so hard in the doorway, catching it on the hard wood frame, that he'd actually broken it. It hadn't dulled his enthusiasm any, he was just careful not to wag in entrances.

Owen hunkered down and opened his arms. Turbo ran right into them and licked him from chin to forehead. "Sorry I couldn't take you out with me." Turbo loved to paddleboard. He sat on the front of the board, the wind in his face, mouth grinning, tongue lolling. "The winds were too much. Tomorrow, maybe."

This got him another lick of forgiveness.

Sami stood there watching this with a small smile. "I took

him for a walk. Cooper scared him so badly that I had to pick him up."

Cooper was eight pounds soaking wet, some mix of cockapoo and the devil. He lived at the boat mechanic's place next door and loved to terrorize Turbo. It'd started last year, when Cooper had run circles around a frozen-in-place Turbo, nipping at the bigger dog's heels. Finally Turbo had lifted a leg and peed on the little guy.

Who'd never forgotten. "He's too heavy for you."

"Excuse me," Sami said, insulted. "I've been weight training. I can lift your dog. I can also kick your ass. Maybe not right now because I had to lift him a second time over the gutters when we crossed the street to come back."

Turbo huffed a sigh.

"It's okay," Sami told him. "I still love you." She turned to the guys. "The local Girl Scout troop is here for the rafting trip they set up a month ago, and no one's on the schedule. Both Braden and Antonio are out with clients. Which of you two bozos are going to take it?"

Owen and Ky did ro-sham-bo, and Owen lost, making him groan. Business was great, and each client was important to them, but the idea of taking twelve sixth-grade girls on a two-hour trip down the river definitely leaned more toward work than fun.

His phone rang, and one glance had him groaning for another reason entirely. It was his aunt's caregiver.

"Ruby's having a rough day," Nan said when he answered. "I'm sorry, but you wanted me to call you when this happened."

"Don't be sorry, I definitely wanted the call, so thank you. What's going on?"

"Today at breakfast, she told everyone she came into contact with that Santa had been in her room stealing things."

This was not the first time this had happened. Ruby didn't have anything of value there, her things were all still at her house. He swiped a hand down his face.

"We've got it handled," Nan said. "She's safe, and nothing else is wrong. I just wanted to let you know."

"I appreciate it." He disconnected, then stood there a moment staring at his phone. He knew how lucky he was that Ruby was being taken care of by people who understood how to handle any issue that came up, but damn, it was still hard that he couldn't do it himself, that he had to rely on others.

"What's wrong?"

He looked up, and both Ky and Sami were still standing there, looking worried. The very last thing he wanted to do was talk about this. Not because it was hard for him, though it was. But his great-aunt had been such a proud woman, it felt like a betrayal to share what her life was like now. "Apparently it's been a rough morning. She's making up stories again. I'm going to have to go see her."

"I get that," Ky said, then sighed. "Fine. I'll take the rafting trip. But you owe me."

"I'll get everything ready," Sami told Ky. She hugged Owen and walked off.

Ky was watching him. "You okay, man?"

"Yeah." He shook his head. "She told everyone that Santa had gone into her room and stolen from her."

Ky let out a low whistle of sympathy.

"Makes me wonder what else she's made up."

"You thinking you're on the wrong side of the investigation?"

He was seriously beginning to wonder. Anna ran on facts and logic, which he appreciated more than he could possibly articulate. "Anna doesn't think her dad had a hand in this, and I'm starting to believe the same."

"She's really got your attention, doesn't she?"

Owen narrowed his eyes.

Ky lifted his hands. "Hey, man, any woman who can make you laugh and is as smart and hot as she is? You better hold on to that."

"Not discussing this."

"Oh, because you already had your emotional meltdown and now you're fine?"

"Because I just remembered you've got a big mouth. You gossip like a sixth grader."

Ky grinned. "Been a long time since you resorted to dumb insults as a misdirection."

"This is about Ruby."

"Uh-huh."

Sami came back and pointed at Ky. "Stop poking at him."

Ky laughed. "Come on, you know you want more info about him and Anna every bit as much as I do."

"Well, duh," she said. "But you know that the more you push, the more he's going to shut up about her." The office phone rang, and she sighed. "Take notes," she told Ky, and left them alone.

Ky looked at Owen. "I'm not going to take notes, so if she kills me, it's on you."

"This isn't about me and Anna. It's about Ruby. I've got no idea how to tell truth from fiction with her anymore. And I don't think she knows either. She'd never want this for herself."

Ky's expression went serious. He didn't have family beyond Owen and Sami. At least not that he wanted to be associated with. "She's rough on you, and outright cruel sometimes."

Owen shook his head. "That's the dementia."

"Still, not many people would step up like you have. You got her into one of the best local assisted and memory care facilities around, and you continuously go to battle with her insurance company to pay what they owe. And what they don't cover, you kick in the remaining balance. You also take care of her house. What more could you possibly do?"

He didn't know, but it didn't feel like enough. "When my dad cleaned my mom out and took off, Ruby took me and my mom in off the street, supporting us when we were completely broke and homeless. It forever changed the course of our lives for the better. I feel like I could never repay her."

Ky looked stricken. "I know everything about you, but I didn't know that—that your dad cleaned you guys out or that you ended up homeless."

Owen shrugged. "Not something I like to think back on, much less talk about."

"Sometimes talking helps," someone said behind him.

Turbo leapt up to greet Anna, who crouched low and wrapped her arms around his dog like they were the best of friends. The relief Owen felt at the sight of her was shockingly powerful. He'd been battling a whole bunch of feelings that he'd tried to write off as sheer chemistry. He'd been so sure if they slept together, it would be gone.

But seeing her standing there, he knew he'd been wrong, very wrong. His attraction to her was stronger than ever, maybe *because* they'd been intimate.

She wore a pair of faded jeans, a tank top the exact color of Lake Tahoe, and beat-up sneaks. She held up a bag that smelled delicious, and his relief turned to a warmth that spread to every deeply buried corner of his soul. Somehow this woman, who wasn't his usual type, who challenged him at every single turn . . . comforted him. More than that, for the first time in a long time he actually felt grounded.

Even if the "hey" she directed his way was a far more muted greeting than she'd given his dog. "Hey back," he said inanely.

"Hey," Ky also said, all chipper, grinning from ear to ear. "He was just thinking about you."

Anna looked at Owen, then back to Ky. "How can you tell?"

"It's the dopey expression, a dead giveaway."

Anna laughed.

Owen didn't take his eyes off her. "Ky."

"Yeah?"

"Go away."

Ky flashed a grin but went away.

Owen smiled at Anna. Then he realized Ky had been right. He could literally feel the dopey expression on his face. "Shit, it's still there, isn't it? I noticed it when I got home the other night, and it hasn't gone away."

She laughed again, and he loved the sound. He wondered if she'd replayed every second of what had happened on the roof as many times as he had. Hoping she had, he leaned in and kissed her softly.

She kissed him back, then stared at him, nibbling on her bottom lip.

Yeah. She was replaying it.

And then, because the two of them were both chronic idiots, they stood staring at each other for another moment.

"You had a question," he finally said.

"I wanted to know if you were free for lunch. I came by on the off chance you were. I brought food." She hesitated. "It's an apology lunch for the things I said after we met with Will at the restaurant."

Right. When they'd shared the world's best kiss and then he'd gotten the kiss-off . . .

"I meant to apologize the other night . . ." She gave a half smile. "But we got distracted."

That they had. "I'd love to have lunch with you," Owen said. "Unfortunately, I don't have long, I've got to go see my aunt."

"Understood."

They headed outside, where Owen dutifully picked up Turbo to carry him across the street—and over the grates—to the lake. When he set the dog down, he found Anna shaking her head and smiling.

"I told you, he's afraid of everything," Owen said. "Especially small stuff, like little dogs. And cats. Oh, and fruit." He shook his head when she laughed. "I'm not even kidding. Pull out a banana or an apple, and I'll have to carry him all the way home."

"No fruit, I promise," she told Turbo as they all sat on the sand side by side and had a picnic with the now gentle wind cooling off the hot day. Anna had brought homemade burritos, and he moaned his way through them. "You're a good cook."

"I learned from Wendy. I don't do it very often, it's not as fun to cook for yourself."

He smiled at her. "Feel free to cook for me anytime. I'll even return the favor—if you don't mind barbecue or mac and cheese. That's about it for my culinary skills."

"Mac and cheese is one of my favorite foods." She put her hand to her mouth. "I just realized . . . I think I'm also wearing a stupid smile on my face."

"Yeah, you are." God, he adored her. "Only on you it's cute."

"Take that back," she said on a laugh. "I'm not cute. I refuse to be cute."

"Well, if it helps, you're also hot as hell."

"I mean, I'm not mad at that." She looked at him for a long beat.

"What?"

"I'm trying to figure out a gentle way to ask you about your aunt and if you're okay."

His feels were way too close to the surface if that simple statement melted him. "I don't need gentle," he said.

"She means a lot to you," she said. "And now I know why. I hate what your dad did to you. I'm so sorry you and your mom went through so much."

"I really wasn't even aware of most of it. That's how good a mom she was." He shook his head. "Hell, I never even knew we were so destitute. Not until I got older."

"You must miss her so much."

"Every day."

Their gazes locked, and he knew that she, unlike most, understood. The high-altitude, hot sun warmed them from above, the sand beneath them keeping them cool. He turned his face to the sun, eyes closed, hearing the water lap at their feet and felt . . . at peace. He tried to keep his life as pressure free as possible, but as she'd pointed out, running the business had its stressors, especially because it wasn't just him. Ky counted on him, and so did their employees. But sitting here with Anna, most of that faded away, leaving him relaxed. Happy.

"Your aunt sounds like an amazing person," she said.

"She is. She deserves better than what she got out of life."

"You're her only relative?"

"Yeah. She married when she was sixteen, but her husband died only a few years later. Instead of sinking into a depression, she defied the times and got herself a job and a house and lived life the way she wanted."

"She never remarried or had kids?"

"No, though she always treated me like her own. The kid she wanted but never had."

"I'm so glad you have her in your life."

"And I'm glad you have Wendy." His eyes held hers. "We've both had a lot of loss. Maybe too much."

"I always felt like it made me different from everyone else."

"Which makes it hard to let people in."

She stared at him. "Exactly." She looked out at the water. "Actually, in my case, it's more like I push them out."

He shrugged. "Because it's safer to be on your own than to stay too long and get hurt."

"Yes." She let out a short, sympathetic laugh. "A couple of weeks ago, I'd never have imagined we'd have something in common."

"Me either."

She drew a deep breath. "There's something you should know."

Well, shit. He should've known the day was too good to be true. "Uh-oh."

She opened her mouth, then shut it. Twice. Turbo, clearly sensing her sudden nerves, climbed into her lap like he was a lapdog and licked her chin. "It's okay," she told his silly dog, wrapping her arms around him. "I just have to tell your owner that he turns me upside down and inside out. Do you think you could tell him for me?"

Turbo licked her chin again.

Owen's heart pinched. "Your secret's safe with both of us," he said quietly. "And, Anna? Same."

She met his gaze over Turbo's big fat head. "My instincts keep telling me you're dangerous."

He pulled her into him, hugging her, enjoying the low, happy sound she made as she cuddled in. "And your heart?" he asked. "What does your heart tell you?"

"That's the thing. It went silent on me." Her hands tightened on him. "Now my body? My body has plenty to say—mostly 'more, please.'" She smiled when he laughed. "I haven't decided who to listen to yet."

"Let me know when you decide."

Her phone rang from her back pocket. Ignoring it, she didn't take her hands off him. In fact, her fingers were exploring a bit, and he barely dared to breathe, afraid she'd stop.

When her phone kept ringing, he started to pull back and was surprised when she dug her fingers in, tightening her grip on him. "I'm not getting it," she said.

He tipped up her chin and looked into her eyes, which suddenly were filled with stress. "What's going on?"

She dropped her head to his chest. "Life."

He palmed the back of her head and held her close to him. "Can you get more specific? And how do you know it's not Wendy trying to reach you?"

"I have a special ringtone for her. And as for the calls and texts, they're from Will." She lifted her head when he tensed. "You sure you want to know?"

"Most definitely," he said grimly.

"He's been calling and texting, demanding to see the coin."

It wasn't often he felt furious to the core, but Will brought out that feeling in him. "I'll talk to him."

"No." She took his hand. "I appreciate the offer, but I take care of myself."

He wanted to argue the point, but he couldn't. She was incredibly self-reliant, resilient, and strong. He wouldn't let her think he didn't believe in her. Which meant, much as he hated it, he had to wait until she asked for help. "You're going to be very careful and let me know if you need me?"

She smiled. "I promise I won't be the stupid chick who goes into the basement alone when an ax murderer is on the loose." She stood and brushed off the seat of her jeans. "Well, that wasn't too painful. Normally, I suck at apologies."

Owen laughed. "You didn't apologize."

"Yes, I did."

"No, you didn't."

She stilled, then clearly ran back their conversation through her mind. "I did. I said I was sorry for what I said the other day."

"No, you said you came to apologize for that, but you didn't actually get to it."

"Oh. Well then." She pulled him to his feet and then stepped into him, leaving zero space between them. "I'm . . ." She pulled his head down to hers. "So sorry . . ." She brushed her mouth to one corner of his. "For the things I said . . ." And then her mouth touched the other corner. "When I was hungry."

With a hand tangled in her hair, he laughed roughly as he pulled her in closer, ghosting his lips over hers. "You're teasing me." He kissed her lightly, then not so lightly, his own version of teasing, smiling when she let out a soft moan.

"You did that on purpose."

"You started it."

"No, I clearly remember you coming into my personal space bubble and giving me that sexy look."

He smiled. "And what, your lips fell onto mine by accident?"

She tossed up her hands. "See, this is why we can't work. We can't even agree on who kissed who. It's a good thing we agreed that this thing ends when we solve the case."

Was it? Not in his book.

"You've got to get to your aunt's," she said. "And I've got to get to work."

He walked her to her car. "Thanks for lunch. And the kiss."

She snorted and then gave him a reluctant smile. "Thanks for doing this with me, even if we are on opposite sides."

"Are we?"

She paused. "Aren't we?"

"We're both passionate about fairness and justice. That's what we're trying to do here, right? Find the truth? No matter what that truth is?"

"Yes." She nodded. "For you and Ruby."

"Not me," he said. "This is about Ruby, which makes it an emotional need, because I think having it back will bring her comfort. I just hate that someone took advantage of her."

"I know. Me too." She looked away for a beat, then met his gaze. "Wendy is still one hundred percent convinced our dad's innocent."

He saw the worry in every tight line of her body. "And you?"

She shook her head. "The evidence is circumstantial but seemingly mounting . . ."

Owen felt for her, he really did. Her good memories of her dad were starting to be tainted by this investigation. Just like his good memories of his aunt were starting to be dulled by the angry, agitated woman she was slowly becoming. "Don't give up on your dad yet."

She looked up at him, shook her head, then went up on tiptoes to brush a gentle kiss to his lips. "Thanks."

"Sometimes it's good to not be an island of one."

"I don't know if I'd go that far."

"A skeptic," he said.

She gave a rough laugh. "Takes one to know one."

Hard to argue with that. Letting someone in often meant making promises, which were emotional strings he'd never wanted to pull.

"You're friends with your exes," she said. "You seem to part amicably with everyone; no harm, no foul, easy come, easy go, no jealousy or weirdness."

"Okay, maybe I have a slight allergy," he admitted.

"I fully understand that I've got a good chance of being devastated at the end of this," she said. "But until then, I appreciate being in it together."

It wasn't until he was watching her taillights vanish around the curve in the road that he realized . . . he wouldn't mind being in it together no matter the outcome.

And beyond.

# CHAPTER 16

That night Owen was slouched on his couch watching a baseball game and thinking about going to bed when a call came through from a number he didn't recognize. "Hello?"

"Owen? It's Wendy."

He sat straight up at the urgent tone in her voice. "You and the kiddos okay?"

"Yes." She paused. "But thank you for asking. I, um . . . You know what? Never mind. I'm sorry, go back to sleep—"

"I wasn't sleeping." He was already standing. "What's wrong, how can I help?"

She blew out a breath. "I'm probably just being silly. But I wanted to tell you that Will showed up here looking for the coin, going on and on about how my dad surely had the rest of the loot and he wanted to see it."

Owen was heading toward the door. "I'm on my way."

"No, it's okay. I shouldn't have bothered you. It's just that Hayden's working late, some sort of quarterly deadline, and I just needed to tell someone. Not Anna, because her trust in our dad is already shaken, and . . . well, I was dumb and screwed up, and now I'm trying to give her the space she asked for."

"Have you tried apologizing?"

"Do you have a sister, Owen?"

Okay, he knew where this was going. "No."

"A brother?"

"No," he said. "But I really think she would want to know about Will—"

"Normally, I'd agree with you, but I know her better than anyone." Her voice was filled with worry. "If I tell her Will showed up here, all bets would be off. She'd go give him a piece of her mind—*alone*. I don't know if you've noticed, but Anna can really tick people off without trying."

He decided to plead the fifth on that one.

"So I personally think it's best if we ignore him," she said.

Owen personally thought it best if he made a little visit to Will to discourage any further visits. "I think that's an excellent decision." *For you . . .*

She sighed. "I can read between the lines on that one. Listen, please, whatever you do, don't tell Anna. He'd been drinking and—"

"Let me take this one worry off your plate, okay? You've got enough going on."

She hesitated. "You're a good man, Owen Harris. Be careful."

"Always." After disconnecting the call, he pulled out his laptop. It was shockingly easy to get Will's address. *Thank you, Google.* Grabbing his keys, he headed out into the night.

Will answered his door in nothing but boxers, looking rough, like he was still drunk and feeling like shit. He scowled at Owen. "Dude, what the fuck. It's the middle of the night."

"Seems like you're used to late-night meetings."

Will blinked slowly. "Is that supposed to mean something to me? I don't have time for this bullshit."

"Make the time," Owen suggested. "And just out of curiosity, what is it that you think Anna and Wendy have?"

"None of your business."

"Wrong answer." Owen might've had two inches on Will, but the guy had a good fifty pounds on him and plenty of mean as his face flushed red with fury.

"Man, what's your problem?"

"My problem," Owen said, "is that you showed up drunk on each of their doorsteps in the middle of the night."

"So? We're old friends."

Owen shook his head. "That's not it. You're up to something."

"Like what?"

"Like maybe you know more than you've let on. Come clean."

Will laughed. "If I had anything to come clean about, you're the last person I'd go to. Do you seriously think if I knew where the loot was that I'd still be a busboy, living in this hovel?"

"You might not know where it's at, but you're clearly looking for something specific."

"Prove it." Will smiled. "Oh wait, you can't."

Owen was tempted to prove something by putting his fist through the guy's smug face, but that would be stupid. And he tried really hard not to do stupid anymore.

"I'm calling the cops," Will said.

"No, you aren't. But stay away from Anna and Wendy, or I will." Owen got into his truck, wondering exactly how many pieces of the puzzle he was missing and if Anna was also missing them or if she knew something she hadn't disclosed. He didn't want to think so, but he wasn't working from just his brain this time. His heart had engaged, and unfortunately for him, his feelings for her ran far deeper than he'd ever intended.

He drove home and got into bed, but sleep eluded him. Instead he stared at his ceiling, picturing the look on her face after he'd made Anna laugh, that vague surprise, like she hadn't had much to laugh about lately.

And then he thought of how, when he had her in his arms, looking up at him like he was a superhero, he felt like he mattered, like maybe he'd become someone she needed in her life long after they figured out this case.

The case. Which wasn't just a case, not to her and definitely not to him. Unfortunately, they'd been spinning their wheels, one step forward, two back.

Because they were too distracted?

Blowing out a breath, he purposely set all emotions aside to concentrate on the facts, on what they knew and what they didn't.

Shady Joe had moved up to the top of his list.

Not two minutes later, he got a text. He could tell without even turning his head and reaching for the phone that it was from Anna by the way his heart took a good hard leap. For a beat, he lay still. Had Will gone running to her, tattling on him for his visit? And if so, how pissed was she that he'd listened to her sister and not told Anna what Will had done? Would she use it as an excuse to shut him out?

And why did it matter? She was right, they were very different people. She lived to work, and he worked to live. At their core, their ways of life didn't align, something he didn't see changing. He needed to take a page from his usual playbook and just enjoy this until it was over, because it would be over. Everything good came to an end, and anyway, this was about getting his aunt her things back and nothing else . . . except maybe a little fun when he and Anna could find it in the quiet moments. That was it. Nothing more, nothing less. And the sooner he committed that to ink inside his brain, the better off he'd be.

He picked up his phone.

**ANNA:** We need to pay Shady Joe a visit.

**OWEN:** You read my mind. Want to guess what else is on my mind?

**ANNA:** Hmm . . . That time YOU kissed ME?

He was smiling as he set his phone back onto the nightstand and set aside his uncharacteristic worry about a future that wasn't going to happen.

The day after Will's visit, Wendy was sitting in bed watching *Friends* for the thousandth time when Anna appeared in the doorway. Her heart surged inside her chest—*not* at the bag from her favorite Mexican food place in her sister's hands, but at Anna herself. There. In person. Even though Wendy had been a first-class asshat. "Hi," she whispered.

Anna came closer to the bed but didn't hop on as she usually did. Her gaze took Wendy in, then her belly. "Babies good?"

Wendy nodded.

"And you?"

Wendy's eyes filled.

Anna sighed and perched a hip on the mattress. "Hayden called to tell me you were upset."

Dammit. "I asked him to stay out of it, I swear! I didn't want you feeling pressured to come back to me."

Anna rolled her eyes. "I never left you. I just needed a break."

"I know." Wendy tried to get herself under control. "I'm so sorry about everything I said."

Anna was shaking her head. "Do not apologize just because you got caught."

"Okay. So how about if I apologize because I was wrong?"

At this, Anna flopped back onto the bed, sharing Wendy's pillow. "You weren't all the way wrong."

"Yes," Wendy said, "I was."

When Anna opened her mouth to say something, Wendy grabbed her hand and gently squeezed. "When you were born . . ." She closed her eyes. It wasn't often she let herself go there, to the hell that day had become, to the pain that had never gone away.

"Wendy, you don't have to—"

"Dad was a mess. He left me with the babysitter to take Mom to the hospital to have a baby and came home with you. Just you." She drew a deep breath. "He handed you to me, told me that the two of us were all you had and that we needed to care for you the best we could, even though our hearts had been decimated."

Anna made a sound of distress. "That was too much to put on you. You were only six! And you'd just lost your mom."

Wendy turned to her sister. Anna's eyes were closed, tears streaming down her face. "So had you," she whispered.

"Taking care of me shouldn't have been on you," Anna whispered back. "It should never have been on you."

"You don't understand. You saved me."

At that, Anna opened her eyes and turned to Wendy. It wasn't often Anna looked anything other than calmly and unassumingly beautiful. But at that moment, her eyes were red and she was as pale as could be as she shook her head. "How? How did I save you? What I did was destroy your whole world. I took Mom from you—"

"No." Wendy shook her head adamantly. "Nothing that happened that day was your fault. *Nothing*," she said fiercely. "And having you to take care of . . . well, it gave me a purpose. It fulfilled a need for me, gave me someone to love. Anna, don't you get it? If you hadn't made it either, I don't know what would've happened to me. Or Dad. You saved the both of us, and for your entire life we've known that you were the glue."

Anna swiped her eyes on her sleeve. "I think you're being sweet so I'll stop crying."

Wendy found a rough laugh. "I don't know, it's kinda nice to see your face all blotchy and not perfect for a change."

Anna choked out a laugh. "Perfect? You're kidding, right?" She sat up and looked at Wendy very seriously. "Tell me something: Do you like me? I mean, I know you love me, but do you like me?"

Wendy stared at her. "Are you serious? Of course I like you. I mean, I'm jealous as hell of you. Your brain, your doggedness to do what's right and not just what's easy. I mean, honest to God, I think half the time you take the hard route just to give me gray hair . . ."

When that tugged a laugh out of Anna, Wendy beamed with pride. But it faded quickly. "I'm sorry," she said softly. "I'm sorry I'm always so bossy. And I don't even know why. I think it's left over from raising you while also being your sister. I never learned to let go of the reins. But I promise I'm going to try like hell, because I get how that must be annoying AF, but you should know, I'm probably never going to be able to let go entirely."

"Good," Anna said softly, squeezing Wendy's hand. "Because on some level, I'll always need you. I'm grateful for you, Wen." And when Wendy gave her a look of doubt, she smiled. "I mean, I'm grateful for you *most* of the time. I'd do anything for you. I hope you know that."

Wendy's heart ached in the best of ways. "Do you think you could go through labor for me?"

"Okay, anything but that."

"Fair."

# CHAPTER 17

Two days later, Anna looked out the window at the prison as Owen pulled into the concrete parking structure, feeling oddly anxious. She tried to never let nerves in on her job. It was a male-dominated field, and since revealing anxieties was the best way to show weakness, she'd gotten really good at never showing too much.

But seeing Shady Joe again after all these years, and inside prison at that, was going to be hard on several layers. "Normally, it takes four to six weeks to get approval for a prison visit," she said. "How did you get us approved in two days?"

Owen turned off his truck and looked at her. "I've got a connection."

Vague, of course. He was good at vague. He was also good at smelling delicious. Not to mention his very male energy, which was so big it took up most of the air space in the vehicle. In fact, if she closed her eyes, she could still almost feel his arms wrapped around her that night they'd taken each other apart and then put each other back together again.

He smiled. "You're thinking about it."

"It?" she asked coolly.

His smile turned carnal. "Don't worry, I'm thinking about it too. Until there's a second time."

"No. No second time." She was already in danger of becoming too attached.

"I don't know," he teased. "The way you're looking at me, I feel like there's definitely going to be a second time."

"It was a momentary lapse in judgment." She hoped he was buying this, because she sure wasn't. "You caught me in a weak moment, that's all."

He laughed.

She opened her mouth, but then she remembered she'd been the instigator. And why the hell was he looking so irresistible just sitting there? He was bossy, stubborn, an immovable stone, never revealing his feelings or emotions, guarding them like his heart was Fort Knox.

No, wait. That was her. *She* was Fort Knox. Annoyed at the both of them, she got out of the truck.

Owen did the same, looking pleased with himself.

"*What?*"

"You like me," he said.

"Do not."

"Do too."

"Do not."

He smiled. "Do not."

"Do too." *Shit.* She smacked her own forehead. "Ugh."

"Let me guess," a woman said, walking past them in the parking garage. "You've been married for more than five years."

Anna let out a little unintentional growl from deep in her throat while Owen just laughed. Then he leaned in and kissed her frowning mouth until she was senseless. Pulling back, he whispered, "Do too," and then started walking.

Jerk.

After a few steps, he stopped, tipped his head back, and stared at the concrete above them as if at war with himself. When he turned to face her, his expression had her stomach sinking to her toes.

"In the spirit of honesty," he said, "I need to talk to you about something."

Oh boy. She had to work to keep her expression even, but nothing good had ever preceded those words.

"A few days ago," he said, "one of my aunt's caretakers said Ruby told her a story about Santa Claus coming into her place and stealing from her. At the time, I didn't think it relevant."

"But it's relevant now?"

He looked at her for a moment. "I've been doing some research on the suspects as I've had the time, just to see if I could learn something new. I couldn't sleep last night and was reading some of what I'd collected when I saw a pic of someone who resembled Santa Claus."

Her heart thumped so loudly in her ears she could scarcely hear herself talk. "My dad only looked like Santa during the last year of his life because self-care was hard for him and he was too proud to let me help him. You've seen pictures of him from the time of the crime. He didn't do this." *God, I hope he didn't do this.* "It's just a coincidence that Ruby fingered Santa. Maybe she dreamed it."

"That's one theory."

"And the other?" she asked, not willing to jump to conclusions on Owen's hidden thoughts. She wanted him to spell them out, hopefully before she passed out from the anxiety of it all.

"Here's the thing," he said. "My aunt can't hold on to short-term memories. If this wasn't a dream, if it's something that actually happened, it would've been a long time ago."

She gave a deep sigh of relief. "Like when the necklace and coins were stolen from her house. Way before my dad couldn't keep up with his own grooming."

He nodded. Then shook his head. "But then again, it could've just been an illusion. Or she was watching old holiday movies. There's really no way to tell. I just didn't want to keep something like this from you." He started to walk again, but she caught his hand and tugged, reeling him in for a hug.

And maybe in what was the best part of her day, he wrapped her up tight. Soaking in his strength and warmth, she closed her eyes, comforted, and hoped he was too. Wait a minute—was she actually signing on to the Trust Owen program? Seemed like it.

The air shifted, and suddenly comfort made way for something else, something sensual and hungry. It sharpened all the more when Owen slowly dragged his mouth up the side of her neck, kissing her just beneath her ear, which threatened to melt her knees. "Owen—"

Footsteps broke through her lust haze, and she looked up to find a woman about her age, model gorgeous even with her hair pinned back in a ponytail and little to no makeup, wearing a guard uniform. She winked at Owen, blew him a kiss, then got into a car and drove off.

"Let me guess," Anna said dryly. "Your connection."

Owen reached for her hand. "I've got a lot of connections."

"Of the been-naked-together variety?"

He wisely ignored this, leading her toward an elevator. When the doors closed, he looked at her, his eyes amused. "Jealous?

Even though you can't make up your mind on whether or not to keep me?"

Ha. Little did he know just how much she *wanted* to keep him.

"Kate and I saw each other exactly twice," he said. "Years ago. She decided I was a flight risk—accurate, by the way—and now we're just friends."

"Again, how is it all your exes still want to be friends with you?"

He shrugged. "Because I'm good at being friends?"

She snorted, and he went brows up.

"Okay," she said. "That's undoubtedly true. But I think something else is true as well, that you've got some sort of man barrier, where you think that you're open, but in reality, you're no more open to letting yourself fall in love than I am."

He tilted his head to the side as he considered this. "I guess I figure it's better to keep someone in my life as friends than to not have them at all. If you could, if things had been different with your exes, would you want to be friends with them?"

"If someone had been friend-worthy."

He nodded, all amusement gone. "Guys are dicks," he said. "Every one of us."

"Not *every* one of you," she said softly, and their gazes locked and held until the elevator doors opened.

OWEN KEPT HIS eyes on Anna as they went through the whole rigmarole to get into the prison. He knew this couldn't be easy for her, facing an old acquaintance of her father's, and when she hesitated at the window, he gently pulled her around to face him. "Hey, you know you don't have to do this. I can go in alone."

"No, I need to see him. I need to look into his eyes when he talks. If he talks."

He respected that. He also respected her for an impressive inner strength. It wasn't going to be easy to enter this hellhole to see someone she'd known once upon a time. And there was something else. While he'd started to doubt Louis Moore had been involved in the theft, he knew Anna's thoughts were going in the opposite direction. She was afraid he might not have been whom she'd thought.

Yes, Owen wanted to find Ruby's necklace, quite badly, in fact, but he didn't want to do it at the expense of her memory of her dad.

Twenty minutes later, they were at a table in a common room when Shady Joe was escorted in. Medium height, with a body gone soft with age, his gaze locked in on Anna as he sat.

"You're my second visitor today," he said. "Thanks to you, I'm a regular socialite now."

She looked confused. "What are you talking about?"

"Ever since that interview with you came out, treasure hunters are hot to talk to me about the Ruby Red's whereabouts."

Anna looked at Owen, then back to Shady Joe. "How did the treasure hunters connect this with you?"

Shady Joe leaned back, practically puffing out his chest. "Gotta be a lucky guess, because I can promise you there's no proof of anything out there."

"That sounds like an admission of guilt," Owen said.

Shady Joe snorted. "I'm not admitting to anything I'm not already doing time for. Besides, there are other suspects." He met Anna's gaze. "Your dad, for one. And for what it's worth, I'm sorry for your loss. I didn't know him all that well—"

"You used to drop Will off at our house when I was young," she said, eyes narrowed. "You don't trust someone with your kid that you don't know well."

Shady Joe shrugged. "You're giving me more credit as a father than I deserve. Truth is, I was crap at it. Ask anyone. Hell, ask Will."

"I'm asking you," she said. "And why do you sound so proud of yourself?"

He shrugged again. "I'm doing the time, getting a clean slate." He smiled, leaning back in his chair like he was a king with a doting audience. "Maybe you should just ask me what you came here to ask."

"All right," she said. "Did my dad have anything to do with the heist or not?"

"Wouldn't you like to know."

She slapped two palms flat on the surface of the table and started to lean in, but Owen quickly put a hand on her arm, directing her attention to the guards watching over the whole room with an eagle eye. "Easy," he said softly.

When she blew out a breath and lowered herself back to her chair, Owen looked at Shady Joe. "Answer her question."

"Or what? You going to call the cops on me?"

Realizing this guy was all arrogance and swagger, he knew they needed a new strategy. "Let's go," he said to Anna. "This guy's full of shit. There's no way he could've pulled this off, he's not smart enough."

Shady Joe's easy smile faded. "Do you know what I'm in here for, son? I pulled off a bank heist."

"Yeah, and you got caught." Owen let his tone say exactly how unimpressed he was.

The man leaned in. "Maybe there's also a lot I *didn't* get caught for." He eyed Anna. "Your dad too, by the way."

"Still don't believe you," she said.

"No? Well then believe this: if someone like me had done this job—and I'm not saying I did—no one would *ever* find where the loot was hidden. Why risk having someone else know where it's at so they could try to steal it out from under me? Hell, I wouldn't have even told my own son. That idiot would do something stupid, like sell it to the wrong person and get caught. Or worse, blow the entire wad. Literally, up his nose."

Anna sucked in a breath. "Will turned to drugs?"

"Will's weak."

"Unlike you," Owen said, appealing to the guy's ego.

An oily smile curved Shady Joe's mouth. "Now you're talking. Listen," he said to Anna. "The only reason I'm in a cell and your dad isn't is because he turned his back on the life he'd been living and went straight." He made a show of looking around. "Can you imagine your dad living out his last days here, sick and weak, an easy target?"

Owen stood up, holding his hand out to Anna. "He's got nothing worth knowing. Let's go."

"Your dad wasn't nearly as innocent as you think he is," Shady Joe said to their backs.

Anna hesitated. Owen tightened his grip on her and kept walking. "Not here."

They were outside before she spoke. "We got nothing from him. We should've pushed harder."

"Anna, he wasn't going to tell us a thing. We'll find another way."

"How?"

"I don't know yet, but we'll figure it out, I promise." He wasn't big on promises and, as a result, rarely made one. But this promise he intended to keep.

# CHAPTER 18

Anna hardly registered walking out of the penitentiary or Owen opening the passenger door for her and getting them on the road. She stared out the window as he drove, taking in the staggeringly high Sierra mountains completely surrounding them as they made their way along the deep azure, whitecapped waters of the lake, which was dotted with sailboats.

What would it be like to be out there right now? With the wind and spray of water in her face, the rush of adrenaline clearing her mind . . .

Why had she never seen Shady Joe for who he was when she'd been younger? Or, for that matter, Will? And what did that say about her dad and her memories of him? Of them as a family?

And then there was the biggie . . . how would Wendy take all of this? Anna drew a deep breath, shaken to her foundation, feeling heavy with a grief she didn't know how to process—all of which left her unsure of who she even was. She could feel Owen glancing over at her with concern, but she couldn't have summoned an I'm-okay smile if there'd been a gun to her forehead.

She stayed in his truck while he made a quick stop at a grocery store, and then he was back and driving to her place. Peering through the windshield, she stared at her dark condo, dreading being alone, dreading even more having to fill Wendy in. She had two missed calls from her and some "you went in without me" texts. Anna had sent her a brief answer, saying everything was okay and that she'd call soon.

But it wasn't okay. Yes, she'd promised to try to be more communicative, but she needed a minute. Sometimes having an older bossy, demanding, caring sister wasn't all it was cracked up to be. But the thought of going through this alone tightened her throat and made her eyes sting.

Only she wasn't alone.

She risked a glance over at Owen, whom she found turned in his seat, looking at her, his expression dialed to serious—intense, even.

"We need a plan," he said.

She nodded her head. "I think the next step is obvious."

"We need to start at the beginning, at the scene of the crime." He said this grimly, clearly not wanting to face it.

Because the scene of the crime was Ruby's house.

He called the memory care facility and asked how Ruby was doing today. He listened, then thanked whoever he was speaking to and disconnected. Lifting his head, he met her gaze. "Apparently, the Tooth Fairy also came by and stole something from her room."

"Oh, Owen. I'm so sorry."

He shook his head. "Me too. I should've known better. Sorry I connected the Santa reference to your dad."

"It's okay, it's totally understandable."

"You're being kind." He gave her a small smile. "I'll wait for a better day and then see if she's up for a visit to the house. Having her with us will be helpful because we might be able to nudge something from her memories. If she's lucid."

Anna couldn't imagine any other man she'd ever met being willing to open up a vein and bleed for her. It put a lump in her throat and made her want to hug him tight, but he'd pulled back, into himself. He started to get out of the truck, but she stopped him with a hand to his arm. Sliding that hand up to his jaw, she kissed him on one corner of his mouth, then the other. And then cupped his face and kissed him properly.

"What was that for?" he asked when she'd pulled back.

Overheated and needing far more than just that kiss, she managed to speak. "It was a thank-you. I don't think I'd be doing this without you."

"Your sister asked you to help preserve your dad's reputation, and you stepped up. You'd definitely have done this on your own. Anna, you're the strongest woman I've ever met." Leaning in close, he kissed her this time, until she could barely remember where they were. "You're amazing," he said quietly. "I hope you know that."

"Stop it. You're discombobulating me."

"Cute." He smiled, but his eyes were intense and never strayed from hers.

"What did I tell you about calling me cute?"

"You are," he insisted. "You're amazing and strong and cute and hot—"

She put her hand over his mouth, making him laugh. "It's just the truth," he insisted. "And you told me I was smart, remember? So you can take all of it to the bank."

"What I told you was that you're a smart-*ass*," she muttered, but smiled against his lips when he leaned in for another kiss.

"Can I walk you in?" he asked.

"You want to check under my bed for the boogeyman?"

"I want to feed you." He smiled at her surprise. "I got some stuff at the store. Can I cook you dinner?"

She looked a little stunned. "Um . . ."

"It's okay to tell me no."

She rolled her eyes. "Well, duh. It's just that you cooking for me feels . . . I don't know." She stared at him. "Intimate."

"Yes," he agreed. "Cooking for someone is intimate. But you've done it for me, and I loved it. I felt cared for, and I want to give you that feeling back. It can be just a friendly thing though. No pressure."

She held his gaze, bit her lower lip to hold the truth in, but apparently, with Owen, the truth couldn't be held back. "And if I want it to feel . . . more than friendly?" she asked softly.

He gave a slow smile. "I won't try to change your mind." He got out of the truck and came around for her, opening the door before she managed to get her limbs in working order.

Taking her hand, he beeped the truck locked. She led the way to her front door, thinking about how easy it'd been to lose themselves in each other that night on the roof. Just thinking about it, remembering how she'd felt wrapped around him, how he'd looked at her, the way he'd said her name as they'd nudged each other over the edge . . . had her dropping her keys.

He scooped them up, waiting for her to step over the threshold. She loved the way his eyes looked in the low, ambient lighting, a deep green, filled with the same hunger and desire that had awoken all the butterflies in her belly.

Clawdia sat in the entry, her eyes narrowed with displeasure and suspicion as she took in Owen. "Mew."

"Who's this?" Owen murmured, hunkering down, balanced on the balls of his feet as he smiled at her cat.

"Clawdia," Anna said. "She's Jennifur's sister. And careful, unlike Jennifur, she's not fond of strangers—"

Clawdia charged at him and . . . headbutted him in the forehead. Surprise had him falling to his ass.

Anna gasped. "I'm so sorry! When I first got her, it took her a long time to understand that me kissing the top of her head was a gesture of affection. Problem is, now she thinks the best way to signal she wants a cuddle is to mash the top of her head against my face. It's like a very affectionate punch in the mouth."

He laughed and stroked her cat along her back. Then the feline love of her life fell over and exposed her belly.

Owen dutifully stroked her there too, and then the loud rumble of a purr filled the air.

"Show-off," she said when Owen rose and smiled at her.

"Don't worry, I'm happy to stroke you too."

She laughed, then dropped her head to his chest.

"What do you need?" he asked quietly. "Tell me and it's yours."

"You."

With a groan, he kicked the front door shut, nudging her up against it so that the wood was at her back, his warm, hard body at her front. Flattening her palms to his chest, she felt empowered when she found his heart racing as fast as hers. Unable to help herself, she took a nibble just beneath his jaw, trying to decide where to touch next. Up?

Or down . . .

"Don't look, Clawdia," she whispered, because down, she decided. His stomach tightened under her touch, while hers hollowed out. She heard the lock click and realized he'd reached around her to bolt them safely in before cupping her face in his hands and kissing her, soft and serious. Then he pulled back, looked into her eyes, and . . . kissed her again, all fiery passion and erotic desire.

When they broke apart for air, he took his mouth on a tour to that sweet spot just beneath her ear, then down her throat, taking a playful bite of her shoulder, making her gasp.

His chuckle sounded both amused and wicked as he laced his fingers with hers. His next kiss was a full-court press and she couldn't get enough. Arching her back, desperate to get closer, she tugged her hands free to get into his jeans.

"Wait," he said, pressing his forehead to hers, breathing ragged. "I wanted to get you into an actual bed this time—"

"Noble goal," she said breathlessly. "Next time." And then she tugged him down onto the soft rug in front of her fireplace.

"Anna—"

"Let me save you some time," she murmured, shoving his shirt up his chest until he tugged it over his head. "I want this. I want you. Clear?"

Crawling up her body, he flashed her a grin. "Crystal." He was pushing her skirt up her thighs while simultaneously dragging his lips down her belly, trailing lazy, open-mouthed kisses in his wake. Her hands in his hair, she moaned his name.

Lifting his head, he took in the sight of her silky black undies and let out a ragged breath. "You're so beautiful, Anna."

She was glad he thought so, but to rush him along, she wrapped her legs around him. For the record, this didn't galvanize him into hurrying. In fact, he took his sweet time, despite how she begged. And she did beg as he gave her everything she'd wanted. When she could uncurl her toes, she rolled him to his back, claiming the top, closing her eyes at the feel of his hands on her, the exquisite stretch as he filled her, the sound of them both breathing heavily. She had no idea how it was possible to feel such a deep connection with someone she hadn't known very long, but it was a very real connection, and that was new for her.

New and shockingly terrifying.

By the time she came back to herself, the last of the bricks around her heart lay in rubble at her feet. They were still on the rug, both of them breathing wildly. Opening her eyes, she found Clawdia staring at them, brow furrowed in judgment. "I told you not to look."

With a half laugh, half groan, Owen rolled to his side and pressed his mouth to the curve of Anna's shoulder. "I like this," he murmured, running a finger over the delicate scripted tattoo she'd gotten on her eighteenth birthday.

## Let it go . . .

"I got it to celebrate exiting my wild-child impulsive days, because of what it represented."

"And what's that?" he asked.

She smiled wryly. "My era of stupidity."

Dragging her to him, he pulled her in close. He cradled her face in his hands, then brought her mouth to his for a tender kiss before resting his forehead against hers. "If anything about your era of stupidity—or mine, because trust me, you weren't the only one—brought us together for this, then I'm grateful for what we've been through."

The words moved her far more than she wanted to admit. He seemed just as overwhelmed as she, and that had a wave of affection rushing through her. Affection and something far more.

He had her splayed across him, his hands trailing lazily up and down her back, his heartbeat steady and comforting beneath her ear.

Tucking a wayward strand of hair behind her ear, he nuzzled his face close to hers. The man was a cuddler. Who knew? Not her. And before now she might've said she wasn't a fan.

Turned out she was most definitely a fan.

With one last sweet kiss, he got to his feet. "Water?"

She nodded and watched him head toward her kitchen, biting her lower lip at the sight of her nail indentions on each ass cheek. "Um . . ."

He stopped and glanced back at her.

"I marked you. I'm so sorry."

He grinned. "Are you?"

"Yes!"

"Well, I'm not."

She smiled as he vanished into her kitchen, followed by Clawdia, who might be suspicious but was no dummy. No doubt she had high hopes of conning Owen into feeding her. "Hey," she called out. "What about Turbo? Will he eat your house?"

"When I stopped at the store, I called Ky, who went and got him for a sleepover with him and Sami."

"Are you okay with that? With Ky and Sami?"

"Of course."

Relaxing, she closed her eyes, delaying reality by replaying what they'd just done, Owen's voice a rough whisper against her ear, his silky hair falling across his forehead as he'd loved her. She'd never thought of sex as being loved before, but she'd never been with a man like Owen either. She was still thinking about that, feeling a little stunned, when he handed her a bottle of water, then scooped her up, carrying her to her bedroom.

"Why does this keep happening?" she asked when he playfully tossed her to her bed.

He climbed onto the mattress and crawled up her body. "Let me explain the birds and bees to you . . ."

# CHAPTER 19

A whirlwind week later, Anna was so exhausted after long, stressful days at work, and then longer, decidedly not stressful nights in Owen's arms, that she was now deep in a dream that she never wanted to wake up from. A man was nibbling his way over every inch of her body. And not just any man.

Owen.

His touch awakened things inside her she hadn't known she could feel, and in this lush, erotic dream, she gave him every inch of her, gave him everything she'd hidden from others, sharing herself with him to the depths of her soul.

"Anna."

"Shh, she's sleeping."

His voice sounded amused when he said, "Anna, wake up."

Whoa. Not a dream. Owen, really in her bed, leaning over her, his white teeth flashing in the dark. "I was having a really great dream," she grumbled.

"I noticed. You were moaning my name."

Oh boy.

He flicked on her lamp and, at whatever he saw in her face,

laughed huskily. "Later, you'll show me what Dream Owen was doing to you so that I can give you a repeat."

Embarrassed, she closed her eyes. "Why are we up at . . ." She cracked open an eye. "Oh dark thirty?"

"Because I need to show you something."

She found a smile. "I believe you've already showed it to me."

He gave a rough laugh. "This is something new. But we have to hurry. It'll take a few minutes to get there." He pulled her from bed, and when she opened her mouth to protest, a pair of her sweats hit her in the face.

He was at her dresser. "Where are your socks?"

"Top drawer. And you forgot a bra and undies."

"I didn't forget."

She went hands on hips. "You want me to leave the house commando?"

His eyes heated as he slowly took her in. "If you keep standing there like that, we're not going to leave at all."

She had to admit, it made her feel incredible to be looked at the way he did. Smirking, she pulled on the sweats over her nude body. "This better be worth it."

He just smiled. Ten minutes later, they were sitting on a dark beach waiting for the sun to come up. She hated to admit this, but the predawn was gorgeous. She could smell the pines, hear the water hitting the sand rhythmically somewhere just in front of them. The water reflected the stars and silver-edged clouds. Dawn was approaching. She shook her head, surprised. "You're a closet romantic."

"Don't tell anyone."

It felt so easily intimate to sit on a beach under the stars, leaning back against him, his arms around her. She didn't realize she'd drifted off until he gently nudged her awake.

"Look," he said softly against her temple.

In stunned silence, she watched the color of the sky change right before her eyes, becoming richer and deeper every second. The air felt cool on her skin, the sound of the water soothing. And then the sun peeked over the mountaintops to the east, silhouetting them against the sky, turning it crimson. Rays of golden light streamed overhead, and the cottony clouds looked like fire.

"Wow," she breathed. "I've never come to the lake for sunrise."

"Never?"

She shook her head. "It's been a long time since I even saw a sunrise. I've never been a morning person."

"I know a way to get you to enjoy them." His voice had deepened to that sexy timbre that made her think of his promise to reenact her dream.

"Owen?"

"Yeah?"

"I've got three hours before my first meeting," she said.

He smiled. "Yeah?"

"Yeah." She smiled back. "Take me home."

ANNA WOKE TO find daylight peeking through the blinds, muting the dark shadows with hints of soft yellow and orange.

Owen was on his stomach, face turned away from her, his hair dark against the ivory of her sheets. She needed to go. A quick shower and she'd head into work, where she could think about anything else. The blanket rode low over his bare back as she gently and very quietly slid from the bed, careful not to shake the mattress as she did. She tiptoed across the cold hardwood floor. At the bedroom door, she stole one last look over her shoulder at the bed. Her bed. With Owen in it. She found it hard to keep a smile from forming.

Or her heart from warming.

This, them, what they'd done last night and this morning . . . it was turning into something she wasn't ready for.

And yet still, she let her gaze linger. Every time they were together, she could feel the change stirring inside her. The change that signaled she was getting in too deep. This wasn't casual. This wasn't a friendship with benefits.

It was more.

She had no idea if Owen realized it. Maybe he did. That gave her pause. She was putting too much into this. Things were changing between them, evolving into something she wasn't ready for and didn't want.

And look at her lying to herself.

Whatever, it didn't change anything. What she felt for him scared the hell out of her.

OWEN STIRRED AND sleepily, eyes still closed, reached out for Anna. He came wide awake when all he found were cold sheets. Sitting up, he looked around. "Anna?"

Nothing from the woman he'd slept with, but he did hear a "mew," and then Clawdia climbed up the side of the bed and sat perched at his hip, staring at him.

He was a light sleeper, very light. Which meant Anna had to have stealthily sneaked out.

On purpose.

The silence of the condo seemed to mock him. He pulled in a deep breath and let it out slowly, taking the pulse of the room. Sunlight slanted in the windows, casting the room in a golden glow. Looking around, he found not one but two clocks on her nightstand. They both read 8:00 a.m. Clearly the morning had started without him. And just as clearly, given the stillness of the place, Anna was gone.

She'd run off. From her own home. Which he figured could mean only one thing—she'd had every bit of an amazing time as he.

"Meow." Clawdia headbutted him, looking for love.

"Your owner's running scared," he said, stroking the cat.

Clawdia's expression said the woman clearly didn't know much.

He couldn't say he was surprised Anna was gone. But he was definitely disappointed. Slipping out from beneath the covers, he stretched and . . . caught sight of his clothes neatly folded on a chair with a handwritten note on top.

Owen,

Thanks for last night. It was fun, but I think we both know it shouldn't happen again.

Anna

He had to laugh. Polite, even as she dumped his sorry ass. Had she gotten called into work early? Or had she left because he'd made her feel something, because she was feeling too much?

"Right back atcha, sweetness," he muttered to himself, then froze because he heard water running. Moving quickly down the hall, he stopped outside the bathroom. She was in the shower. He didn't really want to admit just how relieved he felt, but his knees were definitely a little weak.

He let himself into the bathroom and leaned back against the sink, enjoying the sight of her behind the glass shower door. "Fun, huh?" he asked. Which hadn't been what he'd meant to say. He'd actually planned on not saying anything about the note at all, but apparently he had more feelings on this subject than he'd known.

He had to give her credit: she didn't even jump. Though she did grimace, which faded when she took in the sight of him and realized that he was as naked as she. Her gaze ran slowly down his body and back up again, even more slowly on the second pass.

Flattering. As was her involuntary inhale. The frown lines between her eyes eased, a softer expression replacing them.

"You know," she said, "I might've forgotten the details. Maybe we should do it one more time to remind me."

"Just one?"

She met his gaze. "We can't get too attached, right?"

And wasn't that the problem, because he was beginning to realize he was already very attached, and . . . he wanted more, far more.

As in everything.

In the past, he'd always itched to make his escape. But for the first time, he didn't want to escape at all. He was falling for her.

Hard.

Which was ridiculous. It hadn't even been a month. While he was still overthinking that, she reached out and yanked him into the shower.

Happily crowding her up against the wall, he pushed her wet hair back from her face.

Her expression went wary. She was afraid he would push her on the attached thing. But he had no intention of pushing her.

Either she wanted him or she didn't. And in that moment, she did. He was going to take what he could get. "Why do you have two clocks?"

Surprise replaced wariness. "It's more about having two alarms," she said. "One for the person I want to be and one for the person I am."

He was still laughing when she tugged him down and kissed him stupid.

# CHAPTER 20

Anna was pulling on her clothes while simultaneously stealing peeks at Owen as he dressed. She couldn't help herself.

With a low laugh, Owen shook his head and pulled her into him, pressing his cheek to the top of her head. "The way you look at me sometimes, it makes me feel like Superman, you know that?" He pulled back to see her face, his smile softer now. "You make me feel special, Anna. I honestly can't remember the last time that happened."

She felt her heart squish around in her chest, which she tried to ignore because this was how it had to be. "Don't get too attached to me," she managed to say lightly, in a teasing tone. "Wouldn't want you pining away for me or anything."

He didn't smile. He wasn't playing. "Remind me again why this has to end?"

She stared at him, feeling panic clog her throat. "What other way is it going to end? People leave, Owen. In fact, I've met three of your exes by complete accident, so even if this *was* somehow real—which we both know it's not—it's only a matter of time before I'm the next ex."

He let out a long exhale. "Anna, *this* is real. At least for me."

She shook her head. "We said—"

"I know what we said, that this is just until the case is over. But that doesn't mean it isn't real."

She opened her mouth to argue the point, but . . . she wasn't sure she wanted to. If he wanted this to be real until it was over, then who was she to try to convince him otherwise? Because deep down, and maybe also not so deep down, she wasn't in a hurry to let go of the way he made her feel.

"Look," he said. "I don't have to be at work until one. I don't usually work on Saturdays, but we've got a big group to take river rafting today. I know you said you don't have to be at work until nine, which means we have nearly an hour. Can I take you to breakfast?"

Her stomach growled, making them both laugh. It'd been midnight before he'd made them a chicken stir-fry, but those calories were long gone. "Mari texted me while we were in the shower. The meeting's been moved to another day."

He smiled, slinging an arm around her neck and reeling her in, pressing his mouth to her temple. "Let's feed the beast."

They got caught in beach traffic on Lake Drive. Stopped with nowhere to go in a hurry, she turned to face him, feeling like she knew him so well in some ways, but in others, he was still a mystery.

He glanced over with a what's-up expression.

"Humor me," she said. "Your Kentucky Derby horse name is an emotion you're not good at, plus the last thing you ate. Go."

"Love You."

Her heart stopped. "W-what?"

"An emotion I'm not good at—love. The last thing I ate . . ."

*Her.* She felt her face heat, and he laughed at her expression.

"I've had my mouth on every inch of your body and you can still blush about it? Cute."

She rolled her eyes. "For the last time, I'm *not* cute."

"You're right. You're the sexiest, smartest, funniest woman I've ever had the pleasure of pleasuring." He grinned when she groaned in embarrassment. "And you?" he asked. "Your Kentucky Derby name?"

"Same as yours," she admitted, and he laughed again.

They hadn't moved an inch, and she pointed at him. "You're up. You get to ask a question now."

He thought about it for a minute. "What was awesome as a kid but sucks as an adult?"

"Birthdays," she said instantly. "Not because I don't want to get older. I don't mind that. I just don't like being the center of attention. You?"

"Waking up in another place than you fell asleep. As in when you fell asleep in the car and got carried to bed without remembering, and then panicked when you awoke, because *how did you get there.*"

This made her laugh. "Yes! And eating large quantities of candy in a single serving. Oh, and staying up until two in the morning."

"I'd agree with you, but last night . . ." He flashed her a sexy smile that brought back the night before, the memory of how his mouth had felt on hers, his hands gliding over her body, the way his voice went all low and sexy whenever she touched him . . .

He glanced over at her. "Now I have to know what you're thinking about," he said. "Your eyes heated."

She opened her mouth, but luckily for her, traffic began to move. And two minutes later, he'd turned off the main road.

He pulled up to . . . "A food truck?" she asked, staring at a red-and-white truck parked at an out-of-the-way beach she'd never been to before.

"Best breakfast burritos on the lake," he promised.

They ordered, then took their food to the beach, where they sat on top of an empty picnic bench and ate.

"Okay," she said around a mouthful. "You're right. This is the best breakfast burrito I've ever had." And so was the view, both the lake and the man at her side, sprawled out in faded jeans, a T-shirt advertising some dive bar in Mexico, and mirrored sunglasses that were sexy as hell.

"How did you find this place?" she asked. "I've lived here all my life and I never knew it existed. My dad's buried at the cemetery across the street, and I've visited him a bunch of times and never even realized this was right here."

He'd stopped chewing, swallowed, and pushed his sunglasses to the top of his head to look at her with an odd expression.

"What? Do I have something in my teeth?" She covered her mouth with a hand. "Dammit—"

He caught her fingers. "You don't have anything in your teeth."

"Then what?"

"I found this place when visiting my mom. She's also across the street."

They stared at each other in surprise at the very odd connection. They'd had so many of those she was starting to think the universe was trying to tell her something.

Owen took his last bite, then crumpled up the wrapping from his breakfast burrito and made a three-pointer into the trash bin fifteen feet away. He then took her trash, crumpled it as well, and made another basket.

"Nice shooting," she said.

"We've got a basketball hoop behind our building, and the guys and I play at lunch. How have we never run into each other across the street? Or anywhere."

"I don't know. Maybe . . ." She bit her lower lip on the thought she'd been having for a while but had buried because it felt so foreign.

"Maybe what?" he asked. "Maybe it wasn't meant to happen until now?"

Yes. Exactly . . .

He was still just watching her, thoughts hidden. After a moment, he looked like he wanted to say something.

"Since when do you hold anything back?" she asked.

He gave her a small smile. "You think you know me."

"I think I'm getting there. For instance," she said, "I know you're about to tell me what you were just thinking about. And then after that, you're going to kiss me."

Leaning in, he kissed her. When she was breathless, he pulled back with a smile.

"First of all," she said in a been-kissed-stupid voice, "just because you switched the order doesn't mean I don't know you. Now spill."

He took her hand in his. "When Ruby got her dementia diagnosis a few years ago, she said something to me I wasn't ready to hear. I wanted to move in with her and help out, but she refused to let me, insisting instead on memory care. She wouldn't tell me why, but I knew it was because she didn't want me to give up my life for hers."

Moved, Anna felt her eyes sting. "She loves you very much."

He nodded. "She does. And it's her greatest wish to see me have what she always wanted. Love. A family. She told me I was going to meet someone who was going to change my life, who'd fill a spot inside me that was empty, hollow."

She felt her heart skip a beat. "What did you say?"

A corner of his mouth quirked, his voice wry. "I said I didn't need that. I was fine as is. She told me that was true, I didn't need love in my life to survive, but she knew that deep down, I wanted it. Craved it."

Everything around them seemed to vanish. The breeze, the sounds of the water, everything.

"I denied it," he said. "I was frustrated with her trying to fix my life, which I didn't think needed fixing."

Anna realized she was holding her breath. She told herself she didn't know why, but she did. "And now?"

His eyes never left hers, letting her see everything he felt as he felt it. It was humbling, how he always let her in, even when it wasn't comfortable for him. "And now," he said quietly, bringing her hand up to his mouth, brushing a kiss to the sensitive skin of her palm, "now I think I was full of shit for not admitting that she was right. I'm surrounded by great people, and yet I still get lonely. And . . . someone really great did come into my life."

The air in her lungs whooshed out.

His mouth curved. "Don't panic."

"Why would I panic?" She winced as her voice came out two full octaves higher than usual. "Who's panicking? Not this girl." God, she was such an idiot, and tightened her lips together before more words escaped her.

Owen grinned, but then he let it fade as he looked at her for a long moment, his usual calm patience in play. "Would you like to visit your dad while we're here?"

"If you're up for a visit to your mom."

He smiled. Standing, he pulled her up as well, then kept his hand in hers as they walked across the street.

Caitlin's words echoed in Anna's mind—*every week he'd visit his mom's grave site and never take me. Not one time. He had invisible barriers protecting him that kept me on the outside looking in. Fact is, I wanted more and he couldn't give it to me. He can't give it to anyone.*

But he was taking Anna.

A guy was selling flowers outside the gates of the cemetery. Owen bought two bouquets and offered one to Anna. "I'll leave you to it," he said quietly.

Anna took her time taking the curving path through the beautiful property. It was odd to think of a place where the dead lay as beautiful, but the gently rolling grassy hills dotted with pines and outlined by the stunning Sierra mountains could be described as nothing but.

She looked around and didn't see a soul, not even Owen.

She'd been here many times with Wendy, but she'd never come alone. As she stepped off the path and dropped to her knees in front of her father's gravestone, she sighed. "Hey, Dad."

Throat tight, she set the flowers at the base of his headstone. "So . . . Wendy's about ready to pop." Her dad would've loved being a grandpa. "I'll be there for her," she promised. "And I'll tell the babies all about you." She paused. "But I think I'll leave out some things, if you don't mind." A half laugh that was far too close to a sob escaped her. "I wish you were here, Dad. I've got so many questions. Like, how in the world did I never see Shady Joe for who he really was? And why were you friends with him? And . . . why were you in possession of a coin that belonged to a woman who'd owned the whole set and a million-dollar necklace—all of which are still missing?"

Still on her knees, she drew a deep breath. It was quiet out here, only a slight rustling of the trees and the occasional squawk of a bird. "I love you," she said. "Nothing will change that. But I'm learning some things about you that I wish I could unlearn. Your past . . ." She closed her eyes. "You were funny, kind, adventurous, and giving . . . so giving. You were capable of so much: being a great father, a brilliant businessman, brave in the face of the disease that forced you into a wheelchair . . . But never in a million years could I have guessed your bio included being a thief." She paused. "I didn't want to believe it, still don't, but you've got a record." She pressed the heels of her hands to her eyes. "I don't get it—you *hated* injustice of any kind. You hated it so much that I could've passed a lie detector test claiming you would never, *ever* have stolen a penny from another soul."

She swiped at a rogue tear and kept her eyes squeezed shut. "I want to trust you weren't like Shady Joe. I want to believe that your early past 'mistakes,' as Sonya called them, stayed in your past, that you didn't steal the Ruby Red and the coins. I know I just told you that I still love you, and I do, but . . ." Damn. She couldn't even say it out loud, that if she found out he'd done this, it would, at the very least, tarnish that love—

A hand covered hers where she'd fisted it on one of her thighs. She didn't startle because she recognized not only the touch but the way she felt in Owen's presence.

Safe.

He dropped to his knees at her side, slid an arm around her waist, and brushed a kiss to her cheek. "It's okay to love him how you remember him," he said quietly. "Don't let what we're doing taint those memories."

Turning her head, she looked at Owen and realized he had all the incredible characteristics her dad had possessed. Kindness.

Patience. Adventurousness. Easy generosity. He was strong, both physically and mentally, and never seemed to give in to the doubts that constantly plagued her.

Owen took in her dad's gravestone. "Sir, my name's Owen Harris. I'm a friend of your daughter's. If you're anything like my mom, you worry about her and Wendy. I want to assure you, they're amazing, capable women, but I'll be here if they need me. For anything." He brought his and Anna's entwined hands to his heart and held them there, and for that moment in time, almost unbearably moved, she could almost believe they might actually have a shot together.

Almost.

# CHAPTER 21

The next day after work, Anna stopped by Wendy's house to check on her. She could tell her sister was having a tough day. The signs were smudges of exhaustion and stress beneath her eyes, pale skin, and, maybe most telling, quiet. "You feeling okay?"

"Yeah."

Anna added lethargic to her mental list and did her best to swallow her panic. For all she knew, this was normal, but she couldn't beat back her monthslong fear, the one that had started the day Wendy told her she was pregnant—that something would happen to her sister in childbirth, like it had to their mom. "Can I get you anything? Food? Anything you want."

"No. Thanks."

Okay, now she was really worried. Wendy was always starving. There was only one thing to do—manipulate her the way Wendy manipulated Anna at every opportunity. "Well, *I'm* hungry," Anna said. "Starving, really. But I can't decide what to eat."

Wendy waved a hand in the direction of the kitchen. "Help yourself to anything in the fridge."

"Yes, but I hate it when I go to the kitchen looking for food and all I find are ingredients."

Wendy gave a small smile. "Liar. You love to cook. You just never make time for the stuff you love."

Anna drew a deep breath, reminding herself she hadn't come here to fight yet again—even if Wendy was 100 percent right. "What are *you* hungry for?"

Wendy shrugged.

"Wen, are you sure you're okay? Should I call Hayden? Your doctor?"

"Don't you dare. I'm fine."

But she wasn't fine, or she'd be wanting food. Anna's panic was joined by her old friend Anxiety. "Come on. I know you've got a craving. Let's hear it. Anything."

"Well, if we're talking anything and not just what's in this house, I'd go for an entire bucket of fried chicken. But that's ridiculous, I'm not asking you to go there and then come back here, not when it's closer to your place. I'll just nibble on whatever you rummage up from downstairs."

Anna nodded and went downstairs. Then she quietly went out the front door and back into her car. Five minutes later, she'd bought an entire bucket of fried chicken. Back at Wendy's, she let herself in and placed the bucket of chicken in her sister's lap.

Wendy stared at it and promptly burst into tears.

"Oh no, don't cry!" Anna thrust a stack of napkins into her hands. "I'm sorry! I was just trying to cheer you up!"

"These are happy tears," Wendy said soggily, and started in on the chicken, humming with pleasure, closing her eyes to savor it. After a few minutes, she smiled. "I guess I was hungry."

Anna did her best to not thunk her head against the wall.

Wendy sucked down her bottled water. "Okay, so now that

I've got some protein in me, tell me how it's going with Owen. You're wearing a lovely, enviable, I'm-all-sexed-up glow."

"Well, first of all, I'm not sure there was actual meat, much less protein, in this fried chicken."

"Don't change the subject." Wendy jabbed a wing in Anna's direction. "Talk."

"You want me to admit I know I'm wearing a glow?"

"No, I want you to admit you like him. A lot."

"Fine." Anna chose a biscuit and slathered it with butter. "I like him. A lot. But we've agreed it's going to be over when the case is."

Wendy stared at her. "That's still the stupid plan? Seriously? Why would you even agree to such a thing?"

"It was my idea," Anna said.

"Oh my God." Wendy shook her head. "I take back the smartest sister thing. You're dumb. This is dumb. He's a keeper, Anna. He looks at you like you're the moon and the sun and the stars—*and* lunch. Do you know how rare that is? He's a guy willing to stand at your back, at your side, wherever you want him to stand. Plus, he's got no ego when it comes to knowing just how smart you are, he loves to watch you think, talk, laugh . . . Why are you doing this to yourself?"

"You still want the truth?" Anna asked.

"No, Anna, lie to me." Wendy shook her head. "*Yes, I want the truth!*"

"Okay, well . . . I don't really see myself as a keeper."

Wendy gasped, a hand to her heart. All she needed was a set of pearls to clutch. "That cannot be true."

Anna shrugged. Owen had never thought of himself as a keeper—at least not until now. That seemed to be changing for him, and she knew that if she wasn't the one pushing for this to end as soon as the case did, he wouldn't be pushing for that at all.

But she was scared. That was the bottom line.

Wendy opened her mouth, but Anna held up a finger. "Subject change," she said firmly. "Are you going to tell me what was wrong when I got here?"

"If you're sure you won't tell me more."

"I'm sure."

Wendy sighed. "I love these babies. I do. But today, my maternity stretch pants are too tight, my boobs are sore, and I bent over to pick up my phone when I dropped it—and . . ."

"And what?"

"I farted." Wendy moaned and covered her face. "Like I didn't even know it was coming! Hayden thought it was the funniest thing in the entire world. I told him we have to divorce now, because what was next, us pooping in front of each other? I'll die first."

"You about done?" Anna asked.

Wendy sighed again. "Yeah. But I'm never going to live that down."

"Okay, let me try to touch on all your various and very serious problems. One, your maternity stretch pants were made for one woman and one baby, not one woman and three babies, so you're going to have to give yourself a break there. Two, as for your boobs being sore, look at it this way—you always wanted bigger ones, and now you've got them, so take the win." Then she hesitated.

"You don't know how to make me feel better about the fart," Wendy said dejectedly.

Bingo. "Well, um, guys love farts, right? I've got no idea why, but they do. Plus, you made Hayden laugh. That's not that easy to do, and he has a great laugh, so maybe just try to enjoy that part."

Wendy thought about it and shrugged. "Yeah, maybe you're right. Thanks. And thanks for the food too. You're truly the best, sweetest, kindest sister."

"I'll admit I am the best sister, but sweet and kind are definitely a stretch."

Wendy laughed, and it warmed Anna's heart. "I should've said you're the bestest, smartest, most likely to have my back sister on the planet."

Anna smiled. "I'll take that."

Two days later, Wendy tossed and turned, unable to get comfortable or to sleep. In the dark, she heard Hayden's deep and even breathing and she wanted to kick him for his ability to sleep no matter what. What was wrong with him that he didn't take all their problems and worries to bed like she did? And what was the secret?

Gah. She rolled to her back, which used to be her favorite position to sleep, but now she could only stay there for a minute or two before the babies' weight on her internal organs threatened to cut her off from life itself.

She sighed loudly, really hoping Hayden would wake up.

He didn't, dammit. And since she'd promised not to kick him awake anymore, she couldn't even do that. She briefly considered calling Anna, but she'd already brought her the fried chicken, and she didn't want to be a burden. She knew Anna would be mad at her for doing the overprotection thing, but what she didn't know wouldn't hurt her. Hi, yes, her name was Wendy and she rarely learned a thing from the fights she'd had with Anna.

She'd just have to have a private freak-out party for one all by herself. But babies wriggled inside her, reminding her she wasn't alone at all. There in the dark, she smiled and put her hands on them. At first, it'd been hard to realize her body was no longer her own, instead belonging to these beings she and Hayden had created. Although, to be fair, she'd done far more work than Hayden. Still, the babies had been with her twenty-four seven, keeping her company.

And now, soon, it'd be over. She was thirty weeks pregnant today, which meant in two weeks these babies would be on the outside of her body, their own beings. For so long, she'd been both obsessed with and terrified of this one massive dream of hers actually coming true, and it was almost here. And while that was thrilling, she knew she'd miss this, being alone with them.

Apparently, there really were two sides to having a dream come true.

The babies squirmed some more. Kit Kat, Reese, and Oreo, she decided, so named for her current craving . . . And if Hayden objected, well, he could damn well wake up and talk to her. Or better yet, he could push three watermelons out of *his* hoo-ha.

She reached for her iPad to maybe watch a show, but she ended up in a deep social media dive on Will and Joe. It was still bugging her how Will had alluded to the fact that his dad probably knew more than he'd let on, while at the same time Joe had seemed far too smug.

They were missing pieces to this puzzle, and she couldn't help but feel those pieces were named Will and Joe.

She set down the iPad to think, and the next thing she knew, it was five in the morning.

And something else.

She couldn't have explained it to save her life, but she knew, knew to the depths of her soul, that today was going to be the day. She ran her hands over her body, trying to figure out what had clued her in, but everything felt the same. Same massive boobs, same backache, same constant urge to pee.

Except maybe not the exact same backache. This morning, it felt sharper, more intense.

Unrelenting . . .

She took the next thirty minutes to time the contractions to make sure she wasn't getting out of this cozy bed at the crack of dawn for nothing. But her contractions were six minutes apart.

Holy cow. She was in labor.

She was really going to do this. Damn. Being pregnant was a lot more fun when not facing down imminent labor . . .

Hayden stirred at her side and came up on one elbow. "Need pickles for breakfast again?"

Did she? "Yes. Uh, no. *No.*" Now that she knew she was in labor, she was afraid to eat thanks to the horror stories she'd heard from the moms in her birthing class about pooping on the table in front of their partners and a room full of professionals. Nope. No, thank you. No way, no how.

"Wendy?" Hayden, clearly sensing that something was wrong, came all the way awake. He sat up, a hand going to her belly. "What is it? You okay? Youngest, Middle, Oldest?"

"I think you mean Wilma, Betty, and Pebbles."

He didn't take the bait. His eyes remained calm but piercing as he reached out and put a hand on her wrist, wrapping his warm fingers around her chilled skin. She thought it was sweet, until she realized—he was taking her pulse.

She knew how much he worried, and okay, yes, it meant a lot to know how much he cared about her, as did the fact that he wanted her safe and happy at all times. "Happy wife, happy life," he always told people, with the sweetest, most genuine smile on his face.

She loved that about him, that she was the center of his universe. She truly did. But once in a while, it was okay to not be okay. She was pretty sure he didn't understand that, but there was someone who did. "Can you call Anna?"

He studied her, rubbing his jaw. "Is this like the other night when we were sitting on the couch watching TV and I heard my phone from the kitchen—only when I got up to retrieve it, there was a text from you asking me to please bring the chips on your way back?"

She smiled at the memory. "No, this is different."

He just looked at her.

"I swear! I'm not going to ask her to bring me anything."

He eyed the time. "You do know it's only five in the morning. Anna's not exactly the morning person in this family. She'll kill you for waking her up. And no offense, but I'd rather not have to kill her for killing you. You know how much I love this bed. And playing basketball with the guys. And driving my truck. And—"

"And you couldn't do any of that in prison," she finished for him. "I get it. But don't worry, Anna isn't going to kill me for waking her up."

"How do you know—" He sucked in a breath. "Wendy," he said, incredibly seriously. "You're in labor?"

"If I say yes, are you going to maintain your legendary calm or freak out?"

Hayden leapt off the bed so fast, he dislodged a sleeping Jennifur. The cat hit the floor and sat there shaking her head a moment before giving Hayden a dirty look and stalking off, rigid tail swishing through the air, the picture of a pissed-off kitty.

"Okay, so freak out it is then," Wendy murmured, amused, but also sucking in air because of the latest contraction.

"Stay calm," Hayden said, shoving his feet into his basketball shoes and grabbing her go bag, the one he'd had ready ever since her first pregnancy OB-GYN appointment all those months ago now. He turned to her. "What do you want to wear?"

"More than you're wearing," she said, trying and failing to hold back a smile.

He looked down at himself and she laughed, because he was naked as the day he'd been born, with the exception of his shoes. Still snorting, she reached for her phone on the nightstand, but it wasn't there. She vaguely remembered tucking it beneath her pillow in case her iPad battery died, so she slid a hand around looking for it.

Gone.

She twisted to the best of her ability to search the bed. Meanwhile, Hayden, who'd managed to get dressed in jeans and a T-shirt—inside out, but Wendy figured she was going to need something to keep her amused over the next hours, so she didn't say anything—came at her with a pair of his sweatpants.

Nope. "I am *not* wearing big, baggy, old sweatpants to give birth," she said.

"Babe, hate to break this to you, but you won't be wearing *any* pants to give birth."

Dammit. She hated when he was right. But hey, she found her phone under her own ass, so that was something. She quickly hit Anna's number and waited.

After three rings, Anna answered her cell with a groggy "'Lo? Who died?"

"No one," Wendy said. "Well, maybe Hayden soon since he wants me to wear his ancient old baggy sweats today."

Hayden gave a Wendy-worthy eye roll.

Wendy stuck her tongue out at him.

"If no one's dead, why are we all awake?" Anna demanded.

"I'm in labor."

"Ohmigod! I'll be right there! Don't you dare start without me!"

"Too late," she quipped, but Anna was already gone. Okay then. "Anna will be right here."

There came the sudden sound of pounding feet coming up the stairs. Two seconds later, Anna appeared in their bedroom doorway in just an oversize T-shirt and undies, hair wild, eyes wide. *"You're in labor?"*

Wendy stared at her. "Did you sleep here?"

"She did," Hayden said.

"I had a weird feeling about you." Anna came close, taking Wendy's phone and setting it on the nightstand. She then climbed up on the bed with her, pushing Wendy's probably equally wild hair back from her face. "You okay?"

That Anna was here, that she'd come in silent support, had Wendy's eyes filling with tears. But then she stilled, eyes on Anna. "You had sex."

"What?" Anna asked, clearly startled.

"You totally did it with Owen again, even though you claimed you weren't going to! Dammit, you get to do all the good stuff!"

"Wow," Hayden said.

Wendy waved a hand at him. "Okay, yes, fine, we did it a few nights ago, and you never complain, even though you're trying to sleep with someone who's turned into a Tyrannosaurus rex. And don't think that I don't know it was like trying to thread a needle without glasses. We couldn't do it doggy style because it felt like my belly was going to secede from the United States of Wendy. We couldn't go full frontal because you don't have a twenty-four-inch-long penis. Even playing big spoon little spoon is nearly impossible."

Hayden blinked. "I thought we managed okay."

"I fell asleep on you!" Wendy cried.

"Um . . ." Anna looked at Hayden. "I don't want to alarm you, but your wife has lost her mind."

Hayden wisely didn't respond to this. "Can we go to the hospital now?"

Wendy looked at Anna. "Are you going to deny me details regarding the sexy times with Owen? Throw a starving girl a bone here."

"Seriously?" Hayden asked.

Wendy opened her mouth to say something but froze as the next contraction hit. "Oh. Oh, damn. Shit. *Fuck*."

Hayden tried to scoop her up, but she pushed him away. "Just . . . give . . . me . . . a . . . minute."

Hayden climbed on the bed with her so that she had him on one side and Anna on the other, each holding a hand as she took that minute. The second the pain passed, she looked at Anna expectantly.

Anna talked directly to Hayden. "Can't you control her at all?"

"Not even a little bit," he said.

"*Please* don't make this thing with Owen a bigger deal than it is," Anna said to Wendy. "I told you, this is just a thing until the case is solved."

"She's self-sabotaging again," Wendy said to Hayden. "Fix her."

"She doesn't need fixing."

Anna beamed at him.

"Suck-up," Wendy muttered, then hissed out a breath of

surprise as she felt some sort of internal pop and then a rush of water.

"What?" Hayden and Anna asked in unison.

"I think . . ." Wendy stared up at them in horror. "I think I just peed the bed."

Five minutes later, Anna was on the phone with the OB-GYN as Hayden walked Wendy outside toward his car.

The two little five- and seven-year-old girls who lived next door were sitting on their grass. "Where you going?" they asked.

"To have babies," Hayden said, pointing to Wendy's belly.

"Did you eat them?" the younger asked Wendy.

Wendy was laughing when Hayden helped her into the front passenger seat of his vehicle. He reached for the seat belt to buckle her in, pausing when she curled into herself with a moan as a contraction swamped her.

"Hee-hee-hoo," Hayden said.

Wendy shoved a hand in his face to shut him up as she got lost in the pain. She might've added some choice words as well.

He had the engine started and the car in gear when Anna hopped into the back seat with Wendy's go bag.

"Did you seriously almost leave without me?" Anna demanded.

Wendy laughed through the pain. "Yeah, because this . . . is . . . all . . . about . . . you."

Anna put her hands on Wendy's shoulders from behind and gently massaged them. "Breathe. In through your nose, out through your mouth. Two short exhales, one longer one. Hee-hee-hoo. Hee-hee-hoo."

"That's what I told her," Hayden said. "She threatened to give me a vasectomy. With her nail file."

Wendy put her hands over her sister's and held on tight as she tried to breathe with Anna.

"Doing great," Anna said calmly, turning her hands over so Wendy could entwine their fingers together. "Again. Hee-hee-hoo. Hee-hee-hoo."

"Thanks," Wendy whispered in sincere gratitude when the contraction passed.

Hayden sighed.

"Hey, you were helpful too," Wendy said.

"How?"

"Well, when you nearly ran naked to the car without me, that made me laugh. And laughing is important."

Hayden shook his head.

"I still can't believe I peed on my favorite sheets," Wendy moaned.

"You know it wasn't pee. It was your amniotic fluid," Hayden said. "And I'll buy you more sheets. As many sets as you want."

"He's still worried about the whole vasectomy-with-the-nail-file thing," Wendy said. "Turn right."

Hayden didn't turn right.

"That was the fastest way!" Wendy nudged him in the arm. "Turn right here then!"

"We're going on Lake Drive," Hayden said. "It's the safest route."

Wendy gave him the death stare. "I swear to you, if I have your babies in this car, the vasectomy is the least of your worries."

He didn't look scared. That was the best thing about her husband. He was unflappable, unrufflable—at least when she wasn't in labor. Even now, he was driving calm and steady because in his mind, calm and steady won the race every single time. "Just this once, can't you be the rabbit?" she asked.

"No."

"You're driving like a grandpa."

"I'm not speeding up, Wen."

"But the babies are coming right now!" she yelled.

He glanced over at her. Then shook his head. "That was a lie. And mean."

"How do you know?"

"Because he knows you," Anna said. "You always squeak when you lie, and you totally just squeaked."

"Oh my God," Wendy moaned. "We're not ready for this. We're going to be outnumbered!"

"We're not," Anna said. "Three of us to three of them. We've got this, Sissy. It's going to be okay."

Sissy. Anna hadn't called her that since they'd been little kids. The single word, with warm affection and a dash of worry in Anna's voice, warmed her heart to almost bursting.

"Keep breathing," Hayden said, reaching out a hand for Wendy's. "You're not alone, babe, we've got you. Always."

Okay, so her heart was actually going to burst. Also, her eyes were leaking. She didn't deserve either of them.

"You still okay?" Anna asked. "You hanging in there?"

"Is there another option?" Wendy gave a half-hysterical laugh. "Remember that time we went to Disneyland? We saw that couple with three kids—one of them was screaming, another one was hurling into a trash can, and the third one had taken off running. What happens when that happens to us? Do we console the screamer, clean up the puke, or catch the sprinter?" She started crying, startling all of them, including herself. "And Disneyland is supposed to be the happiest place on earth!" she wailed.

"You'll console the screamer," Hayden said. "Anna will handle the puker. And good thing I was all-state cross-country because I'll grab the sprinter."

"Wait—why do I get the puker?" Anna asked.

"Hello!" Wendy yelled. "Are either of you going to dilate to ten centimeters? Only the dilater gets to freak out!"

Hayden pulled into the hospital, parked, and reached for her, giving her one of his grade A hugs. It was so good, Wendy sighed and relaxed.

"We've got this, babe, the three of us. I promise."

Still crying and also laughing, she hoped he was right.

# CHAPTER 22

Twelve long hours later, Anna felt both exhausted and exhilarated, and she hadn't even been the one having the babies. She sat at a sleepy Wendy's hospital bedside, Hayden on the other side.

All three shirtless—well, Anna was in a sports bra—each of them holding one of the babies skin to skin. Wendy was feeding Baby A. That was what they'd been calling them since they arrived, Baby A, B, and C, until Wendy and Hayden decided on names.

Anna couldn't take her eyes off the cuteness overload in her arms. The way the wrinkly little thing looked up at her, her sweet blue eyes blinking even in the dimmed lights, mouth slightly agape, as if surprised in the very best way to be out of the womb, but also relieved to recognize the voices she'd been hearing for so many months.

"Hey," Wendy said quietly. "You okay?"

Anna looked up, assuming she was talking to Hayden, but she wasn't. Wendy was talking to her. "Me?" Anna shrugged. "Of course."

But she wasn't. She was shaking with letdown adrenaline and something else.

"What's wrong?" Wendy asked.

And Anna . . . burst into tears. "I'm sorry. Ignore me!"

"Tell me," Wendy said, looking deeply concerned. "Are you dying?"

"No! But I was worried you would." Anna was doing that ugly-cry thing where you can't catch your breath. "I've been freaking out that you'd die in childbirth."

Wendy's mouth fell open. "Oh my God." She started crying too. "I wouldn't do that to you!"

"You can't control life and death!"

Wendy said something back that Anna couldn't understand, and Hayden took Wendy's hand and looked at them both. "Guys, only dogs can hear what either of you are saying."

The babies were crying now too. It took Hayden a few minutes to get all the females in his life to stop sobbing, but he managed like a pro.

Wendy finally blew her nose and looked at Anna. "I'm not dying any time soon, but if I ever do—"

"Oh my God."

"No, listen," Wendy said. "When I go, the first thing you have to do is—"

"I know, I know," Anna said. "I have to clean out the top drawer in your nightstand."

Hayden grinned. "That's my favorite drawer."

"I'm dead, Hayden!"

They all laughed, softly now since the babies were back to sleeping.

"Dad would've loved this," Anna said softly.

Wendy's eyes misted. "I know."

Hayden handed out tissues. Again. "So . . . Buffy, Cordelia, and Willow?" he asked, his voice still low and husky and filled with emotion, as it'd been ever since helping Wendy go through birth, making them an instant family of five.

"Oh my God, yes!" Anna grinned at Wendy. "He's *such* a keeper."

"He is." Already softened by motherhood, Wendy gave Hayden a sweet smile. "But we aren't naming our babies from the *Buffy*-verse."

"Eenie, Meeny, and Miney?" Anna asked.

"Boo, Sully, and Mike?" Hayden asked.

"Bacon, Lettuce, and Tomato?" Anna asked.

Wendy just looked at them.

"What?" Anna said. "I'm starving, and a BLT sounds amazing right about now."

"Oh, I know!" Hayden lifted his head. "Chocolate, Vanilla, and Strawberry." And when both Anna and Wendy went brows up, he muttered, "I'm hungry too, jeez."

"The nurse said they always provide a steak dinner postpartum. It should come soon."

Anna's stomach rumbled as she looked down at her bundle, at the perfect little infant, lips pursed like maybe she was hungry too. Proving it, she turned her tiny little capped head toward Anna's chest and, with eyes closed now, began to root around with her mouth open like a baby bird. "Um . . ."

Wendy looked over and laughed.

"How is this funny?" Anna asked. "You've got three mouths to feed. Why aren't you panicked?"

"You know me," Wendy said. "My two factory settings are constant panic over every little thing and . . . it is what it is."

"And right now it is what it is?"

"Yep."

"Okay." Anna nodded. "That's good." The baby was winding up with whimpers. "But what do I do here?"

"Cuddle her closer. I'll swap you out when this one's done."

A few minutes later they all made a three-way shift change and Anna smiled down at Baby B. Or maybe she was Baby C. "Look at us," she said to the triplets' parents. "We're not outnumbered at all."

"Speak for yourself," Hayden said. "It's now five girls to me."

Anna laughed, but quickly stopped when precious Baby B flinched at the sound. Hugging the cutie patootie into her, she nearly melted when the baby sighed in pleasure. "Maybe you are outnumbered," she whispered to Hayden. "But you're a basketball team now."

And truthfully, it was so much more than that. Taking in these wrinkly, alien-looking five-pounders with their worried little frowns and soft little whimpers that made her heartbeat quicken, she felt completely undone. There was just something in the way they looked up at Wendy, and even at Hayden and Anna herself, like they knew they were with their people. Eyes wet yet again, she lifted her head and met Wendy's own wet gaze. "They're perfect, Wen," she whispered.

"My whole family's perfect," her sister whispered back, and looked at Hayden with such love it almost hurt to take it in. "Everyone in this room. You're all I need for the rest of my life."

Anna nodded, but suddenly there was an empty spot in her chest and a pang to go with it. It really made no sense. She'd never been one to dream of a family of her own; she'd never given much thought to having kids. She'd let her work become the most important thing in her life.

But after these past few weeks, her job suddenly didn't feel enough for her anymore. She had a terrifying idea of why that might be, and his name was Owen.

But . . . was it really so terrifying?

*Yes*, because she'd been stupid and made the rule that they'd be over when the case was over. Damn, Wendy had been right after all. She'd self-sabotaged herself yet again.

Leaning down, she dropped a kiss on the downy brunette head in her arms. The baby was calm and, just as her womb-mate had, was looking up at her with big eyes.

Baby C in Hayden's arms was frustrated by the lack of a working nipple and began to make unhappy puppy sounds. Baby B, back in Wendy's arms, was gurgling and babbling, going on and on with a story that no one but she understood. Anna leaned in close. "Just like your mama," she whispered.

Wendy laughed, then sucked in air. "Okay, no one make me laugh. *Ouch*."

Hayden's head came up, eyes sharp. "You're in pain?"

"Well, I'm not *not* in pain."

"Babe." Hayden pushed the button for the nurse.

Anna looked down to find Baby A's eyes back on her, her brow slightly furrowed as if she was concentrating on Anna like nothing else mattered, and Anna's ovaries actually ached. "I know this all seems crazy right now," she told the baby, "but you should know, I'll always have your back. No matter what, I've got you."

The baby's lips curved, and Anna's mouth dropped open. "She's smiling at me."

"It's gas," Wendy said.

"No, it's—" Anna broke off as sure enough, the baby farted right into the palm of her hand. "Never mind." She grinned. "Like mama, like daughter."

Hayden almost fell off his chair from trying to laugh silently.

Wendy narrowed her eyes at both of them, but nothing could erase Anna's smile. She'd never been farted on before, and she didn't even care. In that moment, the love she felt for her niece overruled everything else. "Do you think Mom looked at you like we're looking at these babies?"

Wendy nodded. "I know it. And if she could have, she'd have looked at you like that too."

Comforted by the image, Anna smiled, knowing the love she felt for these babies was forever. And suddenly she realized what she was feeling was the same love she'd seen mirrored in Ruby's eyes when the older woman had looked at Owen. She hadn't understood it then, but she understood it now.

Which made it even more important that they find her things, no matter what that meant for her dad's reputation. "So are we going to name these girls for real or what?" Anna asked. "Maybe Michelle, for Mom, and then Louise, for Dad. And then, of course, you could name the third."

Hayden gave a quiet laugh. "Don't worry. I have no illusions of having any control over Namegate."

Wendy gave him a warm, soft smile, and he returned it. "How about Michelle and Louise?" she said, and Hayden nodded his approval. "And then . . . Annabelle, for my favorite sister."

Anna's throat burned while her heart swelled, so she did as she always did when emotions swamped her and made her feel uncomfortable. "I hope this doesn't mean you want me to take one. Cuz it's not happening until after potty training."

Wendy, not fooled for a second, sent her a sweet, happy smile. "Love you, Anna."

"Love you back."

Wendy turned to Hayden, and they stared deeply into each other's eyes. A whole conversation was going on without either of them speaking a word. Wanting to give them a private moment, Anna stood and handed Wendy the baby, settling her so she could see her sister. Anna then kissed Wendy on the forehead. "Love you. I'll be back."

"Honey, go home and get some sleep," Wendy murmured. "I need you rested."

Anna nodded, and as she turned away and headed to the door, the tears she'd barely managed to hold back were already slipping down her face. She hated to cry, she really did, but she felt frazzled, emotionally spent, and exhausted.

She walked out of the room . . . and found Owen sitting in a chair against the opposite hallway wall, scrolling through his phone. He took one look at her and stood up, closing the distance between them, pulling her in. She allowed herself to relax into him because he was warm and strong, and when he held her like this, she felt safe and comforted.

"How long have you been here?" she asked, throat so thick it hurt to talk.

"Since I got your text that Wendy'd had the babies. She okay?"

"Yes, everyone's good. You didn't have to come, it's been hours."

His arms tightened, and he pressed his cheek to the top of her head. "I would've waited as long as it took."

In the past when he made statements regarding his feelings for her, or what their future might be, she'd ignored them. Or tried. It'd been her own inability to believe or trust that he wouldn't hurt her. And maybe it'd been the emotional last twenty-four hours, but she could feel herself signing the bottom line on the Believe and Trust Owen program.

"You okay?" he asked quietly.

"I'm unraveling and I don't even know why."

He held her gaze, then kissed her softly. "How about I take you home with me? You can unravel there, in my bed."

"Yeah?"

He smiled at the eagerness in her voice. "If that works for you."

"Will Turbo be there?"

"Yes, and he'll be very excited to see you again. That is, if you're interested."

If she was any more interested, she'd levitate there. "Does he sleep in your bed?"

He rubbed the side of his jaw, his day-old stubble making a rasping sound that did things to her she wasn't sure should be happening in public. "I try very hard to keep him off the bed," he said. "But he waits until I fall asleep to join me. For a big guy, he can move like smoke when he wants to. But we can lock him out of the room."

She had to blink away the image of a very sexy Owen sleeping in his bed, his dog lying at his feet. "Don't you dare."

He looked at her for a beat, then smiled. "I've also got ice cream."

"Are you trying to . . . *sweeten* the deal?"

"Hedging my bets," he said. "Doubling down."

"You must really want me to . . . *come* . . . over."

He gave a slow, sexy grin. "I do. I really do."

She laughed.

"So? Yes? No?"

Instead of answering, she started power walking out, loving the sound of his low chuckle behind her.

# CHAPTER 23

The next day, Anna sank into her office chair, exhausted to the bone. She'd had a really long day and night at the hospital with Wendy, and then last night at Owen's . . .

"It's only three in the afternoon," Mari said as she let herself in to drop a stack of mail on Anna's desk. "And you already look done in."

Anna fought a yawn and lost. "I'm fine."

Mari grinned. "Must be hard being kept up all night long by a really hot guy."

Anna refused to take the bait, even if it was true. "Hey, maybe I'm just trying to catch up from Wendy having the babies."

Mari gave her a droll look. "Really? That's the story you want to go with when you have a love bite on your neck?"

Damn Owen's sexy mouth. She put a hand over the love bite in question and, ignoring Mari's laugh, pulled the mail toward her. Unfortunately, most of it was bills and not payments from clients. Damn. Well, at least she'd just taken on two new cases, both possible insurance frauds—her specialty. With luck, she'd have a happier bank account by the end of the month.

Mari took in her expression and sank to a chair in front of Anna's desk. "What can I do to help?"

This was why she loved Mari. She'd do whatever Anna needed, no questions asked.

"I could go through the bills for you." Mari nudged her chin toward the stack. "Prioritize them. Push as many off as possible until you sink your teeth into our new cases and bring in the dough."

"It's okay, I've got this. Plus, I just put a whole bunch of searches I need handled on your desk, and I don't want you to have to stay late when you're having so much fun on that new dating app."

Mari jabbed her thumbs at herself. "This girl's drought is finally over!"

Someone knocked on Anna's office door, and the two women turned in unison to take in Owen leaning against the jamb looking better than any man had a right to look, ever.

"Afternoon, ladies." He turned those deep green eyes on Anna. "You busy?"

"She is not," Mari said before Anna could speak for herself. "She's free. Free as can be. So whatever you had in mind, she's game. And free. Did I mention she's free?"

Anna pointed to the door, and Mari hopped up. "Right. The searches." She winked at Owen as she left.

Anna watched the man walk toward her, his mouth curving as he perched a hip on the side of her desk. "Hey."

"Hey yourself."

"How you doing?"

"I can't stop yawning. Know anything about that?"

He let out a soft, sexy laugh. "Not my fault you're a sex fiend who kept us up all night."

Dammit. And true. "Weren't you taking some clients up to Spooner Lake today?"

"Yep, and we're already back. I was on my way home when Ruby's caretaker called me. She said my aunt's having a really good day, so I should stop by. And if she's having a good day . . ."

Anna stood. "She might be able to talk to us about the coins and Ruby Red."

He nodded. "I take it you have time to come with?"

Time? No. But that wasn't going to stop her. She eyed the stack of mail in her hand. "Mari?"

Mari stuck in her head so fast that Anna knew she'd been eavesdropping. "Just wanted to be close by in case you needed anything, boss."

"Uh-huh." Anna handed over the stack of mail. "I need your help."

"Thought you wanted me to get laid, not pay bills."

Owen grinned. "Wow, what a nice boss."

Anna sighed, grabbed her purse, and nudged Owen out the door ahead of her. She took the time to turn back and narrow her eyes at Mari.

"Have fun," Mari said, grinning and waving. "Don't worry about me at all. Make good choices! Be safe! Oh, and don't do anything I wouldn't." Then she wisely vanished.

"I need new help," Anna muttered.

Owen, the sexy ass, was still smiling when they climbed into his truck.

Leaning in, he clicked her seat belt for her, then used his close proximity to kiss the daylights out of her. When he pulled back and took in her undoubtedly dazed expression, he smirked. "Mari said don't do anything she wouldn't do."

"Except there's nothing Mari wouldn't do."

"Good to know." The heat in his eyes gave her a hot flash, because as she already knew, there was nothing Owen wouldn't do either.

Ten minutes later, he parked in the lot of his great-aunt Ruby's memory care facility. When he hesitated, Anna took his hand. "Are you sure? I don't want to do this if it's going to upset her." *Or you . . .*

"I called ahead and let them know that if she's still doing good, we'd like to take her out for a few hours. We just have to get her back for dinner so she doesn't get upset at the loss of her routine. She's got a few old friends visiting, but according to her caregiver, they'll be leaving any time now."

At the front desk, he signed them in, and they walked down the hall until Owen stopped in front of one of the apartments. He knocked twice and then opened the door with a key. "Hello?"

"Come in!" Ruby called out.

They stepped into a small but comfortable living room area. A trio of elderly ladies stood up from the couch and raced to be the first to hug Owen.

Anna couldn't help but smile as he gamely endured being squeezed tight by each of them, none who came up past his elbow. His aunt, however, he hugged back and held tight to his chest for a moment.

"And who's this?" Ruby asked, smiling at Anna.

Anna didn't let on that they'd already met, just smiled in return. "I'm Anna Moore, Owen's . . . er, um, associate."

Ruby beamed. "Well, any 'er, um' associate of Owen's is an associate of mine. Owen, honey, how are you?"

"He's too skinny, that's how he is." This from the friend with blue hair and a mischievous smile. She patted Owen's butt. "Not enough meat on the bones."

"Definitely needs some fattening up," the second friend agreed, her metal gray hair curled into rows of tiny coils that quivered when she winked at Anna. "How are you going to catch this pretty girl?"

"I think he's already caught her," the third said. Her hair was a mix of firecracker orange and magenta. "Which is a shame because my great-granddaughter's available and ready for kids."

"If I was two decades younger, I'd be first in line," Blue Hair said.

"More like *four* decades," Metal Gray muttered.

"Hey, being a cougar is all the rage," Blue Hair said.

Since Owen was looking uncharacteristically out of his comfort zone, Anna moved to his side. "Sorry, ladies, but Skinny Hot Stuff is all mine."

The ladies all said "Damn" in unison, made all the more amusing because they wore matching velour tracksuits in the same purple with white walking shoes.

"We're on the same bowling team," Blue Hair said. "In fact, we've got a game today, so we need to skedaddle." She leaned in close to Owen, using the excuse to put her hand on his biceps. "She's doing great today. So good to see her."

Owen ushered them all out, thanking them for keeping his aunt company. When he shut the door, he turned and met Anna's eyes. "All yours, huh?"

She shrugged. "Anything for the cause."

He smiled, then turned to Ruby. "You look good."

"Oh, you." She had a hat on her head and her purse hanging off her arm. "Tell me you're breaking me out of this joint for a bit."

"We're breaking you out of this joint for a bit."

Ruby's eyes lit up. "For ice cream?"

"Thought you might want to go to the house for a few hours."

"Oh, yes!" She put a hand to her chest. "Hurry, let's make a break for it before someone catches us."

Owen took her hand. "It's okay. We have approval to go."

"Oh. Well, okay then. Though sneaking out might've been fun."

"We could pretend, if that would make you feel better."

Ruby looked at Anna. "He always did have a smart mouth."

Anna smiled at her. "Still does."

Ruby beamed at her. "Most women don't appreciate that about him."

"I'm not most women."

Owen held the door open for Anna, then leaned in, pressing his mouth to her ear. "Remind me to thank you later. Slowly. In great detail."

# CHAPTER 24

Half an hour later, Owen settled Ruby on the couch in the living room of her home with a bowl of toffee ice cream—her favorite. Anna made her tea and covered her legs with a crocheted afghan.

Ruby beamed. "I hope you're going to marry this one," she told Owen. "It's not like you're getting any younger."

Owen ignored this as he sat on the coffee table facing his aunt, and her smile faded. "What is it?" she asked quietly, her eyes serious now. "Something's on your mind."

He was so overwhelmingly grateful that she was there today, like really mentally there, that he nearly embarrassed himself. "We need to talk to you."

His great-aunt looked to Anna, then back to Owen. "What is it?"

"Have you ever met a man named Joe Shade?" He showed her Joe's mug shot from his phone.

Ruby had her glasses around her neck on a beaded chain. She slipped them onto her face and gasped. "Well, for heaven's sake. I haven't seen him in . . . well, years."

Owen must have looked shocked, because she smiled. "You probably don't want to hear this about your ancient great-aunt, but once upon a time, Joe courted me. What a charmer he was."

Owen's insides chilled. "You dated him?"

"I wouldn't say that exactly."

He did his best to hide his grimace.

Ruby laughed. "He used to visit me here, bring me flowers and candy, that sort of thing." Her face softened with the happy memories. "He made me laugh."

Owen had to take a deep, calming breath. "How did you meet him?"

"We were both at a local fundraiser and had a connection. But then one day he just stopped coming by. This was obviously way before cell phones and such." She shrugged. "We simply lost contact."

Owen had a different theory. Most likely, Joe had purposely run into her at that fundraiser and courted a friendship so he could come by and case out her house, looking for information on her infamous necklace and coin set. And then once he'd found them right there in this house, he'd stolen them and vanished.

"Can you remember when this was exactly?" Anna asked Ruby.

Good thing one of them was thinking clearly. Anna was trying to nail down if this was before or after Ruby's necklace and coins had been stolen, and he should've thought to ask.

"Oh . . . um . . ." Ruby shook her head. "Well, I don't remember exactly, but probably about a decade ago."

Owen was trying to figure out how to speak calmly when Anna put a hand on his arm and leaned past him, smiling sweetly at Ruby. "That's a big help, thank you."

Ruby smiled back. "I remember because I wore the Ruby Red for him a few times. Such a handsome man. I wanted to look my best."

Owen closed his eyes for a beat, knowing deep in his bones that Shady Joe had somehow managed to pull off this job. He was surprised when Anna ran her hand down his arm and entwined her fingers in his, squeezing, waiting a beat for him to feel the grounding connection between them.

"Please don't be upset," Ruby said, surprising him. "I wasn't hurt when he stopped coming by. He was way too young for me anyway." She laughed, but broke off at Owen's expression, sucking in a breath. "Wait. You think he's the one who took my things. That's why you're asking about him, right? You think Joe was a bad guy."

"I think it's possible," Owen said carefully. "But we don't have any proof."

"Is there anything you can remember about that time that might help us?" Anna asked her. "Anything at all."

Ruby thought about it and shook her head. "I told the police everything I knew at the time."

Anna nodded. "Do you think you could look at one more picture?"

"Of course, dear."

As Owen watched Anna scroll through her phone, he knew just how hard this was going to be for her. He could tell when she landed on a pic of her dad because a small smile crossed her face before she flipped the phone around. "Do you know this man?"

Ruby put her glasses back on and bent over Anna's phone, taking in the small picture. She looked for a long time.

Owen leaned in. "Ruby? Do you recognize him?"

Brow furrowed with unease, his great-aunt wrung her hands together.

"It's okay, Ruby," Anna said, clearly not wanting to upset her. And that she would put Ruby ahead of her own need to know the truth about her dad just about undid him. "We can talk about something else."

Ruby shook her head. "No, this is important, I can tell. But no, I'm sorry, I don't think I know him. I'm sorry, I'm just so embarrassed by what I let happen."

"None of what happened was your fault," Owen said. "None of it."

"I guess I know that much, but I still feel foolish. Old and foolish."

Anger burned deep in his gut, but he worked to hide it.

Anna squeezed his aunt's hand. "It's okay. Please, don't worry about it."

"I hate when I can't remember." Ruby sat back. "What's his name?"

"Louis Moore."

Ruby sucked in a breath. "Wait a minute. That name . . . He sent me a letter. Well, his attorney did, on his behalf."

Owen was stunned. "A letter?" This was the first he'd ever heard of it. He looked at Anna, who just shook her head. She hadn't known either.

"I'm sorry," Ruby said, wringing her hands. "I don't know why I'm just remembering. When I got the letter, I put it in a safe spot so I could remember to give it to Owen, but . . ." She shook her head. "Like so many other things, I forgot."

Owen squeezed her hand. "It's understandable. When you moved into the memory care facility, the letter got lost in the shuffle."

She looked at Anna. "Do you know him? Is that why you're asking me about him? Is he somehow related to Joe?" She put a hand to her chest again. "Do you think they were working together?"

At his side, Anna drew a deep breath. "I hope not." She paused. "He's my dad."

Ruby took this in for a beat. "Well, then maybe he could fill in some holes for us."

"I wish he could, but he passed away last year."

"Oh. Oh, honey, I'm so sorry."

"That's incredibly generous of you to say," Anna murmured. "I'm just grateful to you for being willing to talk about this with us. I know it's difficult. I mean, I can't even remember where I left my sunglasses this morning, much less something from a decade ago. Is there any chance you still have the letter?"

Owen's heart ached, impressed as hell watching her talk to Ruby with a sweet, quiet respect.

"I'm almost sure I wouldn't have gotten rid of it," Ruby said slowly. She looked at Owen. "I'm positive I meant to show it to you and have you read it, but . . ." Her eyes went sad, and she turned away. "I clearly forgot. Like I always do."

Owen took her hand in his. "It's okay, Ruby. Like Anna said, everyone forgets things. Do you remember when I first got my driver's license and you let me use your car? I went to the movies and forgot where I parked."

Ruby barked out a laugh. "I'm sure I wasn't very kind about it."

In fact, she'd made him clean all her friends' houses for a month. "Can you think of where you might've stashed it?"

Ruby looked around, shaking her head. Then she gasped. "Oh! My keepsake box."

"If you tell me where it is, I could get it for you."

"I'll show you." Ruby gave a shaky nod and patted him on the cheek. "You've always been such a good boy." She got up, leaning heavily on her cane.

Owen got up with her, following her into her small bedroom, watching as she headed straight for the closet.

"There," she said, pointing to an ornately carved wooden container the size of a shoe box on a high shelf.

He brought it down, coughing as dust fell into his face.

"What a beautiful box," Anna said when he'd brought it to the living room.

"It was my grandmother's," Ruby said. "Her dad gave it to her as a child, when they still lived in Lithuania. After the Ruby Red necklace and coins went missing, it was all I had left of my entire family." She opened the box. Inside were a few stacks of old pictures and other keepsakes, along with a few envelopes. Ruby flipped through them and then held out a sealed white envelope addressed to Ruby from an attorney's office.

Owen opened it. There was a letter inside. By the look on Anna's face, she knew it was her dad's handwriting. He held it out to her, and after a brief hesitation, Anna began to read out loud:

*Dear Ruby,*

*You don't know me, but I know you. Or, more accurately, I know about the theft of your ancestorial necklace and coin collection. It's always bothered me that the police never recovered your things, mostly because I suspect I know who did it. If I'm right, I hate myself for not stopping him.*

*Here's what I know. This man had a plan, and if he did this, I can tell you that he had a hard-to-reach spot where*

*he kept his loot locked away until the coast was clear. As
he wasn't a creative man, I doubt the spot has changed. It
won't be easy to find and will be, frankly, impossible for
you at your age. I'm sorry. You'll have to have help. The
hidey-hole is in a widely unexplored area. To find the right
spot, you go to the fork of roads and go west toward the
sound of water. Look for the stooped trees, as they point the
way to the grottos. Go to the farthest south area that you
can get to without walking right off the cliffs.*

*I'm sorry I didn't go to the police when this first
happened. If I'm being honest, I was protecting myself,
afraid I'd be linked to the robbery, which was me being a
coward. But I'm a better man than that now, or at least
would like to think so. I can thank my daughters for that,
and it's for them that I'm coming clean at all because I
should've become a better man far sooner than I did.*

*You're probably wondering why this letter came from my
attorney, and that's another sign of my selfishness. I'm not
ready to see the look in my daughters' eyes when my past
comes to light, so I've asked my attorney to wait until I'm
gone. I hope you can forgive me . . .*

*Signed,*
*L*

There was a long beat of stunned silence during which Owen's
mind spun. He could tell by the look on Anna's face that she was
spinning too.

And doubting her dad about his claim to not know more than
he'd revealed.

Owen actually wasn't. Sonya had said Louis declined helping

Shady Joe do this job, and he believed her. And then there was the fact that Will had seemed far more furious at his dad than at Anna's, not to mention certain that Joe *had* done this.

And then there was something else. Something about the careful way Louis had worded his letter. Why would a guilty man send a letter that could be used as evidence against him, even a year later?

He wouldn't.

Because he wasn't guilty, at least not of this.

Anna leaned back, her mouth even more grim than it had been. "He was protecting himself, even to the end," she said. "He knew he'd be implicated."

"No, honey," Ruby said. "He did it for you."

Anna drew a shaky breath. "You're kinder than I am. He didn't write this letter until he knew he was dying."

"You think he knew?" Owen asked her.

She nodded. "I know it. The doctor told us after he'd passed that he'd known for many years, and at the time Wendy and I were so overwhelmed with grief, we didn't really question why he didn't tell us. I think we assumed he was trying to protect us. But now I think he was protecting himself."

"Don't be too hard on him," Ruby said. "If it turns out he's right, it means I'll get my things back. That's all that matters."

Anna looked stunned at her generosity and got up to hug her. After, she turned to Owen. "Fork of roads? Stooped trees? Grottos? It sounds so vague. The greater Tahoe area is made of hundreds of thousands of square miles of rugged, hard-to-reach mountains. It will be like finding a needle in a haystack."

Owen pulled out his phone. "I've heard the term 'fork of roads' before . . ." He thumbed something into his search engine. "Okay, so there's a fork of roads in the Mojave Desert.

Too far . . . And—" He looked up and smiled. ". . . And another at Mount Lion."

Anna shook her head. "Where's Mount Lion? I've lived here all my life and I've never heard of it."

"It's a remote—extremely remote—place where thrill seekers hike up and then backcountry ski down. The reason you don't know it is probably because it was closed off years ago. People kept dying up there."

"But not you," she said.

"Not me," he agreed. "Ky and I have been up there several times, though not since we were stupid teenagers."

"Dear God," Ruby said. "I'm glad I didn't know."

"Can it be accessed by anyone?" Anna asked.

"Not easily."

"But *you* can get in."

"Yes."

Anna nodded. "Good. But you're not going without me. We're a we, remember?"

Owen's heart took a good hard leap at that, but he could tell by the look on her face that the words had slipped out without permission. "Anna, I can bring Ky. You don't have to do this, it's incredibly dangerous—"

"Let me repeat myself," she said. "I'm going."

He knew by the familiar look of obstinance that there was no use arguing with her. "Depends."

"On what?" she asked in disbelief.

"On whether you promise to do exactly what I say, no arguing."

Anna made a show of looking around. "Did we step back into the 1950s when I wasn't looking?"

"Anna," he said on a short laugh. "I'm not one to exaggerate, so when I tell you this place is closed off because people died out there, and died *horribly*, you have to understand the danger. Some people went into that area and never came back, and their bodies have never been found."

She stared at him, then slowly nodded. "Okay. I hear you."

"But you're still going."

"Yes."

Ruby smiled at her. "I like the way you can't be bossed around. Oh, to be young again in these modern times."

After putting the box away, they drove Ruby back to the memory care facility, walking her to her room. Owen held her close, not sure if when he came by in the next day or two she'd actually be . . . herself.

"I love you, Victor."

Owen closed his eyes at his grandpa's name. And so it began. "I love you too."

Outside in the parking lot, Anna stopped and hugged him. Overwhelmed by emotion, knowing that once Ruby was gone, he'd be completely alone, he dropped his head to her shoulder and held on for a long moment.

Back in the vehicle, Anna pulled on her seat belt and said casually, "You know there are only two places where I'd let you be the boss of me."

"Mount Lion," he said. "And . . . where else?"

She flashed a smile. "In bed."

He laughed and realized he wasn't alone at all. Damn, he loved her. It should've felt too soon, it should've terrified him, but instead of feeling the need to ruin what they had, he wanted to do the opposite. He wanted to nurture it, accept it, and for once let his heart lead.

# CHAPTER 25

Anna tried to get a grip but couldn't. It was dawn, and Owen had just parked at the base of Mount Lion. Apparently they could hike in two miles, up to the locked gate that prevented people from going any farther up the mountain.

But hopefully not them.

From there it would be another two miles of a straight-up climb. Owen seemed confident. Ky had stayed behind to run Tahoe Adventures for the day, but he would be in radio contact, tracking their movements.

Owen, a long-range two-way radio on his hip, backpack on his shoulders carrying supplies, smiled at her. "You okay?"

"Yep." It'd been two days since Ruby had pulled her dad's letter from that beautiful wood box. Wendy and the babies were still in the hospital but doing well. Anna had gone by every day to love up on them all. So far, she'd been puked on, pooped on, and cried on. She'd loved every minute, but each day as she left, she checked her birth control pack to make sure she'd remembered to take her pill, because no way did she feel ready for what Wendy was happily dealing with.

Anna had worked as many hours as she could manage during the day, and then each night she and Owen met up at one of their places to make their plans for their trek.

And when they'd been done planning, when it'd been late and their guards had lowered—okay, her guard, because Owen had never had a guard up against her—they'd gone to bed.

Together.

And there, in the quiet dark hours between dusk and dawn, they'd come together in the way they did best.

She had to lean forward to be able to see the entirety of Mount Lion out Owen's windshield, which was tall, majestic, rugged, remote . . . dangerous. Intimidated, she swallowed hard but refused to let her nerves get ahold of her for what still was ahead—a tough hike and then, for the entire last leg of the climb, a scramble up and over massive, ancient rocks that had been there since the Ice Age.

This, of course, had triggered all her nightmares from when Adam had deserted her in Desolation Wilderness, years ago now. She told herself this was different. Owen was different. He didn't go off half-cocked, he was always prepared and knew what he was doing, seemingly at all times.

And he'd never leave her out here.

Never.

"I can do this alone," Owen said quietly, watching her think too hard. "You could wait in the truck."

She knew he meant it. She could let him go do all the work, and he would, no questions asked. Not proud of the small part of her that wanted to let him do it, she firmly shook her head. "I'm going with."

With a nod, he adjusted her backpack for her. Hers was smaller and lighter than his, which also contained climbing gear. She was trying really hard not to think about it as they started walking. But just like that, her feet felt like two concrete blocks.

Owen met her gaze. "Anna—"

"No, I've got this. Truly."

"You do," he said. "We're going to be safe. We're only going to go as far as we can while remaining safe."

"We're going all the way."

He looked into her eyes, and at whatever he saw, probably equal amounts of obstinance and terror, he gave her a small smile. "We're going all the way. Ready?"

She nodded, and he lifted his radio. "We're hitting the trail. Over."

"Good copy," came Ky's voice.

Anna eyed the mountain, somehow even more imposing now. "Let's get this over with."

They started walking, and for the moment, their pace felt doable. Under any other circumstances, she'd have enjoyed it. Fallen pine needles crunched underfoot. The pines towered above them, with sunbeams slanting through, dappling the forest floor.

They didn't speak much. She didn't know what kept Owen quiet. As for herself, she couldn't have talked to save her life, because as the going got harder, all the oxygen she sucked in went straight to her already taxed lungs.

Forty-five minutes later, they stopped in front of the locked trailhead to Mount Lion. Owen once again pulled his radio off his hip. "At the gate," he said.

"Good copy," came Ky's voice. "You made good time so far. Keep moving, don't want you trying to come down once dusk hits."

Right. Because it would take them hours to make the second part of the trek, and then they had to get all the way back down before dark.

No fewer than five signs had been nailed to the gate, all variations on the same theme: *Do not pass Go!*

She stared at the signs, and a very small smile crossed Owen's face.

"Fine." She tossed up her hands. "I don't like that we're breaking the rules."

He gave his head a shake, but the hint of a smile stayed. Then, before she could change her mind, she climbed the gate. At the top, she jumped down, incredibly aware of Owen moving far more agilely and gracefully than she. But she'd actually done it.

*Anna Moore: new and improved and fearless.*

She had to be, had to succeed, both for Ruby and her dad, and by extension, Wendy. Anna had no idea who she'd be after this journey, but she did know she wouldn't be the same person she'd been before finding that coin.

She knew Owen no longer believed her dad had been involved, but—and it killed her to even think this—she still had doubts. In her experience working in insurance fraud, most people who got caught had priors. Yes, her dad's record had been for petty theft, but he'd been *suspected* of other crimes as well, including this one. How many cases had she been on where people got off scot-free for lack of enough evidence?

Too many.

Aware of Owen standing at her side, she drew in a careful breath.

"Anna—"

"I'm good." Sheer force of will had her feet moving. The trail started out steep but not impossible. Or so she told herself.

Almost immediately they came up a large boulder installation at the apex of the pass. Oh boy. "We're going up this?"

"Yes."

She swallowed hard. "Oh good, because I was afraid this would be too easy for me."

He smiled at her attempt to lighten the mood. "It's nature's way of thwarting and discouraging people from going any farther."

She had to tip her head back to see the top of the stacked boulders. "Definitely a deterrent. Was it this way when you were here with Ky?"

"Yep."

"How does anyone get over it?"

"Not easily," he said. "But we're not going over. We're going around."

Going around was even harder than she'd imagined, and she'd imagined it pretty hard. An hour later, they came to a stop. In front of them the trail separated four different ways. She stared at the possibilities. There was no sign, no way to know which path they should take— "Wait. This is the fork of roads!"

Owen had been watching her, and he smiled that she'd caught on. "Yeah." He checked in again with Ky, who warned them winds would be picking up in the next half hour.

Great. Anna looked on either side of the trail, at the thousands-of-feet drop-off, and told herself that fainting right now would be bad for her life span. Then she was distracted by the sound of running water. "I hear water! Just like my dad's letter said. I don't see it, but we need to go west."

He nodded.

She shook her head. "I have no idea which way is west."

He pointed to the far right path. They began moving again,

surrounded by thick, towering trees, the earth beneath their boots spongy with fallen pine needles and recent rains. The occasional bird squawked at them, and squirrels chattered away. The day was stunning, but more than that, for the first time she actually thought maybe they could really do this, find the hidey-hole.

After a while, they came to a natural sinkhole, a large one, maybe the size of a football field, and she stopped short in wonder. A waterfall cascaded down a cliff a hundred feet above them, forming a beautiful if small lake. The azure blue water was so crystal clear, she could see all the way to the bottom. Gray rocks stuck out of the lake's surface, and tall pines shaded the water, deepening the water's edge to cobalt.

They stopped to drink from their water bottles, and Owen handed her a protein bar, waiting to make sure she was going to eat it before he took one for himself. Then they continued, slower now, making her aware that he'd tempered his pace to hers. Wiping her sweaty brow on her sleeve, she kept putting one foot in front of the other.

Until they got to the tree line.

Owen turned in a slow circle, then stopped and pointed.

She followed his finger to . . . "The trees," she murmured. "They're all bent from the wind. It's the stooped trees! We go where the trees are pointing!"

They headed that way, and not surprisingly, it was much harder going now. She couldn't have explained it to herself if her life depended on it, but sudden panic hit her hard and shockingly fast, stealing the air from her lungs, making her heartbeat thunder in her ears and her feet refuse to go another step.

*What am I doing?* She'd promised herself no crazy adventures, not ever again. On top of that, she'd also told herself she wouldn't fall for someone who adventured for a living.

And yet there she stood, doing both—which yes, had been her idea, but that just meant she'd lost her damn mind. Because not only was she falling, she had fallen, and hard. And even worse, she'd made it clear that they were over when they solved this case.

Which meant walking away from him. How in the world was she going to do that without losing a huge chunk of her heart? She thought she was doing a great job of hiding her distress and didn't even realize she was closing in on hyperventilating until she felt Owen's hand grip hers, turning her to face him. She tried to say she was fine, but she didn't have enough air for words.

He bent his knees a little to look into her eyes. "Breathe in through your nose and then slowly out your mouth." He exhibited what he wanted her to do, and she stared at his mouth, doing everything he did until the little black dots dancing across her vision faded away.

"Talk to me," he said softly.

"It's just that I realized this is it," she breathed. "This, today, could be the end of it."

He didn't ask her to clarify what this would be the end of exactly. He was smarter than that. He knew she was talking about them. Only what he didn't know was how much she regretted making that damn deal in the first place.

His sunglasses had been resting on top of his head, but at her words, he slid them down over his eyes. For a full moment, he was still as stone. "It is what we agreed upon, isn't it," he finally said.

She nodded, and even though she couldn't see what he was thinking, she had to look away.

"Anna."

With an inward grimace, she turned back.

He flashed a small smile. "It was great while it lasted."

She swallowed hard. "Yeah. It was." The words felt scraped over a throat cut by glass while anxiety butterflies took flight in her belly. She'd miss being with him and around him. She'd miss the feeling of contentment, the flutter in her heart and soul whenever he so much as looked at her. "Owen—"

"No, I get it. If after all we've shared and done you still believe that I'm nothing more than a reckless wanderlust adventurer, then you're right. We aren't meant to be." His voice wasn't cold or even angry. Just calm. Quiet. "So if you want to wait here, or even go back down to the truck while I finish this, I'll find you. I won't leave without you."

Because he wasn't Adam. Or Michael . . .

When she didn't, *couldn't*, respond, he gave a nod and turned away. "I'll be back. Give me a couple of hours."

And then he walked away.

# CHAPTER 26

Anna watched Owen go a moment, then hurried to catch up to him.

He didn't look at her. "Be sure, Anna. It gets harder from here."

Honestly? She couldn't imagine anything being harder than knowing it was over between them.

When he finally looked over at her, his mirrored shades in place, she could tell nothing from his carefully blank face.

"I'm sure," she said.

And with a nod, he kept going.

They didn't speak for some time, until out of the blue, he said, "You do realize that your job is often far more dangerous than mine."

She thought about that and had to admit that at times, it might be true.

Another ten painfully long minutes went by with nothing between them except huffing and puffing, during which she thought about her dad and what he would think of what she was doing.

Reading her mind, Owen said, "Even if we find the necklace and coins, it's still circumstantial evidence at best."

Still trying to make her feel better . . . "You used to be so certain he was the thief."

"Yes, until I was reminded by this amazing, brilliant woman I know to keep an open mind. It was good advice, Anna. You should try it."

She rolled her eyes. "In my line of work, it's not about gut feelings, it's about proof. And it's not *all* circumstantial. There's that pesky criminal record I never knew about. Plus, he's also suspected of other crimes."

"Suspected. Not proven. And we don't even know if we'll find the necklace and coins. But if we do, there will still be no proof he led us to them."

"What are you talking about? The letter—"

"Was destroyed."

Their gazes locked and held, and she knew he'd done it for her. "Owen—"

"Even if we find everything and I bring the coins and necklace back to Ruby, there's still every chance she won't remember they were missing."

"So then you'll keep bringing them to her until she does," she said firmly.

He looked at her for a long beat, clearly fighting with his emotions. "I'm going to ask you again: Would you like to stay right here while I go the rest of the way? Whatever I find, or don't find, you won't ever have to know."

She nearly melted on the spot because he meant it. And she realized that everything she'd thought she'd known about him early on had been so wrong. He wasn't a selfish man-child who liked to charm his way through life. He was genuine and real.

Honorable and loving. He would always protect the ones he loved, at any price. "We're *both* going to do this. There's no way I'm going to let your aunt down, whether she ever knows or not."

They kept going, with each tight turn in the trail revealing more mouth-dropping vistas of nothing but the wild Sierras spread out before them as far as the eye could see.

Then the going suddenly turned far more difficult.

She was seriously winded by the time they came to the first rock face, which turned out to be a series of huge Ice Age slabs of granite that got increasingly hard to climb. They lost the trail several times.

Luckily Owen knew what he was doing, and he pulled out a paper map. Even with that, several times they also needed Ky's help and twice had to backtrack.

"Are we lost?" she asked.

Owen shook his head.

"Did we go too far?"

"We're going south, as far as we can get without walking right off the cliffs. We haven't gotten to the cliffs yet."

The higher they went, the more the wind whipped at them. Several times she'd have been knocked to her ass if Owen hadn't grabbed her. He'd kept very close since they'd gone past the tree line, which she took as a lack of faith. Not unfounded, but, well, embarrassing. "I'm okay."

"Anna, I'm not doubting your ability. When I'm at work and guiding people through challenging situations, I always stick close. Novice or expert, it doesn't matter, not if you're my responsibility."

"I get that," she said. "But I'm *not* your responsibility."

"Today, on this trail that's closed because people kept dying on it, you are. Don't fight me on this. I intend to keep you in one piece and in working order, because I enjoy you in one piece and in working order."

She snorted. "You mean in bed."

"In bed. On the kitchen counter—" He stopped to laugh softly when she bit her lower lip, remembering that particular—and extremely memorable—adventure from a few nights ago.

"And the club chair in the corner of your bedroom. And my shower—"

She put a finger to his lips because while she was glad and grateful they were back to teasing each other instead of the painful silences, if he kept talking, they'd be adding "and on the trail against a massive rock" to the list, no matter if they were still together or not.

He nipped at her fingers, smiling when she jumped. "Against a rock, huh?"

Great. She'd said that out loud.

"You good to keep going?"

"Yes." It only took about twenty more minutes for her to regret it. They were now having to climb up and over granite slab after granite slab, each feeling a little more unstable and slippery than the previous. Owen stopped and hunkered down, pulling off his backpack and taking out ropes. "If you trip, this will avoid you sliding backward."

She glanced behind them and felt a little sick. The height was staggering. They were thousands of feet up. She couldn't even see the area where they'd parked anymore. But that wasn't her real problem. Her real problem was that she already missed Owen and he was right there. "Oh my God, what was I thinking?"

He climbed up the next slab and squatted low, reaching a hand down for her. He pulled her up onto the rock with him and wrapped his arms around her, brushing a kiss to her sweaty temple. "It's going to be okay."

Was it though?

"I've got you," he said. "You know that, right?"

"Because . . . you're friends with all your exes, including me?"

He shook his head. "You're different."

Her heart skipped a beat. "Does that mean you won't stay friends with me?"

"It means you'll always be more than just a friend to me."

She stared at him. She wanted to say "same," but that age-old fear trapped the word in her throat. "This is very new for me, someone besides Wendy and Hayden wanting to keep me in their life." It was an embarrassing truth. She'd never really felt understood or fully accepted for who she was. But here, in possibly the most dangerous situation she'd ever been in, she'd never felt more safe or secure.

"Hey," he said, dipping down a little to see into her eyes. "Never doubt it."

Unbearably moved, she leaned in and kissed him. At his surprise, she shrugged. "Well, we haven't found the necklace and coins yet, right?"

He laughed low in his throat, a sexy sound that had her thinking about the up-against-a-rock thing again, but she controlled herself because she was too winded to follow through.

As they continued on, he helped her locate good hand- and footholds, and she found herself feeling secure and far more confident than she'd imagined possible. Owen had probably done stuff like this a thousand times or more, but he never gave any hint of irritation at her slower pace or that he wished he'd done this without her. Somehow, when she was with him like this, she felt exciting and fascinating and interesting. Like a new and improved Anna.

A couple of hours later, he boosted her over the last massive granite slab. She landed gracelessly and rolled to her back, panting. When she could, she got to her hands and knees and offered Owen a hand just as he boosted himself up and over, landing at her side.

"I think we found the cliff," he said.

No kidding. With a three-hundred-and-sixty-degree vista laid out far below, it felt like they were on top of the world. The wind was wicked and relentless. They both sat, trying to catch their breath as Owen checked in with Ky and consulted the printed map in his hands. He eyed the area around them, narrowing in on something slightly to his right. "There," he said, pointing about a hundred yards off, to what looked to her like just another bunch of stacked rocks.

"There what?" she asked.

"There are the grottos."

She started to stand up, but he stopped her. "Stay low. People have died trying to walk around up here."

Anna gulped.

It was no easy task to go that last hundred yards, and even as they moved, she could only see one possible cave. It wasn't until they made it closer that she realized it wasn't just one, but a series of caves, almost all too small to crawl into.

Grottos.

She wasn't claustrophobic by any means, and yet she still didn't want to climb inside any of them. "Do you think we're in the right place?" she asked, having to talk loud over the roar of the wind whipping around them. All she could think about was how many bugs and snakes probably lived in the caves. Maybe bears too, or even mountain cats.

Owen was carefully crawling around openings, peering in with the use of a penlight he'd pulled from one of the pockets of his cargo shorts. "I'm hoping we're in the right place," he said. "We won't know until we search this entire area."

That was one of the things she loved most about him. He never pandered to her fears, but he also always told her the truth, even when it was something she might not want to hear. "Divide and conquer?"

With a nod, he pulled another penlight from his backpack and handed it to her.

She went right and he left. In the first cave she came to, the opening was only a foot wide, so she had to get really low. Her beam of light revealed some rocks and dirt, nothing else. Same for the second and third, but on the fourth cave, the opening was larger, maybe two feet, and when she peered in, she caught sight of the largest spiderweb she'd ever seen. She covered her own mouth to hold in her startled gasp and quickly backed away.

"Anna? You okay?"

"Fine!" she yelled. She took a deep breath, then whispered to herself, "You *are* fine." She went back to searching, coming across a cave slightly larger than the rest, not quite four feet tall. When she flicked the light inside, she got a reflection of something shiny, and her heart skipped a beat.

Unfortunately, whatever the shiny thing was, it sat at least ten feet inside the cave. Probably it was nothing, maybe a treasure of some sort that an animal had dragged in there. She craned her neck and saw Owen methodically checking everything near him, then turned back to the cave opening. "You got this," she whispered to herself. "You're okay, you're okay," she chanted softly on her hands and knees, moving through the damp dirt, the penlight leading her toward whatever the thing shining back at her was. It seemed small, and she couldn't make it out until she got close enough.

And once she did, she gave an involuntary gasp. It was a flat black metal box, the kind that was sometimes used as a cashbox. The flat black didn't reflect any light, but the silver clasp did, which had been what she'd seen from outside.

The box was locked. Before she could figure out what to do, she heard Owen calling for her, his voice urgent.

Getting out was far trickier than going in. She had to crawl backward while dragging the surprisingly heavy box along with her. "I'm coming!" she yelled, and as soon as her head cleared the cave, she stood up and whirled around. "Owen! I've got a—" She broke off because he was crouched low beside what looked suspiciously like . . .

A body.

An incredibly still body.

She blinked and was at Owen's side without even realizing she'd moved. "Oh my God. Is he—"

"Badly decomposed?" he asked grimly. "Yes."

Shocked and filled with horror, Anna shook her head in disbelief. "Who is it?"

Owen picked up a stick and used it to nudge the wallet that had fallen out of the guy's nearly deteriorated jeans pocket. Still using the stick, he flicked it open and bent in closer to read the ID. "Rico Edwards." He looked up. "Why does that name sound familiar?"

She stared at him. "Oh my God. Because he's one of the five original suspects, and when I researched him, there were rumors he'd been linked to Shady Joe around the time Ruby's things were stolen. Nothing concrete, so I had to let it go."

Owen reached for the radio. "Ky, we've got a DB where X marks the spot. Call it in—" He broke off and sucked in a sharp breath.

"What?" Anna asked.

"What?" Ky also asked.

Owen very carefully used the stick to nudge the man's pants pocket, from which the most gorgeous necklace she'd ever seen had slid from. A huge red ruby surrounded by diamonds twinkling in the late-afternoon sun in spite of layers of dust and dirt.

Owen looked up at Anna, eyes wide with surprise. She was pretty sure she wore the same expression.

They both startled at a sound, just a slight rustle, really, but they both whipped around—

—To find Will standing there pointing a gun at them. "Well, look at what I found," he said. "This must be what Christmas feels like."

Anna glanced at Owen, who gave her a pointed look. Right. Her job really *was* more dangerous than his.

"What are you doing?" Anna asked Will.

"Same thing you are."

"I don't have a gun in your face," she said.

"For which I'm grateful because now I can take over this crazy ride." He winked at her. "Better buckle up, buttercup."

# CHAPTER 27

Owen's life had flashed across his eyes before. Many times, in fact. In his adrenaline-fueled line of work, it happened. But nothing compared to this. He hated being at a disadvantage, and right now, on his knees with a gun in his face and Anna shifting restlessly like she was going to make a move, he was in the middle of the biggest disadvantage of his entire life.

Anna's eyes dropped to the necklace, and he knew she was going to try to grab it. Heart stuttering in his chest, he rose to his feet, yanking her up along with him, shoving her behind him. He could feel her shaking. Or hell, maybe that was him.

"Cute," Will said. He eyed the dead guy and shook his head. "Wow. Dad got sloppy."

"Your dad did this?" Anna asked. "How did he even get up here?"

"The promise of money is a powerful motivator," Will said. "And remember, he used to be in good shape. Before the booze, and then of course jail."

"You told me he'd never discussed any of this with you."

"I lied. Didn't want you to know I knew anything. Didn't want to tarnish your view of me." He laughed, clearly not really caring what she thought. "Plus, I didn't know much at the time of the theft ten years ago. In fact, I didn't know anything until I went to visit Dad after he'd been stupid enough to get caught for that bank robbery. Apparently he'd squandered away most of the fortune he'd made—"

"You mean stolen," Anna said.

"Glass houses, princess." Will shrugged. "Anyway, I guess after your dad, who'd been out of the life for a while by then, refused to do the job, Dad found himself someone else."

"Rico Edwards," Owen said.

They all looked at the decomposed dead guy.

"Yep," Will said. "Poor bastard. Tried to sneak away with the necklace."

"Your dad killed him?" Anna asked.

Will shook his head. "That's the crazy thing. I'm not sure he did. Supposedly they did the job together, hid the loot. Then Dad ended up in prison before he could find a fence, things were too hot. So maybe Rico took the opportunity to come back up here, maybe planning on stealing it all out from beneath my dad." He shrugged. "My dad told me several times that Rico had a lot of health issues. A bad heart. Maybe the coins were too heavy for him and he decided to take just the necklace, but died before getting too far."

Convenient . . . "Or . . . your dad killed him before going to prison."

Will shrugged.

"Or you did Rico yourself," Owen said.

Will shook his head. "I didn't know where he'd hidden the loot, he wouldn't tell me." His face darkened. "He didn't trust me, can you believe it? I'd long ago given up looking for it. So thank you for your service." He nudged a chin toward Anna. "Get the necklace and bring it to me. Slowly. That black box as well."

"How did you even find us?" she asked.

"After your visit to my work, I put a tracker on your truck. I've been watching your dot, knowing you would make a move eventually. The necklace, Anna."

Owen started to reach for it, but Will shook his head. "Not you. Her. *Now*, Anna."

She started to move, but Owen tightened his grip on her. Anna met his gaze, her own filled with worry, stress, and fear. Fear for him. "He won't shoot me," she said softly.

Owen wasn't willing to take that risk. "Put the gun down, Will. This is more trouble than you want, and the authorities are already on their way."

Will laughed. "Even if that was true, I'll be long gone before they manage to get up here." He moved a few steps closer, gun aimed at Anna's head. "Move it."

Owen didn't let go of her as he spoke to Will. "So far you've only been stupid but haven't committed an actual crime. You willing to end up in a cell next to your dad for the next few decades?"

Will snorted and eyed Anna. "I bet you don't even know that this self-righteous prick came to visit me."

With a start of surprise, Anna looked at Owen.

Owen winced inwardly. "Anna—"

"Oh, this is gonna be good." Will laughed, pleased with himself. "Can't wait to hear the lies come out of Mr. Perfect."

Owen watched uncertainty come into Anna's eyes, and damn if that didn't sting worse than having the gun in his face. "He's full of shit, Anna."

Will tsked. "Lying to the little lady already? Not a good sign, man." He smiled at Anna and flashed her his phone. "I've got him on my doorbell cam."

"That's because I did go see him," Owen said.

"Without me?" she asked in disbelief. "Were you ever going to tell me?"

"Look, there was nothing to tell." Shit, he knew the moment the words were out of his mouth, he'd stepped in it. "I went to see him to tell him to back the fuck off of the drunken, late-night visits."

Anna stared at him. "I told you I could handle myself."

"I know," he said tightly, incredibly aware of how much Will was enjoying this. "And later, we can discuss it at length."

"Seriously? You could've just said, 'Hey, I went to Asshole Will's house to tell him to back the fuck off.'"

"Wow," Will said. "That hurts."

Anna, not taking her eyes off Owen, ignored Will. "This isn't over."

Oh, but it was. She'd even told him so on the way up.

"I think you should dump him," Will told Anna. "If he'll lie about the small stuff, why would he be honest about the big stuff? It'll be your dad all over again."

She sucked in a breath and looked at Owen.

God, he hated the doubt on her face. "You really believe after everything you've been through that I'd lie to you?"

"Omitting is lying."

"Couples counseling's over, kiddos. The necklace, Anna."

She turned to Rico's body. Her face was pale, her eyes glassy, but her hand was steady as she reached out and grabbed the necklace, then glanced at the cliff.

"Throw it and I'll blow your boyfriend's head off," Will said.

Owen could see in the guy's eyes that he was going to kill them anyway, so he did the only thing he could. He turned to the woman of his heart. "I love you, Anna." And then he lunged at Will.

The last thing he heard was a deafening bang and Anna's scream.

# CHAPTER 28

Ears ringing from the report of the gun, Anna watched in horror as Owen fell heavily to the ground and didn't move. When Will started to turn to her next, she reacted without conscious thought, throwing herself at him. They rolled a few times, but she had fear and fury on her side. Breaking free, she got to her feet, but Will reached out for one of her hiking boots and tugged.

They hit the ground again, her on top this time. He had his hands around her neck, which meant somehow he'd lost the gun. Buoyed by that knowledge and fueled by panic, she punched him in the throat.

Coughing, holding his throat with one hand, Will rolled toward her and wrapped his palm around her lower leg. But she was done with this, done with him, and she kicked out. Hard. She was still kicking his unconscious body when someone wrapped their arms around her and wrestled her away.

Owen, covered in blood, looking ashen, held her against him, so tight she could feel him shaking. "Are you . . . laughing?" she asked in disbelief.

"I hope you never get this mad at me," he said. "I'm not sure I'd come out the winner."

"I *am* this mad at you!" Whirling to face him, she patted her hands down his torso. "There's so much blood, where are you hit?" She yanked the radio off his hip and yelled into it. "Ky! Owen's been shot!"

"What?" Owen looked down, seemingly surprised. "Huh. You're right. I am bleeding." He hit his knees.

"Help's on the way," Ky said through the radio. Calm but serious. "Is he breathing? Is it a through and through? Can you slow the bleeding? Keep the wound clean?"

"He's breathing, I don't know yet, and I'll do my best." She crouched before Owen, shoving his shirt out of her way to see a hole just below his collarbone, blood seeping out of it. Craning her neck, she looked at his back. Another hole. A through and through, then. "You put yourself in front of me!" she yelled at him, ripping off her own shirt to press it against the exit wound, which was bleeding much more profusely than the front. "That was stupid!" Tears were pouring down her face. "You're so stupid!"

He let out a low half laugh, half groan. And then he collapsed in her arms.

ANNA EYED THE clock on the wall of Wendy's hospital room. The hands moved so slowly she wanted to scream. Her head hurt from where she'd hit it on a rock attempting to take down Will, who was at this very minute in custody, hopefully sitting in a jail cell. She hadn't even realized she'd been bleeding until she'd gotten here. Five stitches later, she was fine.

Except for the going crazy part.

It'd been four hours, twenty minutes, and five seconds, and

Owen was still in surgery. He'd better not die on her. She wasn't done yelling at him.

Because . . . *he loved her?*

One of the rescue team's first responders had said it was possible the bullet hadn't hit anything vital. But she couldn't get past the image of Owen lying on the ground in a puddle of his own blood.

He'd been medevaced here and rushed into emergency surgery. Ky was in the surgical waiting room, and he'd promised to come get her when he heard something.

But there'd been nothing but radio silence.

She drew a deep breath. It'd been a crazy day and night, and she'd had a shocking number of revelations, some spoken, some unspoken. But the biggest thing she'd learned was that Owen would lay his life down for her.

No questions asked.

"Anna, he's going to be okay," Wendy said.

She looked at her sister holding one beautiful baby, and then at Hayden holding another, and finally down at the one in her own arms—she had no idea how to tell them apart yet and didn't want to admit that out loud—and found herself stunned at the juxtaposition of life and death. "You don't know that," she whispered.

Just saying it out loud made her chest ache. Closing her eyes, she bent over the precious baby girl in her arms and cuddled her close. But the problem with closing her eyes was that everything that had happened on that mountaintop played across her eyelids in high-def.

Her, begging an unconscious Owen not to die.

Ky, talking to her through the radio, telling her to get the gun, keep it close in case Will woke up.

She'd lived five lifetimes before help had arrived . . .

"Do you know what the last thing I said to him was?" she asked the room. "I told him that he was stupid."

Wendy choked out a laugh. "Sounds about right. He is a man, isn't he?"

Hayden went brows up.

"No, you don't understand," Anna said. "He'd been shot and I *yelled* at him. I told him he was stupid for taking that bullet for me. And he . . ." She swallowed hard.

*I love you, Anna . . .*

She closed her eyes again. "He lost consciousness. So he's lying on that surgical table with his last memory being me yelling at him that he was stupid."

Wendy grinned. "Aw. You love him."

Anna opened her mouth, then shut it again. Dear God. In spite of herself, it was true.

Wendy grinned knowingly.

Hayden looked confused. "If you love him, why did you make that ridiculous deal about this being over once you located the necklace and coins?"

"Babe," Wendy said, shaking her head at her husband. "Just sit there and look pretty." She turned to Anna. "So? Why did you?"

Anna sighed. "Because as you just mentioned, I'm ridiculous."

"You could always recant," her sister said with an annoying older sibling vibe. "When he wakes up, which he will, tell him just how ridiculous you've been and recant the deal."

Anna hesitated.

"Okay, what aren't you telling me?" Wendy asked.

"Owen went to see Will and didn't tell me." Embarrassment had her raising her voice. "Will had a video!"

The baby in her arms jumped, and she winced guiltily, kissing the furrow in her tiny little brow, lowering her own voice with effort. "He lied, Wendy. Lied by omission. And look at Dad! Neither of us could've in a million years imagined he'd been a thief! So it's not a stretch to believe Owen could be a liar. He went to see Will without me. Why would he do that? He was the one who said we were an us and that he had my back. Not that he'd go *behind* my back!"

Hayden gave Wendy a pointed look.

Wendy grimaced.

"*What?*" Anna asked.

Both of them suddenly became enthralled with their babies.

"One of you needs to start talking and fast."

Wendy sighed. "He went to see Will because of me, okay?"

"*What?*"

"Will showed up at my house," Wendy said. "The night after he showed at yours. He was drunk, threatening, angry, and I got scared. Hayden was working late that night, so I called Owen."

Anna's mouth was literally hanging open. "Why didn't you call *me?*"

"Because I didn't want you to end up in jail."

Anna sucked in a breath, trying to rein in her anger, but she couldn't. Wendy had called Owen, not her. How was she supposed to get over this? "You clearly told Hayden about it."

Wendy grimaced again. "Yes."

"But not me."

"Yes. I'm sorry!"

"You're not, or you would have told me!"

"I'm telling you now," Wendy said.

"Yeah, because Hayden made you." Once again she was the odd person out. "I can't believe this. Now I can't trust you right along with Owen."

"Focus!" Wendy yelled. This time it was the infant in her arms who jumped. Wendy cuddled her close. "Shh. I'm sorry, shh, it's okay, baby."

Anna managed to find a rough laugh. "You don't know which one you have either."

"Hey, I'm still getting the hang of this mommy thing. And you're just mad because you realized you love Owen and a little part of you is totally panicking inside."

Actually, it was a pretty big part of her panicking inside, thank you very much. Owen hadn't told her something big, but . . . Wendy had asked him to keep it a secret. Which pretty much deflated her anger. Owen had been between a rock and a hard place, aka her and Wendy, but at the end of the day, he'd had their backs in the only way he could. He hadn't betrayed her.

He *wouldn't* betray her.

Yes, they'd started out on opposite sides of the fence, and yet . . . and yet he'd never shied away from the possibility that he could be wrong about her dad. He'd kept an open mind. He'd stood at her side. He was capable, resilient, smart, strong in both spirit and body, and he'd been an amazing partner. He thought things through, and while he was capable of acting on impulse, he never acted rashly.

Unless he was trying to put himself between her and a bullet, that was . . .

Most of all, he was calm, and he'd used that calm to help her feel brave. That made him something else—a friend, a great one. But he was also far more than that, and if she was being honest, he was also more than just a boyfriend or a lover.

He was the kite string that both anchored her and yet kept her flying.

And he loved her.

She had no idea how to handle that. Okay, so he hadn't told her about protecting Wendy. The truth was, she was so incredibly grateful to him for being there for Wendy when she'd needed him. And what had Anna done to show that gratitude? She'd reminded him that they were over, then let him take a bullet for her and, oh yeah, had called him stupid.

All in the same day.

And he was currently in life-threatening surgery to which she could lose him.

Everything else seemed trivial, and she could scarcely breathe. "I'm sorry. I'm not upset you went behind my back. I'm upset because I'm afraid to lose him. I'm just so terrified of opening up my heart, and it doesn't even matter because he wormed himself in there whether I like it or not." She wiped her nose on her sleeve. "And for the record, I don't." Her eyes filled. "And if he dies, I'll kill him."

"Is that my sweatshirt you're using as a tissue?" Hayden asked.

She looked down at her arm. "Yes."

He looked pained.

"Do you want it back?"

"Not even a little bit."

Wendy smirked. "You have worse on your shirt from changing Annabelle earlier."

Sonya poked her head into the room, looking unsure of her welcome.

Wendy's face lit up. "Sonya! Come in! Anna told me she

called you—you're so sweet for coming! I wanted to thank you for being such a help a few weeks back when Anna went to see you, but—"

"You've been a little busy." Sonya smiled. "I get it. Congratulations. I just wanted to leave you a basket of goodies in case the food sucked."

Wendy gave her the gimme hands, and Sonya set the basket on the table by her bed before looking at the baby in her arms. "Oh my goodness," she said softly. "She's precious." She turned and took in the other two as well, and her eyes widened. "Triplets?"

"Yep," Wendy said. "Three times the fun."

Sonya's eyes got misty. "Your father would've loved this so much." She put a hand to her heart. "I know how much I miss him. I can only imagine what you're all going through."

Hayden passed the tissues around again.

"It's because of you that we're going through a lot less than we could have been," Anna said. "You sent me on the path that ultimately allowed us to learn he didn't steal the Ruby Red or the coins."

Wendy looked at Anna. "Maybe now his name can remain on the buildings he worked so tirelessly to give to the public."

Anna didn't know how to tell her that while he hadn't stolen from Ruby, he still had that early record, which was now out there to the public.

Sonya swiped at a tear that had escaped down her face. "He was just such a wonderful, loving man who, yes, maybe made a few desperate, questionable decisions, but when he turned his life around and went legitimate, he really did try to talk Shady Joe into doing the same. But Joe wasn't interested in legitimacy. He was far too consumed with greed." She paused. Bit her lower lip. "There's something I didn't tell you before. I hope you can understand why. I needed to know you wouldn't stop loving him no matter what you found out."

"Of course not," Wendy said. "What is it?"

"Joe sent your dad that coin, the one you found in his things. It must've been shortly after the theft. Joe sent it as a taunt, a sort of 'screw you, I got the whole thing even though you said I couldn't do it.'"

"Why do you think he never got someone to recover Ruby's things and return them to her?" Anna asked, bringing up the question that had been bothering her for some time now.

"It came down to being too high of a calculated risk."

"To who?" Wendy asked.

"Us," Anna said softly, watching Sonya as the woman nodded sadly.

Anna looked at Wendy, who had a hand pressed to her heart, which was presumably aching every bit as much as her own was.

"Your dad spent the rest of his life correcting course," Sonya said. "Even when he knew putting himself out there in such a public way with the philanthropy might come back to haunt him." She paused, clearly weighing her next words carefully. "He was filled with guilt over feeling like he knew *exactly* what had happened to the Ruby Red and the coins. There was no escaping that. Knowing where Joe liked to hide things and how hard it was to get up there, he wanted to find a way to tell Ruby where her belongings might've been hidden, but he was also afraid of what Shady Joe might do if he revealed the hiding place or the fact that he had the coin."

"He was afraid Joe would come after him," Anna said.

Sonya shook her head. "He wasn't afraid for himself. He was

afraid Joe was unhinged and would go after his one vulner-ability."

"Us," Anna breathed.

Sonya nodded. "He was also afraid for Ruby, because Joe had been able to charm his way into her life once before. He knew the guy could do it again. At the time, your dad knew Joe was being watched by the authorities, who were very close to putting him away for some other crimes, several of which were for elder abuse." She paused. Hesitated. "Lou also knew about his MS and that he was on borrowed time."

"That's why he didn't have his letter sent immediately. He was waiting, hoping Shady Joe would be locked away and unable to hurt anyone, but also he was looking to keep himself out of it and safe from prosecution. Only Joe didn't get locked up for years, and Dad . . . he didn't get sick and pass for nearly a decade after that."

Sonya winced but held eye contact. "I'm sorry."

Anna shook her head. "I don't blame you for keeping his se-crets." And she truly didn't. She'd had a loving father who'd made some wrong decisions for the right reasons. He'd changed the course of his life, and by extension, hers and Wendy's as well.

Someone knocked on the hospital door and Anna's friend Nikki peeked in. "Hey there." Nikki took in the sight of the babies and beamed. "Oh wow, Wen, you and Hayden sure do make cute kids!" She turned to look at Anna. "I'm really sorry to do this now, but I need to ask you some questions about what happened."

"What happened to Will?" Wendy asked. "And will anything happen to Joe?"

"Will's being held without bail since he's considered a flight risk. He'll be charged for several crimes, including aggravated assault with a deadly weapon and unlawful installation of a tracking device. Rico Edwards will be getting an autopsy. If it turns out he didn't die of a health issue and Joe killed him, he'll be charged for that as well." She looked at Anna. "Can we go somewhere private to talk?"

"Don't you dare go somewhere private," Wendy said. "I mean it. I'll just get up and follow, and then the nurses will yell at both of you."

Anna sighed. "We can do it here."

Nikki nodded. "So . . . what happened up there? In your own words."

Anna let out a breath and looked at Wendy. "I know how much Dad's reputation means to you, and what it will mean to the girls, and all the good that he did, all the love he had for us, that still stands. You know that, right? It'll never leave our hearts. I need you to say you know that because I'm going to tell the whole truth so we can be done with it, so nothing can come back to haunt us, or these precious babies, ever."

Wendy's eyes were shiny when she nodded. "I know."

"Even if it means his name isn't on buildings anymore?"

Wendy sniffed. "I thought that was what mattered, but I was wrong. All that matters is our own memory of him and what a wonderful dad he was."

So Anna told Nikki everything, the whole crazy story from start to finish.

Nikki had been taking notes, at least until Anna got to the part about Louis being an associate of Joe's, when she held up a hand. "Stop," she said. Paused. "You know that anything you tell me about your dad is going to end up in the report."

Anna looked at Wendy again, who nodded. "The truth's more

important," she said. "I get that this might hurt his reputation. We know he made mistakes, but he's atoned for that as much as he could. Do what you have to do. It's okay."

When Nikki was gone, Anna looked at Wendy. "You okay?"

"Getting there. You did the right thing. Dad was amazing. The end. *That's* what I'm going to tell the girls."

Anna nodded. And if Wendy was brave enough to admit all that, then she could be brave enough to go make an admission to Owen as well.

She realized that there were moments in life that were tipping points. Fixed moments when you realized that things would happen that would fundamentally change you, and maybe there'd be no going back, but that was okay.

She'd had more than a few of those moments since meeting Owen. But the one that scared her the most had been watching him throw himself in front of her to save her. He'd had to have known with terrifying certainty that he could die doing so.

He'd done it anyway.

And that had been the moment she'd known exactly how much she loved him—with her entire heart and soul. If she lost him now, if he died, he'd do so without knowing how she felt. She hadn't been brave enough on the mountain, but she would find the courage now. She couldn't live with herself if she didn't.

# CHAPTER 29

Even before Owen opened his eyes, he knew something was wrong. He could hear a rhythmic soft beeping and the unmistakable scent of antiseptic.

Shit.

Hospital.

He opened his eyes and stared up at a stark, sterile ceiling. He felt his heart speed up as he tried to think past the fuzziness of the meds he'd clearly been given. Lifting his head, he eyed himself. Hospital gown. An IV pumping something into him that had dulled pain but not eradicated it. And a thick, heavy bandage covering the right side of his chest and shoulder, with his arm held to him by a sling.

Thinking was a challenge, but he closed his eyes and pushed himself. His eyes flew open as he remembered going after Will, and then . . . a blinding pain. He remembered lying on the ground and hearing a struggle. He'd lifted his head to find Anna kicking Will's ass, which had been the hottest thing he'd ever seen.

And then nothing.

*Is Anna okay? Has she been hurt?*

He wracked his brain for more info, but it didn't come. His heartbeat pounded in his ears, and then his monitor began to beep. He tried to sit up, but pain slashed through him, making him gasp out loud. "Holy shit—"

A nurse peeked her head in and smiled sympathetically. Her tag read *Hi, my name is Judy!* "Yeah," she said. "Moving is a bad idea. Just stay still, I'm going to check your vitals. How you doing?"

Well, let's see. He'd told Anna he loved her *after* she'd dumped him, he'd been shot, and as a bonus, he couldn't remember what happened to Anna. "The woman who was with me on the mountain. Is she okay? Anna Moore."

"I'm sorry, I haven't seen her." She finished checking his vitals and made some notes. "The doctor's on his way in to talk to you. Your friend Ky was here for your surgery, but once you were brought to your room, he had to go. He said you guys had a bunch of clients booked today and they're stretched so thin he couldn't get out of work, but that he'd be back as soon as he could. I don't want you worrying about a thing. Is there anyone I can call for you?"

Owen looked around for a clock but didn't see one. It was dark outside, but there was a slight lightening of the sky. He'd really been here all night? "I need my phone—"

A doctor strode into the room. "Good morning, how are you feeling?"

"Like I was shot."

The doctor gave him a grim smile. "There's a good reason for that. You remember what happened?"

"Mostly."

He nodded. "We've got good news and bad news. Good

news: no broken bones, nothing major hit—a miracle in itself, because if that bullet had hit a centimeter over in any direction, we'd be having an entirely different conversation."

"And the bad news?" Owen asked.

"You lost enough blood to require a transfusion, and there's still a chance for persistent deficits in the shoulder and arm as far as sensation and movement go. And, of course, infection. But we're watching over you carefully. You've got a lot of physical therapy ahead of you, but all things considered, I'm pleased."

Owen drew a breath. "And the woman who was with me, Anna Moore. How is she?"

The doctor looked up from his chart. "Is she family?"

"Yes," he lied. Or . . . was it really a lie? Anna certainly felt like family. Or at least she had until she'd dumped him on top of Mount Lion. Remembering that part was as painful as being shot. "Please. I just want to know that she's okay."

The doctor nodded. "She had a few bruises and scrapes, one that needed stitches, but nothing serious. She was released hours ago."

For the first time since he'd woken up, Owen felt like he could take a deep breath. She was okay. But . . .

She'd left.

When he was alone again, he stared at the ceiling some more and tried to talk himself into believing that she had a lot on her plate. Wendy had just had the triplets. Plus, she was slammed at work.

And then there was that one pesky fact about this thing between them being over.

Only it didn't feel over, not for him.

He told himself to sleep, heal, and once he got out of here, then they could figure things out. But the room around him felt large and devoid of anything humanizing and . . . empty. So damn empty. And it wasn't like he could call his aunt. She didn't handle phone calls well. For whatever reason, talking on the phone was a trigger for her, even on a good day.

It was okay. It was fine, and *he* was fine. Totally fine. Totally and completely *fine*.

Yeah, and even he wasn't buying what he was selling.

He looked around for his phone, but he didn't see it. Bracing himself, he once again attempted to sit up. He was swearing and sweating when the door opened.

"What are you doing?" asked his favorite voice in the world.

Anna.

"Ohmigod, are you serious?" she demanded. "Don't you dare try to get out of bed. In fact, don't you dare move so much as a muscle!" In opposition to her practically yelling at him, her hands were gentle as she pressed him back to the bed.

Unable to stop himself, he lifted his good arm and pulled her in, burying his face in the crook of her neck, and just breathed her in for a long moment, willing himself to let go of the fear. The future could be full of misery or full of happiness. It would be what it would be. No use spoiling the here and now by running ahead. And the present, with Anna pressed close to him, alive and breathing, happened to be pretty damn awesome.

"Hey. Hey, I'm okay," she whispered, turning her head to brush a kiss to his jaw. Then his throat, just above the hospital gown. He took another deep breath and tightened his one-armed grip on her.

She lifted her head. "Are you in pain?"

"No."

She snorted, but then her eyes went suspiciously shiny. "I was so scared for you."

"Eh, I'm hard to kill." He tried to smile but wasn't sure he managed it. "But my heart stopped when you stepped in front of me."

"I'm not the one who got shot!"

"'S'okay. I've got good drugs in me." Very carefully using his good hand, he slid his fingers into her hair, gently pushing it back from her temple so he could see the bandage there.

"It's nothing. Just a few stitches."

"Will?"

"Arrested." She dropped her forehead to his. "I nearly had a stroke because you had to go and be all heroic."

She was holding on to him tight enough to hurt, but he didn't care. There was something in her grip and in her voice that had a little tendril of hope unfurling within him. "So . . . you don't want me to be heroic?"

"No. I mean, well, yes." She lifted her face and met his gaze. "In the bedroom for sure—"

The rest of his tension left him, and he grinned. But it faded quickly. "How is it that you can just look at me and make me feel like I'm worth something?" he whispered.

She seemed to melt a little at that, which he figured had to be good, right?

"Seems fair," she whispered back. "Because you can give me one look and melt my clothes off."

They both smiled. Then he drew a deep breath. "I thought you left," he murmured. Something he'd meant to take to the grave, but there it was. Everything about her made his mouth run free from his brain.

She looked horrified. "I would never have left the hospital while you were in surgery. Ky was in the surgery waiting room, and he promised to tell me the minute he heard about you so I could check in on Wendy and the babies. He called me a few minutes ago on his way out. It took me a moment to off-load the baby I was holding. Don't ask me which one."

"Michelle and Louise . . . and Annabelle." He smiled. "You got your way."

"I mean, it was just a matter of time," she said modestly.

He laughed and then grimaced. "Oh shit." He pressed his good arm against his chest as black dots danced in front of his eyes.

"Oh my God." She cupped his jaw and stared into his eyes. "Don't laugh! Don't move. *Are you okay?*"

"Getting there," he murmured.

"Wait—how did you know the babies' names?"

"I didn't get a chance to tell you on the way up the mountain, and then I was pretty busy sleeping while the doc patched me up . . . But yesterday . . ." He paused. "Maybe the day before? Hell, I don't know what day it is. Anyway, I texted Wendy a congrats and we had a little chat."

She pulled back. "About me?"

"Let's just say she assumed I needed advice."

Anna sucked in a breath, looking more panicked than she had facing down a damn gun. "What did she say?"

"She said if I can't handle you at what I have mistakenly assumed is your worst, then I should be prepared to be unpleasantly surprised in the immediate future."

Anna stared at him. "I shouldn't be surprised, she can't help herself."

"She was trying to help me win you over."

That got him a half smile as she perched a hip on the side of his bed and gently pushed his hair off his forehead. "I know. And, Owen?"

"Yeah?"

"The reason I never would have left the hospital? It's because I'd have waited on you for as long as it took."

That she'd mirrored his exact words to her after Wendy had given birth had something warm and wonderful sliding into his chest.

"Are you really okay?" she asked, eyes filled with worry and stress.

"Getting better by the minute." He lifted a hand and gently brushed his fingers over a blooming bruise on her cheek. "You?"

"Same." She let out a long exhale, and a good amount of the tension in her released. "I didn't even know a person could lose as much blood as you did and live, and—" She burst into tears.

"Hey. Hey, it's okay. C'mere." Somehow he pulled her onto the bed with him, and even when she bumped his wound and he saw stars, he didn't care. "I told you, I'm hard to kill," he whispered, holding her as tight as he could, never wanting to let go. She was flush against his side, her hair all in his face, a strand or two sticking to the stubble on his jaw.

Before he'd met her, he could never have imagined such an intimate embrace having nothing to do with lust and yet somehow still being *everything*.

With a light brush of her fingers, she traced the thick bandaging around his shoulder and chest. "I just can't stop reliving it," she said softly. "The gun going off, you hitting the ground . . ."

He lifted her chin. "And I can't stop thinking about the look on your face when Will told you I'd gone to see him. I'm sorry I didn't tell you, Anna. I should have. I knew it at the time, but I was doing the stupid guy thing and trying to protect you."

She shook her head. "I don't need protection, Owen. I just need you."

He gently swiped away a few tears with the pad of his thumb. "Right back at you." He brushed a kiss to her temple. "So . . . we both feel overly protective of each other."

"Seems that way." She snuggled in closer, and he couldn't quite hide his wince. Her head came up, eyes filled with concern. "Did I hurt you?"

He hurt from head to toe, but he was taking that one to the grave. "I'm fine."

"You're not, but you will be. I plan to bully you back to health."

He smiled. His eyes drifted closed, because God, he was tired.

She took his good hand between hers. "I told the cops everything."

His eyes flew open and met hers. "Even about your dad?"

"Yes."

He searched her gaze, trying to decide how she was really doing, but he didn't see any regret in her eyes. "And . . . you're okay?"

"I will be," she said with a smile.

He nodded. Paused. "I think we should talk about something."

"Um . . . now?"

"I think so."

Her mouth curved slightly. "You don't sound positive."

True story. He wasn't positive at all. "I usually put what I need ahead of what I want. That gets confusing with you because I can't always separate the two. So, about what I said to you up at Mount Lion—"

"Yeah, about that," she murmured. Bit her lower lip. "Do you think you could say it again? You know, when we're not about to die?"

He blinked. "You want me to say it . . . again."

"Very much."

He was pretty sure her smile made his heart skip a beat. "I love you, Anna."

HER HEART. IT both ached and rejoiced as she drew in a deep breath.

"I know it hasn't been that long, and that we're complete opposites, and we don't make any sense at all, but I'm tired of fighting it."

"It," he repeated carefully.

"Yes, it. Us. I love you too, Owen. *Ridiculously.*"

He stared at her. "It's not the pain meds, right? You're really here, telling me you love me?"

"I am. I don't want to ever look into the eyes of another madman before he shoots you and wish I'd told you how I felt sooner."

His gaze never left hers. "Sidenote, let's never look into the eyes of another madman."

With a rough laugh, she carefully hugged him. "You should know, I love you *way* too much for my own good. I was so afraid you wouldn't love me back and I'd get hurt. Because you *can* hurt me, Owen. Far more than anyone else ever could—" She broke off when he slid a hand to the nape of her neck, pulled her in, and kissed her.

"I will never intentionally hurt you," he murmured. "I should've listened to my gut and never gone along with the 'just until the case is solved' thing. I should've told you how I was really feeling from the very moment I started to fall for you."

"To be fair," she said, "I wasn't ready to hear it."

He drew a deep breath. "I told myself I could let you walk

away, that I didn't trust anyone with my heart anyway, not even you. But I keep thinking about what came to me after I was shot. You were yelling at me to keep my eyes open, yelling at me that if I died on you, you'd drag me back to the land of the living—"

"Uh, maybe you could go back to forgetting that part—"

He shook his head. "Don't you dare make me laugh, it will hurt like a red-hot poker." He paused, clearly trying to gather his words. "In that moment, I could see how you felt about me, the truth of it, how deep it went, and I realized it wasn't about not trusting you. It was about believing that"—he closed his eyes and turned his head—"believing I deserved to be loved."

If it hadn't already, her heart would've cracked right open. Cupping his face, she brought it back to hers. "Owen," she breathed.

He opened his eyes. "It was about having everything I'd ever wanted—*you, Anna*—right in front of me. I've always had to work for everything I ever wanted. And because of that, I've always trusted that what I have is mine because I knew I'd earned it."

She smiled. "You don't think you earned me? After everything you've done for me?"

But he wasn't playing. He made a low, very male sound of frustration, like he couldn't pull the words he needed out of his drugged-up brain. Instead, he kissed her, slow, sweet, loving, before he met her gaze. "I'm going to ask you to give yourself to me because I love you more than life itself, Anna Moore, and in return, I promise to do the earning every day for the rest of my life."

She felt her eyes fill, but she blinked the tears away because she wanted to see his face. "And I promise you the same, Owen Harris."

From the doorway came the sound of carefully muted cheers. Wendy in a wheelchair holding two sleeping babies. Hayden standing behind her, the third sleeping baby strapped to his chest.

"I missed something good," Wendy said. "Start over! Say whatever you've just said to each other to make you both look so happy! Well, Anna looks happy. I mean, Owen does too, but he also looks a little gobsmacked."

"She loves me," he said.

Wendy grinned. "You're on good drugs, right?"

"Yes, but she really did say it." He looked at Anna with sudden concern. "Right?"

"I said it," she promised. "I meant it."

"Say it again," Wendy begged. "Please!"

Anna looked at Owen, who had laughter in his eyes. He loved her sister too, which was amazing in its own right. "I love you, Owen. More than I thought possible."

"Um, thanks?"

She grinned. "Obviously, I'm really new at this." Her smile faded. "I was so afraid to fall."

His eyes never left hers. "I'll catch you, I promise."

Anna's heart melted, and Wendy sighed dreamily. "Quick, Hayden, divorce me so we can start over and get that new in-love feeling."

"The problem with that is I've never been more in love with you than I am today."

Wendy stared at her husband and then appeared to melt. "Because of the babies?"

"Because of you."

"Oh," she breathed. "You're good too."

Hayden started laughing.

"I love you," Wendy said. "I do. But if you wake the babies, I will kill you where you stand."

He worked to get himself together. "Understood."

Wendy kissed him, then turned to Anna, who was busy kissing Owen. "Hey, so they've sprung us from this joint. Owen, take your lips off my sister's for a sec and ask her if she wants a ride home."

Owen grinned up at Anna. "Does Anna want a ride home?"

She shook her head. "No, Anna doesn't."

Owen's eyes were filled with amusement, affection, and love . . . and not a single iota of her panicked. "Anna's home is wherever you are," she said.

He kissed her again and Wendy muttered, "Sheesh, you two, get a room."

"Hellooo!" Anna said, waving her arms around the room.

Owen started to laugh, then sucked in a breath, holding her close, and just like that, the chaos in her chest settled. She could feel his heart beating beneath her fingers, strong and steady, sure. He smiled up at her, his gaze promising everything she ever wanted. And for once and for all, she was going to accept it.

"Love you guys," Wendy said, and waved as Hayden wheeled her away.

Owen looked at Anna. "How long can you stay?"

"Forever." Stunned by her own bold admission as it sat in the air between them, she tried to pull back.

But he held tight and smiled. "Works for me."

Judy came in, along with another nurse, holding a small plate that held a piece of chocolate cake and one of those fake flame candles.

"I was going over your chart," Judy said, "and realized it's your birthday."

Anna looked at him in surprise. "It is?"

He shrugged.

"Oh my God, I got you shot on your birthday?"

"No, you got me shot on the day before my birthday. And it's no biggie, I got cake out of the deal."

Judy grimaced. "We got the cake from the cafeteria, so I can't actually recommend it, but thought you might wanna at least make a wish with our fake candle." She flicked on the flame with a toggle switch.

They all sang the happy birthday song, and Owen pretended to blow out the candle before grinning at Anna. "Going to ask me what I wished for?"

She smiled. "What did you wish for?"

He threaded his fingers through her hair, pulling her closer. Just as his lips met hers, he whispered, "You . . ."

# EPILOGUE

*Three years later*

Anna had never been the girl to dream about getting married or having the house and the white picket fence and two-point-five kids. It just had never seemed realistic for her.

So that she was currently at her own small, intimate wedding reception at a beautiful restaurant right on the lake still didn't seem real. On one side of her sat Great-Aunt Ruby, smiling and bobbing her head to the music, watching Ky and Sami and also Wendy and Hayden dance on the small dance floor. On the other side of her sat Owen, with Michelle and Louise in his lap.

Anna had Annabelle in hers.

Her new husband smiled at her. "I'm pretty sure your sister thinks this is her wedding."

Anna watched Wendy shaking her groove thing and laughing at Hayden, whose idea of dancing was to stick one hand high in the air, bend his knees a little, and sort of weave from side to side.

"It's nice to see them out and having fun. Three toddlers have been hell." Anna turned her head to Owen. "The past few years were hard for everyone."

He rolled his shoulder, something that took him nearly a year after being shot to be able to do. He ran his finger along Anna's jaw. "You look worried. Don't be. It feels good." He touched the necklace around her neck. The Ruby Red. Her something borrowed. Ruby had insisted.

Owen's great-aunt had been taking a new med that hadn't made her better, but she'd not declined any more either, a huge relief. They'd known they'd have to play it by ear whether she could attend today, and after a few questionable weeks, they'd been thrilled when she'd woken up that morning clear as a bell. Owen had paid to have a caretaker there for her just in case she needed or wanted to go home. So far she'd been so happy to just sit and be a part of the day.

Ruby met Anna's eyes, her own misty. "My mom's necklace looks beautiful on you," she said with a warm smile. "And my grandnephew has never looked happier. I hope he knows how good he's got it."

Anna grinned. "He should, I tell him daily."

Owen snorted. "True story."

Ruby cackled. "You're perfect for him. You don't take his crap, and you keep him on his toes."

"Aren't you supposed to be in my corner?" Owen asked, not looking worried.

She smiled. "Always."

"What they doing in dat room?" Annabelle asked from Anna's lap, pointing to the restaurant's restroom.

"That's the potty. Do you want to try going?"

This got Anna an emphatic headshake. Annabelle wasn't sold on potty training yet. But when Ky walked by, heading to said potty, Annabelle yelled, "You gonna poop?"

Ky looked startled.

Owen was laughing so hard he couldn't speak.

Anna gave him a nudge to the gut with her elbow. "Sorry," she told Ky. "Carry on."

A minute later, Sami came through.

Annabelle straightened up and asked her new favorite question. "You gonna poop?"

Sami blinked. "Uh . . ."

Anna waved Sami on. "Save yourself."

Ky came out of the bathroom, and Annabelle shouted, "So did ya? Did ya poop? You get a candy if you did! Ask my mama!"

Owen dropped his head to Michelle's little shoulder, gasping for air since he was laughing so hard.

Wendy plopped on the other side of Ruby. "I legit thought my thirties would be way more exciting than me contemplating whether eight p.m. is too early to go to bed." She reached for the kidlets. "Hand them all over and go dance."

Didn't have to tell Anna twice. Two minutes later, she and Owen were on the dance floor and he had pulled her in close. Anna closed her eyes, smiling at the feel of him against her, knowing in her heart of hearts it would never get old.

Owen tilted her chin up so he could look into her eyes. "What are you thinking about? The candy you'd get if you went poop on the potty?"

She laughed. "No!"

"What then?"

"That there's no one else for me."

"Glad to hear it, since you just vowed to give me forever." He dropped his forehead to hers, then kissed her softly. "There's no one else for me either, Anna. You're the best choice I ever made."

With an agreeing smile, she kissed the man she was going to spend the rest of her life with.

Now for an early peek at

*Better Than Friends*

by *New York Times* bestselling author Jill Shalvis

# CHAPTER 1

Olive had three pet peeves: loud chewers, the use of the word *moist*, and love. She'd given it a try, several times in fact, but it hadn't worked out, the end.

Too bad she couldn't do the same with her past.

"You're breathing funny," Katie said. "What's wrong? Did you eat something with nuts in it again?"

Another example of how love hadn't worked out for her: Olive *loved* peanuts, so of course she was allergic. "No, and I'm fine," she said into her Bluetooth. Look at her, the master of the misdirect. Sure, it'd taken years, but she could fool just about anyone, even her lifelong BFF. "In fact, I'm great. Totally great. Like one hundred percent great."

"That's sarcasm, right?"

Katie Turner-Brooks had an eidetic memory, could solve complicated mathematical problems in her head, and could recite years-old conversations verbatim, but being neurodivergent meant sarcasm eluded her.

"It's me manifesting," Olive said. "Because I really *want* to be great." And *not* halfway to a panic attack . . .

"Then you will be."

"Like it's that easy." Olive had been a seriously awkward kid who'd been desperate to belong, and driving along the north shore of Lake Tahoe toward Sunrise Cove, she became that kid all over again. "I made a stop and bought salami, espresso, and a chocolate cream pie, if that helps explain my emotional state."

"Look, hardly anyone remembers that time you ran over the town hero, ruining his chances for a pro baseball career."

Olive sighed. The "town hero" was Noah Turner, and he was a lot of things, including Katie's twin brother and also Olive's onetime pretend boyfriend.

"Dammit," Katie said when Olive didn't laugh. "I read a book on how to act normal while living with autism, and I *still* can't tell a joke right. Listen to me—who cares what anyone thinks? You saved my life—"

"I didn't."

"You did," Katie insisted. "I used to be weird and antisocial—"

"Used to be?"

Katie paused. "Okay, fine, so *that's* how you tell a joke. And you did save my life. No one but my own family liked me. They were always so worried for me, until you moved into your grandma's house right next door to me and declared yourself my best friend."

"Well, someone had to do it."

"Okay, now you're just showing off. Anyway, all those stupid kids who used to torment us every single day—they peaked by our senior year. They were the best they were ever going to be. But you and I, we're *just* peaking."

Olive sighed. "We both know I don't have my shit together."

"Gotta fake it to make it, babe. You told me that once. You also said that no matter how many times you break, you still put yourself back together."

"Yeah, well, past me was stronger, full of hope. And do you remember everything I ever said?"

"Yes."

"Well maybe you should forget any of the dumb stuff."

"How do I differentiate?"

Olive laughed. "You did it! You told a joke!"

"Who said I was joking?"

"Ha-ha."

"Hey," Katie said, "thanks for coming to help me with little Joey so I can spend the days in the hospital with Joe."

"Of course I came." Katie had rarely asked her for anything, even though she'd given Olive so much: a family, acceptance, unconditional love . . . "I can't imagine what you're going through."

Noah and Joe were work partners, both ISB special agents—Investigative Services Branch of the National Park Service under the Department of the Interior—working out of Yosemite. They'd been investigating a series of car burglaries and thefts and had ended up in a high-speed chase. One of the suspects in the car had opened fire, blowing out their windshield and then two of their tires, which had caused them to flip.

Joe had been transported to the ICU in their local hospital. Noah had been released, though he was still healing from an injury to his right leg. Actually, that was a reinjury, since thanks to her it'd been badly wounded years ago.

Things she'd put away in the *Don't Think About It Right Now* file.

"How is Joe?" she asked. "Any change?"

"Still in a coma," Katie said, "which is the short story. The long story is that he's in a state of unarousable unconsciousness due to a dysfunction of the brain's ascending reticular activating system, or ARAS, which is responsible for the maintenance of wakefulness."

Katie's voice never showed much inflection, but that didn't mean she didn't feel things, because she did, deeply. She just couldn't show it. "He's going to be okay," Olive said softly.

"Yes, because if he's not, I'll climb into his coma and drag him out myself."

"I'll help."

"Misfits unite."

Olive laughed softly. "Misfits unite." It'd been their mantra since she'd moved in with her grandma at age fourteen. Up until then, she'd been homeschooled on an off-the-grid farm. As a result, she could build a fire in three minutes flat, but didn't know the first thing about kids her own age. Nor had Katie. This had made them an easy target at school. Poor Noah—not troubled, not different, not "weird"—had been their reluctant protector.

"Where are you exactly?" Katie asked.

"Passing the high school."

"Then you'll be here in ten and a half minutes. Don't get lost."

Olive laughed. "It hasn't been *that* long. And I never get lost."

"Not true. Remember when you were taking your driver's license test, and the DMV guy said turn right, but you always mixed up your rights and lefts, and you turned left—"

"I've got that down now," Olive joked, hoping to ward off the whole tale; unlikely, since Katie couldn't stop in the middle of a story.

"You ended up on a one-way street going the wrong way and totally freaked out, so you rushed to make a right turn, but it wasn't a street, it was a trail, and since it was posted everywhere that no cars were allowed, you failed your test—"

"I remember—"

"And your instructor got chest pains and had to take an ambulance to the hospital, but it turned out to be just indigestion because he'd eaten four hot dogs at that food shack at the lake, which had been shut down the day before for giving dozens of people food poisoning. Do you remember that part?"

"It's ringing a bell," Olive said dryly.

"You made the front page of the local paper. It's rare to make the front page, but you managed it again a few years later when—"

"Let me save you some time. I remember *all* the stupid stuff I did." And she wanted to talk about none of it. "I'll see you in a few—" She broke off when a limping jogger stepped off the sidewalk without looking. Slamming on the brakes, she nearly had heart failure before her car skidded to a stop a foot from the guy.

When he turned to face her, she sucked in a shocked breath.

"What?" Katie asked.

Olive's car was half in the crosswalk, slightly crooked, the smell of burnt tires assaulting her senses. The person she'd nearly hit yanked out an earbud and lifted a hand up to shade his eyes, clearly trying, and failing, to see past her windshield into her rental Mini Cooper.

A miracle, because she knew him, which didn't help her anxiety any.

Noah Turner mouthed *sorry!* and continued moving across the street in an uneven gait.

"Olive?" came Katie's worried voice in her ear.

"He can't be serious," she muttered. "He's *sorry*? I almost had a heart attack, but hey, as long as he's sorry—"

"Who are you talking to?" Katie asked.

Olive grimaced. "I just almost ran over your brother."

"*Again?* He's not going to like that."

She resisted the urge to thunk her forehead against the steering wheel. "I'm pretty sure he couldn't see my face, and I don't plan on enlightening him. You can't either."

"Oh, I don't talk about you. You're like the One Who Shall Not Be Named."

Olive felt her eyes widen. "What?"

"Don't take it personally. He's got a whole list of things Mom and I can't talk to him about. Item number two is women and/ or marriage. All women, not just you."

Olive choked out a laugh. "I'm afraid to ask what number one is."

"It's kids. We're not allowed to ask when he's going to settle down and have kids. But really, he should've made a rule about getting set up, because Mom's been trying to set him up with every even vaguely single woman she hears about."

Olive found her first smile for the day. Here she'd been dreading coming back and having to talk to him about what happened all those years ago, but it sounded as if he had his hands full.

"Oh, and you'll be staying with me," Katie said.

"I'm not going to put you out at a time like this. My grandma's got plenty of room—"

"She's been renting her extra rooms out to supplement her social security checks."

Olive felt her heart squeeze. "What?"

"You didn't know?"

Guilt swamped Olive. Had she been so busy keeping her PR firm afloat that she'd neglected to make sure Gram was okay? They were close, really close, even with Olive living in London. They spoke on the phone every week without fail. "No, I didn't know."

Katie was quiet a moment, as she always was when trying to think about how to say something without being too harsh or blunt. "Maybe she didn't want to worry you," she finally said.

Gram had been a nurse for forty years. She had a pension and her house was paid off. *Why was she renting out rooms?* "You've got enough going on, I'll get a hotel room."

"No." Katie paused, then said softly, "I need you, so promise me."

Katie had been there for Olive through thick and thin, and there'd been a lot of thin. "I promise." Gram's house came into view, and she turned into the driveway she shared with the Turner house.

"You're here, late as always," Katie said. "Your ETA was twelve thirty-two, and it's twelve thirty-eight. But then again, you did almost hit my brother. That added a few minutes to your time."

Olive turned her head and smiled at Katie's face pressed up against the window. Next to her stood a shorter mini-Katie—her five-year-old son, and Olive's godson, Joey.

Olive's heart warmed at the sight of the house, at seeing Katie and Joey, at everything, including Holmes, the family's twelve-year-old basset hound snoozing on the porch, snoring loud enough for her to actually hear him from her car.

"Uh-oh," Katie said.

Olive saw her pull her phone from her face to read the screen. "What's wrong?"

Katie sent her a grimace through the window. "Noah just texted that he's almost here too. He wasn't supposed to get back from his run until one twenty-four, which would've given you enough time to see me before going to see your grandma. He must've cut through the woods even though he isn't supposed to jog on uneven turf yet thanks to his reinjured leg. That's going to set his recovery back."

Olive didn't want to think about how he'd gotten injured in the first place, or it'd make her sympathetic toward him, and she really needed to hold on to her self-righteous anger in order to stay sane. Leaping out of the car, that anger turned to anxiety. It was important to be flexible in life whenever necessary. "Let me know when the coast's clear and I'll come over."

They disconnected and Olive turned to Gram's house just as the front door opened.

"Olive, oh, honey, you're finally here!" Gram cried, wiping her hands on the same floral apron she'd worn for as long as Olive could remember. In the blink of an eye, she was being hugged in arms that were much frailer than they'd ever been, but no less fierce or short of love. She held on tight, smiling because as always, her grandma smelled like roses and vanilla and childhood dreams.

"I'm so very glad to see you, Olive, but about your room—"

"It's okay. Katie told me about your renters. I'll sleep at her place, but are you okay? If you need money, I'll find a way to help." Everything she made went back into her company, but for her grandma, she'd figure something out.

"No, I'm good. *Really*," she added at Olive's worried look. "It's just the bunco girls are planning a trip to Hawaii this winter. Renting out the extra rooms seemed like a great way to get the money to go. I hear they make great mai tais, and you can go to luaus and watch hot men dance while twirling firesticks every night." She smiled. "I missed you so much."

"Missed you more. Oh, and hey, have you talked to Mom or Dad? Yesterday was our monthly check-in call, and they didn't answer or call me back."

Gram shook her head. "No. They're probably traveling to some festival or craft fair to sell their wares and forgot the date. Remember last year when they went to Burning Man and forgot to tell us? It was two weeks before they remembered to check in." Holding on to Olive's hands, she spread her arms out so she could take in her appearance. "Wow! You didn't have to dress up for me."

In her sundress, denim jacket, and wedge sandals, Olive wasn't all that dressed up. But she supposed, when compared to the hand-me-downs she used to wear, she looked very different. In the past ten years, she'd learned to look like the polished, elegant, self-reliant, successful woman she'd wanted to be. In her line of work, image was everything. Image and confidence. Which, let's face it, she still had to fake.

"You look fantastic, but you're not sleeping well."

Olive smiled. "Is that your way of saying I look like crap?"

"You look like a sight for sore eyes. But you also look worried and stressed."

"I am. For Katie."

"Of course. But it's also more."

Olive didn't bother denying this, it wouldn't work. She was a grade A-plus liar when she needed to be, after all she was a public relations specialist, but she'd never been able to fool her grandma.

Proving it, Olive found herself being pulled through the house and out the side door to the patio, where she took her first deep breath in . . . she had no idea. She hadn't realized until this very moment just how much she'd been missing the stability her grandma always provided.

"Sit," Gram said. "I'll be right back with the cure."

"Mew."

Olive looked down and found herself being stared at by a tiny orange-and-white kitten. "Well, hello." She reached down, but the little thing hissed at her and backed away. "Hey, I come in peace."

"Maybe you do, but she most definitely doesn't," Gram said. "She's a stray, just appeared out of nowhere yesterday. I'm calling her Pepper because she's so spicy."

"She's very thin."

"I know. I put out food and water for her. And I'm about to do the same for you."

Olive turned to Gram and laughed, because she had a tray of milk and cookies, just like the old days.

Gram grinned. "I do love the strays."

Olive eyed the cookie she'd dipped into her mug of milk. It was a fine line between not enough soakage and too much soakage, which would cause the cookie to fall apart all over her.

"Is it your job you're worrying about?" Gram asked. "I thought you loved living in London, running your own company."

Olive thought about that as she leaned over her mug, and yet *still* managed to dribble milk down the front of her dress. She didn't know how many cookies it would take to be happy, but so far it wasn't six. "I do love it, both the UK and being my own boss."

With a smile, Gram expertly lifted her perfectly soaked cookie to her mouth without getting a single drop of milk on herself. "I could use your skills at the senior center. We're trying to expand and need funding."

"I'd be happy to help."

"That will be lovely. And the boyfriend? What's his name again? Ian? The one who gave you a pretty bracelet, right?"

No, Ian had given her emotional whiplash and a headache,

with a splash of trust issues, after he'd cheated on her with someone she'd thought had been a friend. She'd bought herself the bracelet when she'd dumped him last year. "I'm . . . seeing someone new."

"Oh, that's nice. What's his name?"

"Matt." Matt was funny, sweet, kind, loyal, had a great job, great family, and was . . . pretend. Which really made him the perfect boyfriend.

"He didn't want to come with you?" Gram made a show of looking at Olive's ring finger. Her *ringless* ring finger . . . "I'd have loved to meet him."

"He's been super busy lately, so—"

"Poppycock. Who's too busy for love? You deserve it, more than anyone I know."

Olive didn't want for love. She wanted for structure, which had always been missing from her life. As a result, she operated in relationships like that young kid she'd once been, always accidentally re-creating the chaos she'd lived with growing up.

A truck drove up the common driveway, parking at the very top, on Katie's side. The man who got out was everything she remembered: tall, lean muscled, his dark, slightly curly hair peeking out from beneath a ballcap, his eyes hidden behind mirrored sunglasses. Once upon a time, he'd always had a smile, but not today. Today his mouth was set to grim. He rolled his shoulders like he was in some pain, then stilled at the sight of the Mini Cooper, the one that had nearly hit him. With a frown, he headed to it and peered inside.

Olive sucked in a breath and slouched in her chair. She was still holding her breath when he removed his sunglasses and stared inside the car for another long beat before lifting his head, unerringly finding her gaze with his own.

# ABOUT THE AUTHOR

*New York Times* bestselling author **JILL SHALVIS** lives in a small town in the Sierras full of quirky characters. Any resemblance to the quirky characters in her books is, um, mostly coincidental. Look for Jill's bestselling, award-winning novels wherever books are sold, and visit her website, jillshalvis.com, for a complete book list and a daily blog detailing her city-girl-living-in-the-mountains adventures.

# Read More by
# JILL SHALVIS

## THE SUNRISE COVE SERIES

## THE WILDSTONE SERIES

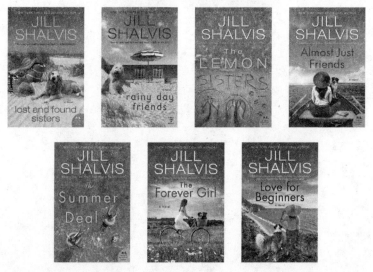